MAR 17

CH

Man on the Run

OTHER NOVELS BY CARL WEBER

Lookin' for Luv

Married Men

Baby Momma Drama

Player Haters

The Preacher's Son

So You Call Yourself a Man

The First Lady

Something on the Side

Up to No Good

Big Girls Do Cry

Torn Between Two Lovers

The Choir Director

She Ain't the One with Mary B. Morrison

The Family Business with Eric Pete

The Man in 3B

The Family Business 2 with Treasure Hernandez

The Choir Director 2: Runaway Bride

To Paris with Love with Eric Pete

The Family Business 3 with Treasure Hernandez

Grand Opening with Eric Pete

Man on the Run

CARL WEBER

GRAND CENTRAL
PUBLISHING

NEW YORK   BOSTON

Copyright © 2017 by Carl Weber

Cover design by Claire Brown
Photography by George Kerigan
Cover copyright © 2017 by Hachette Book Group, Inc.

Grand Central Publishing
Hachette Book Group
1290 Avenue of the Americas, New York, NY 10104
grandcentralpublishing.com
twitter.com/grandcentralpub

First Edition: January 2017

Grand Central Publishing is a division of Hachette Book Group, Inc. The Grand Central Publishing name and logo is a trademark of Hachette Book Group, Inc.

The publisher is not responsible for websites (or their content) that are not owned by the publisher.

The Hachette Speakers Bureau provides a wide range of authors for speaking events. To find out more, go to www.hachettespeakersbureau.com or call (866) 376-6591.

Library of Congress Cataloging-in-Publication Data.

Names: Weber, Carl.
Title: Man on the run / Carl Weber.
Description: First Edition. | New York : Grand Central Publishing, 2017.
Identifiers: LCCN 2016035909| ISBN 9781455505272 (hardback) |
    ISBN 9781478909583 (audio cd) | ISBN 9781478909590 (audio download)
Subjects: LCSH: Escaped prisoners—Fiction. | BISAC: FICTION / African
    American / Contemporary Women. | FICTION / African American / General. |
    FICTION / Contemporary Women. | FICTION / African American / Urban Life. |
    FICTION / Urban Life. | GSAFD: Suspense fiction.
Classification: LCC PS3573.E2164 M363 2017 | DDC 813/.54—dc23 LC record
    available at https://lccn.loc.gov/2016035909

ISBN: 978-1-4555-0527-2 (hardcover), 978-1-4789-7395-9 (large print hardcover),
978-1-4555-0528-9 (ebook)

Printed in the United States of America

LSC-C

10 9 8 7 6 5 4 3 2 1

This book is dedicated to my fans who read *Lookin' for Luv* and *Married Men* and fell in love with my writing style. Thanks so much for the years of support.

Man on the Run

Kyle

1

"Oh my God!" Lisa moaned repeatedly as she squirmed around in the Jacuzzi. My wife was in the middle of a toe-curling orgasm, with her legs locked around my neck like a vise, making sure I didn't go anywhere.

Normally this would have had me beating my chest like King Kong. Except this time, my head was submerged underwater, and I was on the verge of blacking out. If I didn't do something soon to stop her, she was going to have a whole lot of explaining to do, both to my kids and to the police. With the understanding that I was not going to break her death grip, I desperately made one last attempt to free myself by lifting her completely out of the water and onto the Jacuzzi's edge. She landed on her ass with a loud thump, her wobbly legs releasing me.

"What the—" I said after taking a moment to fill my lungs with air. But I couldn't be mad, because one look at her shuddering body told me my wife was completely oblivious to the fact that she'd almost drowned me. She blinked her eyes opened, a satisfied grin on her face as her feet dangled in the water.

"Fuck, that was amazing," she whispered, staring at me as if

I'd just performed a magic trick. Words could never express how much I loved to make her happy. "I didn't know you had that in you."

"I may not ever have it in me again," I teased half-seriously, giving her a mischievous grin. She didn't get the joke, so I moved on, pulling her in close. I kissed the wetness from around her neck, and despite the saltiness of her sweat, she tasted sweet to me.

I stared into her eyes and whispered, "I love you."

"I love you too," she murmured, running her hands gently up and down my back. "I can't believe we're in the backyard, in the middle of the day, making love. Do you know how long I've wanted to do something like this?"

I didn't reply, not verbally anyway. We rarely got moments like these, and I wasn't about to waste this one talking. I could show her how much I was enjoying this better than I could tell her, so that's what I did. I pulled her back in the water, spinning her around. Taking a fistful of her hair, I bent her over the Jacuzzi's edge, sliding my dick into her from the rear.

Lisa and I had a good life together. As a matter of fact, we were looking forward to the kids getting out on spring break so we could all go on a cruise to Jamaica. But that was a family thing, where once again we'd have to find stolen moments for ourselves. Right now it was all about us. With one in college around the corner at St. John's and the other a senior in high school, romantic moments like this between the two of us were few and far between. In fact, our sex life was starting to become somewhat uninspiring. It had boiled down to me waiting until the kids were in bed before rolling over and begging her, "Can I get some tonight?"

Finally, one night she sucked her teeth and told me how unromantic and predictable my actions were. Of course, that didn't stop her from giving me some. She knew she had to get it in where it fit in too, but I heard what she was saying loud and clear. Hell, I agreed with what she was saying. It was hard to get quality, unrushed time together for a little lovemaking. Our time alone had to be strategically placed where we wouldn't get caught or interrupted by the kids. What better time than in the middle of the day when they were at school?

When I entered her, I was gentle at first, but my wife liked it rough when the kids weren't around, so that's exactly what I gave her. I plunged into her hard and deep, and just to make it exciting, I pulled on her hair a little. She squealed with delight, encouraging me to pull it even harder. I tried my best to remain in control, but when she started throwing them hips back at me, working her magic like only she could, I just went for broke, thrusting my dick in her like it might come out the other side.

"That's it, baby. You know how I like it. Yeah, right there. Make her come! Oh, shit!" She encouraged my every thrust with her words.

The more she talked, the faster I stroked. I could tell by the way she tightened around me that she was on the verge of orgasm, which was good, because I was too.

"I love you," I said into her ear as I held her hips, pumping her against the side of the Jacuzzi. "And I damn sure love this pussy."

"You love it, huh? Show me how much you love it. Oh, yes, yes, make me come!" Lisa began moaning and shouting louder. "Oh, shit! Yeah, right there, baby. I'm 'bout to explode," she yelled, her entire body shuddering, letting me know that the time was now.

In one deep stroke, my back stiffened up like a board, and I let loose inside my wife, then collapsed right on top of her.

I'm not sure how long I lay on top of her with my eyes closed, but it felt like eternity—until her body tightened up and I thought I heard applause. You know you've done your thing when your wife starts to applaud your performance.

"Kyle...Kyle...Kyle!" she repeated, louder each time.

"Yeah, babe." I figured I was probably getting heavy and she wanted me to move, but I did not want to break our connection. I just wanted to lie there and enjoy that feeling for the rest of my life.

"Ahhhhhh, we've got company!" She tried to lift herself and me up, but I was too heavy.

"Company?" I muttered. I still had my head on her shoulder with my eyes closed. "What are you talking about?"

"She's talking about us." The snickering male voice scared the shit out of me.

"What the fuck—" I blinked open my eyes only to come face-to-face with what looked like a small army of armed men. I felt like I was at the end of *Scarface*, when all those guys came over the wall after Tony Montana. Thank God my daughters weren't home.

"Anyone else in the house?" a tall white man asked with authority. He was the only one not pointing a gun at us, so I could only assume he was in charge. When Lisa and I didn't respond, he snapped, "I said, 'Is anyone else in the house?'"

His voice rattled me, but it scared the shit out of my wife, who was now in tears. I positioned her behind me as I answered him. "No, no, we're the only ones here. Please, man, if this is about money, you got it. Just don't hurt us." I knew I probably sounded like a scared little bitch, but they had twenty guns, and all I had was a limp dick. At that moment, I would have admitted to being a scared little bitch if it could save the life of my wife and me.

"Nobody's going to hurt or rob you," the man in charge said, showing us a five-star badge. "My name is Deputy Donald Franklin, and we're with the U.S. Marshals Service."

"Marshals Service?" Lisa mustered the courage to speak up. I could feel her moving around behind me, trying to use my body to hide her nakedness.

"What do you want?"

"Sorry. We didn't mean to scare you. We're just being cautious. First time we ever barged in on anyone in a Jacuzzi. Looks like fun." He chortled, then reached down and picked up a towel, tossing it to my wife. "Why don't you folks get dressed?"

He didn't have to tell Lisa twice. She wrapped that towel around herself and scrambled out of the Jacuzzi to retrieve her clothes.

"What is this all about, Deputy?" I asked, angrier now that I knew I wasn't being robbed.

He reached inside his suit jacket and pulled out some official-looking papers. "I think this will explain it, Mr. Richmond. You are Kyle Richmond, aren't you?"

"Yeah, I'm Kyle Richmond." I stepped out of the Jacuzzi, picked up a towel, and wrapped it around myself as he handed me the papers. "What exactly is this?"

"That, Mr. Richmond, is an arrest warrant, along with a warrant to search these premises." His men started to disperse toward the house like they'd practiced his line and their response a thousand times.

"Arrest warrant?" Lisa, who was now half-dressed, squealed. "What are you saying? Are you here to arrest my husband?"

She had said what I was thinking, and I could feel butterflies taking flight in my stomach, despite the fact that I hadn't done anything wrong—other than be a rich black man with a white wife.

"No, Mrs. Richmond, we're actually looking for your husband's friend." Franklin stared at Lisa for a moment, then turned his attention to me. "Fourteen hours ago, Jay Crawford escaped from Danbury Federal Correctional Facility. You do know Jay Crawford, don't you?" He was asking a question I was sure he already had the answer to.

I looked up at the man, then over at Lisa and back to him, swallowing hard. "Yes, Deputy, I know Jay Crawford very well."

"Good, so why don't you tell me where the hell he is?" the deputy asked, staring at me, stone-faced.

Jay

2

I foraged around the outside of the quaint ranch-style house, lifting everything that wasn't nailed down. It had always been my experience, from hanging out with my well-off buddy Kyle, that one out of every five summer-home owners left a key hidden somewhere on the property, just in case they had to send a repairman, had a friend coming by, or simply didn't want to take a chance of being locked out when they forgot the master key in their city house two and a half hours away.

So far I'd come up empty. I'd been to multiple houses that didn't have an alarm sign in front, and I still hadn't found a key. Not that it mattered. I'd go through a hundred if I had to. You see, breaking out of prison was the easy part; it was staying free in the middle of a manhunt that would prove to be difficult.

Nevertheless, I'd done what most would have thought impossible: I'd escaped from a maximum security prison and was far enough away that I didn't have to worry about dogs being on my heels. Unfortunately, I hadn't slept or eaten in almost two days.

I guess I should have thought this whole thing through just a little bit more. Escaping prison was something a man could do on his own. You don't really need anyone to plan an escape if you're truly motivated, which I was. But now that I was out, I realized that I definitely should have considered asking for help. I really wasn't looking to put in jeopardy the few friends I had left—at least not yet, not until I started working on the bigger picture. Besides, it was less of a risk asking folks to help you when you were face-to-face. You know, when there was no one around to read your mail or eavesdrop on your phone calls and visiting-room conversations.

I finally found what I was looking for under a flowerpot at the sixth house I checked. Six had always been my favorite number.

"Come to Daddy," I said with a smile, bending over to pick up the dirt-covered key. Once it was in my hand, I headed straight for the front door.

"Fuck!" I exhaled, trying my best to keep it together. I can't even begin to explain my frustration when the key wouldn't fit into the lock. After managing to sneak onto one of the ferries from New London, Connecticut, to Orient Point, New York, and then finding my way to East Hampton without rousing any suspicion, I had finally found a key, but it didn't work. It was demoralizing.

With a shrug of my shoulders, I walked around to the back door. It was a long shot, but maybe my luck hadn't quite run out yet. When the key slid into the back door lock and I heard it click, my heart wanted to sing *Hallelujah*.

Taking a quick check of my surroundings, I pushed the door open, waiting a full minute before I entered the house to see if some sort of alarm was going to go off, then locked the door behind me. The stale odor told me nobody had been there since the fall, which was a good sign, because it probably meant they wouldn't be back until late spring, and it was only March. I went straight for the fridge, where I found nothing of use, only some condiments and salad dressing. The freezer, however, was a different story. I found frozen vegetables, a whole pack of chicken parts, and a small box of Omaha steaks, all of which I removed. It was going to take them a few hours to thaw out, but I was going to eat good that night. Regrettably, I was hungry now, so I microwaved the vegetables, doctoring them with spices I found in the cabinets. I swear, until you spend ten years in prison, you never know how good something as simple as Green Giant vegetables can be.

After my stomach was full, I located the master bedroom and went straight to the closet. To remind me that I was caught up in a real-life drama, the clothing belonged to a man who had to be at least half a foot shorter than me, about two sizes smaller, and his feet were just as small. I exited the closet and went for the dresser. I fished around in a couple of drawers until I found something that was workable.

"Well, Jay, old boy, you can't lose with a sweat suit," I said, pulling out the navy blue fleece. Then I went through each room, randomly looking through drawers, closets, and dressers for any loose cash or more appropriate clothing. The only thing I found that would be remotely helpful was an old mayonnaise jar full of change. Not exactly a windfall, but at least it was filled with mostly silver coins, and not all pennies.

By the time I finished ransacking the place, it was dark and I was tired as hell. For now, this was a safe place, but eventually I'd have to formulate a plan to avoid being captured. I was not about to let that bitch who had me locked up in the first place hurt my son. I just hoped it wouldn't be too late.

Wil

3

I let out a long, aggravated sigh as I watched two United States deputy marshals walk out of my office. They'd just drilled me for the past hour about my friend Jay, who had apparently escaped from prison. I eased my 290-pound frame back behind my desk and into my chair, waiting until both men disappeared into the elevator before I picked up my phone. I dialed the only person who could possibly make sense of what the hell the deputies had just told me.

"Big Wil, what's up?" Kyle, my best friend of more than thirty-five years, answered. There was a tentativeness to his voice that made me think he'd been expecting my call.

"Jay escaped from prison," I told him. I was sitting on the edge of my seat, waiting to hear his reply. Kyle, Jay, our other friend Allen, and I had always been close, more like brothers than friends, but Kyle and Jay had a different kind of bond. I knew this news was going to hit him hard.

There was a slight pause on the line, which spoke volumes. Kyle wasn't normally one to hold back his opinion. "Yeah, I know," he finally responded. "The deputies raided my house about two hours ago. I'm still trying to calm Lisa down from the trauma of having all those men with guns seeing her naked."

"Raided your house? What the fuck is going on?" I shouted. His wife being naked registered, but I didn't want to touch that with a ten-foot pole. I did want to know why they felt the need to raid his house. I mean, couldn't they have stopped by his office like they'd done to me? Or did they know something I didn't?

"Jesus Christ, Kyle. You didn't help him escape, did you?"

"Come on, Wil," he growled angrily. "They raided my house because I'm the only one who has visited Jay regularly. I'm pretty sure I'm the prime suspect to have been his accomplice." There was a hint of annoyance in his tone, and I understood the reason for it. He was sending me on a little bit of a guilt trip.

Kyle had been on my ass for the last year to go see Jay more often, especially since he'd pulled some strings to have him transferred to Danbury, Connecticut, closer to us. I'd gone a few times, but the truth was, I hated all the bullshit I had to go through. The guards treated us visitors like we were the damn inmates. I wasn't about to get into that "you don't visit him enough" argument with Kyle again, so I ignored his comment. Besides, we had a much more important issue to discuss at the moment.

"You didn't answer my question, and those deputies who left here made it very clear that they think he had help. So right now, I need to know it wasn't you."

"No, Wil, I didn't help him...but I'm not saying I wouldn't if he'd asked," he replied in a dead serious tone that quite frankly scared the shit out of me.

"What the fuck? That's aiding and abetting a fugitive! They lock people up for shit like that. You could lose your family, your business, and more importantly your freedom behind Jay's bullshit."

"Wil," he said in a low, calm voice. "He's been in prison for ten years, and we both know he's innocent."

"Do we?" I asked. I wanted to believe Jay was innocent, but I had my doubts.

"What do you mean, do we? Of course we do. He's our best friend, remember? He wouldn't do anything like that."

"Look, Kyle, I'm just saying, none of us know what went on behind those closed doors, but you've seen the evidence. That girl Ashlee was beaten up, there was evidence of vaginal injuries, and she had his semen inside her. Who are we to say she was lying?"

"I can't believe what I'm hearing. Wil, Jay didn't rape that woman. She set him up." His voice rose with his anger.

"If you say so, man." I really didn't want to continue the conversation, and thankfully, I was given an out when I spotted a dark-suited figure headed toward my office. "Look, my director is headed this way. I'll give you a shout after work."

Malek Johnson, my boss of two years and fifteen years my junior, barely acknowledged my secretary Barbara as his short ass walked past her and into my office. Malek was one of those smooth-talking, brown-nosing Negroes who talked a good game to the white boys upstairs so that they thought he was a fucking genius, but he didn't know shit. If it weren't for me and the other department heads saving his ass all the time, he'd have been gone a long time ago.

"Everything all right, Wil? I heard you had a couple of cops come to see you." He lifted an eyebrow in a fake gesture of concern, which made my stomach turn a little. Guess he was on a fishing expedition.

"Yeah, two U.S. marshals wanted to ask me a few questions about an old high school buddy who escaped from prison yesterday." I laughed, trying my best to keep the mood light, in spite of the seriousness of the situation. Just the fact that I knew someone who had escaped from prison was embarrassing as hell. I swear I could see Malek's smug ass suppressing a smirk. "But it's nothing," I told him. "They just wanted to know if he'd made contact with me."

"And has he?" Malek asked sternly as he settled into the chair across from my desk.

"No, and I don't think he will."

"Good." He nodded, folding his hands in front of him. "Have you taken a look at our stock price today?" I tried to read his facial expression and his body language, but he was impenetrable.

I shook my head. "Not since the merger rumors."

There were a few rumors floating around about a possible merger or a buyout, but I had tried not to pay attention to them. Some type of shift was definitely in the air at the pharmaceutical company, but whether the change would be for good or for worse, I wasn't sure. I just knew I couldn't get sidetracked from what I was supposed to be doing. The best thing for me to do—the best thing for any of us to do—was to just keep doing our jobs and doing them well. That way, if a merger did happen, there was a chance we could remain employed.

"It's no longer rumor," Malek said. "The VP told me about it a week ago, and CNBC reported it today. Stock's up almost ten bucks and climbing. A company guy like you probably made out well on your profit sharing alone."

"I'm sure I've done all right." I smiled, because he was right. I'd held on to every share I'd been given or bought since the day I walked in the door twenty-five years ago.

"And I'm sure you'll continue to do all right, but there are a few people around here who won't." I wasn't sure what he meant by that, but I was relieved that it seemed the bad news wasn't directed at me. Either way, I didn't want to jinx my apparent good luck, so I kept my mouth shut.

Malek continued, "Wil, I need you to do something for me."

Even though I wanted him to think I was cool, calm, and collected, inside I was starting to become tense. Given the topic we were discussing, I could imagine several things he would ask me to do, and none of them were good.

I shrugged. "Sure, what's up?"

His eyes were cast downward. That was not a good sign. It's never a good thing when a man can't look another man in the eyes. Finally, he made eye contact.

"Like I told you before, the merger is going to happen. At least that's what they are calling it; but ultimately, we're being taken over. It's their CEO who's going to run things, which means his people. Upper management is going crazy trying to look lean so they keep their jobs." He looked out through my glass wall at several employees, the ones that I supervised, seated in their cubicles.

Dear Lord, if this man was in here to do what I thought he was about to do...

"What are you trying to say, Malek? Am I out of a job?"

He turned to me and shook his head. "No, but some of your people are going to have to go. I know you've been with the company awhile. Some of your employees have been working with you just as long. Which is what makes this so difficult."

I swallowed hard, trying not to throw up. My stomach was doing so many flips.

"I need you to cut half your staff."

"What?" I said in shock as I stood to my feet. I'll be honest and admit that a part of me was overjoyed it wasn't me being axed, but to have to deliver bad news to half of my employees—that was asking a lot.

"You can't be serious," I protested. "We barely get things done with the staff we have."

"Well, figure it out, 'cause I'm serious as hell," he replied, his tone all business and no sympathy.

"When do I have to do this?" I was beside myself.

"Tomorrow. Severance packages are being worked up as we speak, but we want all their IDs and computer passwords by tomorrow, end of day." He stood up from his chair. "I'm sorry, Wil. I know it's tough. Hell, it was tough for me just to come in here and ask you to do it, but our hands are tied."

I looked out at my employees. Some of those guys were like family. I'd been to their homes for barbecues, they'd been to mine; I'd gone to lunch with them, and they'd shared some of their personal problems. A couple of them even looked to me as a friend. I couldn't do this to them.

"Malek," I said to my boss as he was headed to the door. "I can't do this." I pointed to the window. "I can't do that to them."

He looked at me with not even a hint of compassion in his eyes. "It's part of your job, Wil, and if you can't do it, then we can find somebody who can, if you know what I mean."

The underlying threat did not go unnoticed. As much as I didn't want to see my team out of work, I had to look out for number one first, so I was quick to say, "If that's what you want me to do, then I'll do it."

The corners of his mouth raised, and then he said, "Thought so."

Allen

4

"I don't understand. I thought he was up for parole. Why would he do something stupid like this?" I asked Kyle, who'd picked me up from the subway and driven me home just to have this conversation.

"That seems to be the million-dollar question, Al," Kyle replied, pulling up in front of my house. His smooth, dark-skinned face was tense, like he was carrying the weight of the world on his short, muscular frame. "I just hope Jay doesn't do anything stupid and get himself killed."

"Tell me about it." I sighed, genuinely concerned. Jay had always been a wild card, even as a kid. "You, Wil, and Jay are the only family I have left, other than Cassie."

Kyle and I sat in his car silently, each of us lost in thoughts of our fugitive friend, until I reached for the door handle and he grabbed my wrist.

"Hey, there's still a chance the marshals might be contacting you like they did to me and Wil. You be careful. These guys have orders to shoot first and ask questions later." He gave me the sternest of looks.

"I will, but I doubt I'm even on their radar," I told him, and he nodded his agreement. The only reason we could both be so confident was because, unlike him and Wil, I'd never gone to see Jay in prison or spoken to him on the phone. I'd wanted to. Hell, twice I even drove down to North Carolina, where he spent his first three years incarcerated, but I just couldn't bring myself to see the closest person I had to a brother locked up like that. I did, however, give Kyle money to put in his commissary every month and a gift package every holiday, but nothing was ever in my name or official.

"Oh, and Al, if by chance Jay tries to contact you, tell him to stay away from my house and my office if he doesn't want to get caught. Wil's too. They've got people watching us."

I nodded, then stepped out of the car, heading up the walkway. I hadn't gone five feet before Kyle beeped his horn, rolling down his window with a goofy grin on his face. "Hey, on a happier note, how are things in paradise?"

"Everything's great. Couldn't be better." I was now grinning too. Kyle and Wil were always teasing me about my eight-month marriage. Cassie and I were the butt of every newlywed joke you could imagine. "Cassie's home. Why don't you come on in? I'll throw a couple of steaks on the grill and we can throw back some cold ones like the old days."

"Wish I could, but Lisa's been on the warpath ever since the marshals showed up at the house. I spend any time away from her and she'll think I'm conspiring with Jay. I'm going to take her and the girls out to the Melting Pot for dinner, see if I can get her off my back. Besides, don't nobody wanna be around you and Cassie with all that over-the-top kissy-face shit y'all be doing." He laughed, joking about how affectionate we were in public.

"What's the matter? You jealous?" I asked with a smirk.

"Damn right I'm jealous." He shook his head, looking disgusted. No man loved his wife more than Kyle loved Lisa, but my friend was an ass man, and no one had an ass like my wife. Fuck, nobody had a body like Cassie, period, that we knew personally. She was one of those women who had really big tits, a tiny waist, and shapely oversized hips that almost looked cartoonish, like Jessica Rabbit. Not to be bragging on the missus, but when she walked in the room, she turned heads—men and women.

"She's still sucking your dick without being prompted, isn't she?" he asked.

"Of course. She loves giving me head."

"Well, brother, you better enjoy that shit while you can, 'cause I'm here to tell you, it's not gonna last forever." There was no hiding the jealousy in his tone. "My wife ain't sucked my dick without being encouraged in fifteen years, unless it was my birthday, our anniversary, or she's pissed me the fuck off real bad."

"Stop hating, Kyle." I laughed.

"I'm not hating, Al. I've been married twenty years. I'm just predicting your future. You're no different than the rest of us, and neither is your wife."

I could hear him laughing as he pulled out of the driveway, and I made my way to the house feeling good about my current situation—at least the sexual part. The rest of it, well, that was something I needed to talk to my wife about.

"Cassie," I called out when I entered the house. I was home early, and I was actually a little surprised she wasn't laid out on the sofa watching Maury, Steve Wilkos, or Jerry Springer. My wife loved herself some trash TV.

With no sign of her on the first floor, I went directly to our bedroom on the second floor. I entered just as I heard the shower stop. The idea of Cassie being naked behind that door sent half the blood in my body straight to my groin.

I'd met Cassie a little less than four years ago, when she was working at the Library on Liberty Boulevard. She was this exotically beautiful biracial woman who really seemed to have her shit together, not just a pretty face with a dynamite body. I was so impressed that I'd gone to see her almost every day after work, and eventually we started going out for some very expensive dinners. Despite her being sixteen years younger, Cassie had won my heart right away, and I pursued her like I'd done for no other woman.

Not that she reciprocated my desire. For the first year, she made it very clear we weren't dating, although we did hook up a few times after a late night of partying. For the most part, it was more like we were hanging out and I had to pay. Not that I minded. Just being around her made me feel special; that is, until other guys started showing up and making their presence felt. Some of them were like me, hopelessly in love with the finest woman they'd ever seen, while others were just straight-up players after her body.

After a year, I finally worked up the courage to ask her where things were going between us. That's when she gave me the "I love you like a brother" speech and dropped the bomb on my head that she was moving in with some thug from Hollis, Queens. Well, to say I was devastated is an understatement, but that didn't stop me from continuing to visit her at work. What stopped me from seeing her was when her boyfriend's jealousy got out of hand. I tried to ignore him, but eventually an altercation ensued. I would love to call it a fight, but he whipped my ass so bad it would have been unfair to him to call it anything other than a massacre. I didn't get in one punch.

Needless to say, that was the last time I saw Cassie, until she showed up at my doorstep two years later, beaten half to death. She wouldn't let me take her to the hospital or call the police. It took me almost two months to nurse her back to health, but she finally recovered, telling everyone she could that I had saved her life. On Valentine's Day of that year, she slipped into my bed, told me she loved me, and then asked me to marry her. I accepted, on one condition: that she stop working and that we start a family. I was quite a bit older than her, and I didn't want to be paying for my kid's college education when I was eighty. She reluctantly agreed, and neither of us had regretted that decision—until today.

"Allen." The sound of Cassie's voice, along with the jasmine-scented steam flowing out of the bathroom and seducing my nostrils, snapped me out of my memories.

Cassie stepped into the bedroom wrapped in an oversized white towel, with her head wrapped in another towel. She reached up with her right hand and removed the towel covering her head, shaking out her dark, shoulder-length hair. At that moment, she looked like she could have been on a *Sports Illustrated* photo shoot. Every time I saw my wife, I was still stunned by her exotic beauty, as if I were seeing her for the first time.

"I wasn't expecting you home so early," she said.

"I wanted to surprise you."

She took a step into my personal space, kissing me with those succulent lips of hers. She slid her tongue into my mouth, and I could taste mint. As much as I wanted to, I just couldn't resist. I kissed her back, enjoying the sensation for a minute before I pulled back to speak my mind.

"Yeah, I wanted to surprise you the same way I was surprised when I went to take my boss out to lunch this afternoon and my debit card didn't work."

"Oh, shit." Her eyes opened wide as she took a step back, her body language screaming her guilt.

I may have acted like everything was fine for Kyle, but I'd come home to deal with what was becoming a constant problem.

"Allen..." she started.

"*Oh, shit* is right. Pretty fucking embarrassing, huh?" I snapped, raising my voice just enough to hold her attention.

If there was one thing I hated, it was confrontation, especially with Cassie, because I really did love her. But this time she'd left me no choice.

"So I called the bank to see what the problem was. You know what they told me?" I studied her face, and her expression revealed that she definitely did know. "They told me that I didn't have any money on my card because my beautiful wife—oh, and they mentioned how beautiful you were continually—withdrew five thousand dollars from my checking account."

She started gushing desperately, "Don't be mad at me, baby. I'm sorry. I'm so sorry. I should have called you. Let me make it up to you, please." Cassie took hold of my wrists, placing them on her hips so the towel she had wrapped around her fell to the ground. My eyes traveled up and down her nakedness, resting on her most distinctive feature.

My wife's smooth, almond-colored body was not just beautiful and sexy; it was a flawless canvas that had appeared on the covers of both *Maxim* and *Inked* magazines because of the bright green serpent tattoo that wrapped around her right leg, then made its way up her thigh and across her ass and back, over her left shoulder, stopping on her left breast as the head of a cobra. Her right breast was tattooed with a bright red apple.

I'm not really a tattoo guy; it's just not my thing, but her snake was like nothing I'd ever seen before, and even when I was mad, the damn thing seemed to hypnotize me. I couldn't help but stare as she reached between my legs and began unbuckling my belt.

"No, no, no. I know what you're trying to do, and we are not going to deal with this in the bedroom. I'm not going to allow it," I said, forcing myself to resist what my body wanted so badly.

"Not going to allow what?" She laughed, sliding to her knees as she held my erect penis in her soft hands.

"Stop. I mean it, Cassie," I protested weakly, placing my hand on her forehead. My palm barely made contact with her head, communicating just how conflicted I was about really wanting her to stop.

"So what are you saying? You're not going to allow me to suck your dick?" She shook her head at me pitifully, not giving me a chance to react before my penis was completely engulfed in her mouth. At that point, all I could do was let out a moan.

Less than five minutes later, I was laid out on the bed with my pants around my ankles, moaning like a little boy as my wife worked to bring me to orgasm. I opened my eyes and looked down. It just so happened to be the same time Cassie was looking up at me. The sensual look in her eyes as I watched her lips around the head of my dick sent electric shocks throughout my body. How had I ended up with such a stunningly beautiful, bright woman who was great in bed and great at giving head? It was a question I'd asked myself a million times.

"Oh, God." My chest was heaving as I threw my head back and looked up to the heavens. Call it blasphemy if you want, but I had to thank God as my body exploded in pleasure.

"Mmmm," Cassie moaned as she kissed and licked her way up my belly and to my chest. Once she made it past my neck and chin, she pressed her lips against mine, then pulled back and said, "You're not still mad at me, are you?"

Until she brought it up, I'd honestly forgotten that I'd come home to confront her. Cassie's head game was just that good. "I don't know what I am. Why would you take my money?"

"Allen, please, I'm sorry about your lunch, but I didn't take your money. I took *our* money." She tried to kiss me, but I resisted. "But if it will make things better between us, I'll put every nickel back in the account," she said sadly.

"No." I was so damn frustrated. She made me so weak with almost no effort on her part. "I want you to tell me why you stole my money."

"Stole? Is that what you call it when a wife takes money out of a joint account to try to better herself? Stealing?" She glared at me angrily. It was a look I almost never saw from her. She was usually a pretty agreeable person, which made for a peaceful home. But not now. Now she was pissed. She walked over to the dresser and brought back an envelope. "Here."

"What's this?" I asked, opening the envelope.

"It's a cashier's check for five thousand dollars made out to York College. They have a special program I got accepted to for people like me who are misplaced in the workforce. I wasn't going to bring it up until tonight, because I wanted it to be a surprise. I wanted to make you proud. You did say you'd pay for me to go to school and further my education, didn't you?"

"Yeah, I did." My shoulders sagged with regret. I shouldn't have jumped to conclusions.

"Well, don't worry about it. I don't need you to pay for me to go to school. I can get my old job back any time I want. I thought you were different, Allen." On that note, she walked out of the room, making me feel like a horse's ass. All I could do was jump up with the check in my hand, following after her, begging.

"Baby, baby, please, please! I'm sorry. You can have the money. You can have all my money."

Kyle

5

I left Allen's house feeling pretty shitty for lying to him about taking Lisa and the girls to dinner, but I didn't really have a choice. My wife and Wil's wife, Diane, had made it pretty damn clear they didn't like or trust Cassie and expected us to stay as far away from her as humanly possible. This bad blood stemmed not only from Cassie being so much younger than us, but from Allen's bachelor party, which neither Wil nor I, as co–best men, had anything to do with planning. Believe it or not, Cassie had hosted and set up Allen's bachelor party. A bride hosting her future husband's bachelor party was a first for me, and I was pretty skeptical, but I will say this much: If by chance I ever get married again, I'm going to have her host mine too, because that shit was off the damn chain. I'd never seen so many fine naked women and lewd acts in my entire life. It was like a virtual reality porno, and if I hadn't been there to witness it myself, I wouldn't have believed it.

What fucked everything up was that some idiot filmed it on his phone and his wife found the recording. Of course, she decided she needed to share it with everyone else's wives, and the next thing we knew, the rest of us were in the doghouse, some worse than others. It took me almost a month before Lisa calmed down, two months before Diane spoke to Wil, and we were only watching the action. I knew a couple of guys who were getting divorced right now because they were filmed with their dicks inside the pussy. Thank God I hadn't been that stupid, because Lisa would have seen divorce as letting me off too easy. She would have killed me.

Speaking of Lisa, her ringtone chirped and I answered it via Bluetooth in the car. "Hey, hon."

"Hey, you still at the office?" she asked.

"No, I just dropped off Allen. I'm headed home."

"Okay, I'm at Trader Joe's. You want anything?"

"No, I'm good," I replied. She stayed silent. "Lee, you okay?"

"No, I'm not. I don't think I'll ever be okay," she admitted. "Every time I close my eyes I see men pointing guns at me."

I bit my bottom lip. I hated that she felt that way. "Hey, this is going to end soon."

"Is it? Kyle, they have a Con Ed truck parked across the street. It hasn't moved since it pulled in front this morning."

Her words set off an alarm in my mind. I'd seen a Con Ed truck parked in front of my office too, which hadn't seemed unusual to me, until now. I suppose I shouldn't have been surprised. It made sense that they were going to be on me like flies on shit, considering I was the only person who'd visited Jay regularly.

"Kyle, I need to know. Have you heard from him? Have you been talking to Jay?" Lisa asked me.

Now it was my turn to get quiet. It had been one long day. Operating a chain of beauty supply stores in a beauty-obsessed world was hard work, and the last thing I wanted after such a hectic day was to be interrogated by my wife. Hell, I might have almost preferred another visit from the feds.

"No, babe," I said for the thousandth time, wishing she would realize that my answer was not going to change.

"Don't you lie to me, Kyle," Lisa pressed. I could just imagine her pointing at me through the phone, her other hand situated on her hip. "You expect me to believe that Jay's been on the run the past twenty-four hours and he hasn't tried to hit up his personal ATM machine? I'm sorry, but I don't believe it. I heard what you said to Wil."

"Look, Lisa, what the hell do you want me to do? I'm telling you the truth, so give me a break, a'ight?" I slammed my hand on the dash. Usually I tried to control my temper when my wife and I had disagreements, but I was under a lot of pressure, and she was starting to get on my nerves.

"Don't play with me, Kyle. This is serious. Lie to me and you're just sleeping on the couch, but you lie to them, and you and Jay might end up cellmates. Is that what you want, Kyle? Huh? Is that what you want?"

I sighed. Once Lisa got worked up, there was no getting her to pump her brakes. All I could do was allow her to keep going until she ran out of gas.

"No, Lisa. You know that's not what I want," I said as I turned onto my block.

"Then what do you want?"

"I don't know, peace on earth...goodwill to all men."

"Can you be serious for a damn second?"

On the corner across from my house, I spotted the Con Ed truck Lisa had told me about. That was enough to sober up my mood for sure. "Look, I'm pulling up to the house now. I'll be there in a minute, and when you get home we'll finish this conversation. Okay?"

"Yeah, whatever, Kyle," Lisa said.

"Love you," I said, hoping to end the call on a good note.

"Mm-hmm. Sure you do." She hung up.

I shook my head as I parked in the driveway, thinking, *Where the fuck is Jay, and what is it going to take for my life to get back to normal now?*

Jay

6

"In a daring daytime jailbreak, Jay Crawford, a convicted rapist, escaped from Danbury Federal Correctional Facility yesterday. Crawford, who is considered to be armed and dangerous, has ties to the Queens area, where he is suspected to be hiding. Officials are asking anyone who might have seen this man, or who has information on his whereabouts, to contact authorities immediately. Police say he is armed and dangerous, and they are advising that if you see him, do not approach him."

"Armed and dangerous my ass," I spat, throwing a steak bone at the TV, then picking up the remote to turn off the news. I couldn't watch that bullshit one fucking minute more. It was hard enough being on the run without those assholes plastering my face across the TV like I was some rabid dog who needed to be put down.

I got up and stormed into the bathroom.

"Ugghhh!" I walked over to the sink, slamming my hands down on the basin as I stared at myself in the mirror. I had dreamed about my freedom for so long that I'd conjured up this idea that it was going to be easy. I'd neglected to consider the reality that being a fugitive was much harder than being an average free citizen. With my picture all over TV, my chances of remaining free were now slim to none. I hadn't planned for them to be on my ass this fast. Now I understood what a mistake that had been.

I stared at myself for a moment, feeling stupid and hopeless, until an idea popped into my head. I needed to change my appearance from the picture they'd shown on the news. In that photo, I looked a little like Rick Ross. I wore my facial hair identical to how he wore his. The only difference was that I wasn't bald, but that could easily be fixed.

I sifted through the medicine cabinet and the drawers in the bathroom until I found a pack of Bic razors. Turning on the water, I lathered my face with a bar of soap and got to shaving. In a matter of twenty minutes, my head and my face were as smooth as an ice rink.

"Who the fuck are you?" I laughed as I looked at myself, turning my head left to right to check out my profile. My own children wouldn't have recognized me. So those million folks who'd just watched the news surely wouldn't be able to recognize me either. I burst out laughing again. I almost felt sorry for every Rick Ross–looking man who was going to get stopped by the police thanks to the media. Their efforts were now all in vain. As a matter of fact, I was so sure no one would recognize me that I felt confident enough to test it.

I took a shower, enjoying the feeling of the warm water pouring over my head and down my body. I truly wished that I could stand there forever. Finally, a shower where I didn't have to watch my ass, literally. Once I finished cleansing all the grime that had built up over the last day, I put on the sweat suit. I wasn't about to wear no other dude's underwear, even if we had been the same size, so I went commando, washing mine out and leaving it on the sink to dry.

I walked a mile to the small Main Street in town, carrying the jar of coins in a knapsack I found in a bedroom closet. I felt bad stealing the money, but I was desperate. I found the grocery store, which, to my relief, had a Coinstar machine. After dumping all the change into the machine, I was surprised to end up with $155.60. It was more than enough to buy myself something that I hadn't had in a very long time and had been dreaming about. It was time for a beer. I slipped out of the grocery store and went to find a bar.

It didn't take me long to spot one on the corner. In fact, there seemed to be bars up and down the street in this tiny town. I guess all the summer residents liked to get their drink on or something. I picked a bar that looked relatively dark inside. Sure, I had changed my appearance, but this would be the perfect way to test my new look. The dim lighting would make me feel a little more secure as I took this chance of being around people for the first time since my picture had been posted.

I walked into the bar and took a moment to check out the atmosphere. It wasn't too crowded, and the few patrons sitting at the bar didn't look like the type of people who'd be trying to make small talk with me. One guy was sitting with his head hung so low that his face was practically in his glass of beer. Whatever he was depressed about, I doubted he would even notice my presence, so I approached the bar near him to order a drink.

"What can I get you?" the bartender, a white woman in her mid-forties, asked as I sat down on a barstool.

"Beer, please," I said, feeling my heart pounding against my ribs.

"What kind?" she asked, motioning to the vast array of beers on tap. Nothing about her demeanor made me think she recognized me, so I relaxed slightly.

Of course, I wasn't about to tell her that after ten years behind bars, I didn't care what kind it was as long as it was alcoholic, so I just shrugged. "You know what? Why don't you pick one for me?"

She laughed. "Okay, one bartender's choice, coming up."

As I waited for the beer, I listened to the song playing from an old CD player above the bar, smiling when I realized that it was one of 50 Cent's earlier hits. That song was on the radio almost constantly during the year before I was sent to prison. I wondered if the bar had bothered to update its CD collection in the ten years since then.

"Here you go." The bartender slid the beer in front of me. "One Blue Moon."

"Thanks." I wrapped my hands around that cold one and savored the moment. I didn't want to rush this long-awaited experience. I looked down and stared at the tiny bubbles bursting in the foam for a minute.

"Everything okay?" the bartender asked.

I nodded and quickly raised the glass to my lips. No need for her to think I was a freak. That would only cement me in her memory if anyone ever came in here asking about a fugitive. I got a whiff of orange, which seemed strange but good, and then, after just a taste on my tongue, I knew the whole thing about savoring was out the window. I guzzled that beer down like a frat boy and didn't come up for air until the last drop slid down my throat.

"Ahhhh." I set the glass down on the bar, pounding my fist on my chest to release the air bubble that was stuck. Had I been home with my feet kicked up, I probably would have let out a loud burp, but I was not trying to attract any unnecessary attention at the moment. "Wow, that was nice. I could have sworn I tasted a little bit of orange."

"You did," the bartender said with a smile as she placed another beer in front of me.

I held up my hand, shaking my head. "Oh, no, I'm good with one right now."

"This one is on—" She stopped speaking suddenly.

"The house? It's on the house?" I finished her sentence with a cocky smirk.

Jay, you still got it, bruh, I thought. I might have been locked up for a while, but I always did have a way with the ladies. This one wasn't really my type—I preferred my women a little darker—but shit, I'd fuck her for sure, just to end my ten-year dry spell.

She picked up on my vibe, but it turned out she wasn't hitting on me after all. "No, sorry, honey. It's from the, uh, lady over there." She nodded toward the other end of the bar.

I glanced left down the bar to see a heavily made-up blonde with a huge pair of tits, waving at me. I couldn't really make out her face, especially since the bar was so dim, but her titties alone had me intrigued. I lifted my drink in her direction, and she did the same.

"Don't do it, bro."

I turned around and saw an average-looking black woman of average height, standing there with her hands on her hips. No acrylic nails, just plain, normal-length nails. As a matter of fact, everything about her was pretty plain. She wasn't a beauty queen, but she wasn't a dog either. Life hadn't been too hard on her. Seemed like an ordinary girl who lived an ordinary life.

She was rocking back and forth from one leg to the other. "She gets you motherfuckers every time," she said.

"Gets us? What are you talking about?"

"Can't you motherfuckers tell a man from a woman? I swear if you weren't black I would've just sat back and watched, laughing my ass off."

"Man from a woman?" I glanced over at the blonde, who had now stood up. She had to be at least six foot three in those heels. The Amazon started to walk over to me, and when she lifted her arm to wave at me again, I noticed just how huge her damn hands were.

I looked back at the woman who'd given me the warning, and she folded her arms over her chest, eyebrows raised, as if to say, *I told you so.*

"Oh, hell no!" I said to the bartender, pushing the beer right back at her. When the dude who had been slumped in his beer before lifted his head and looked in my direction, I realized I'd been a little louder than I should have. I dialed back the volume a little and said, "I can pay for my own beer."

"Elle is harmless. Ain't that right, Elle?" the black woman said as the giant approached us. She was definitely getting a kick out of watching me squirm in front of this dude in a dress.

"That depends," Elle replied with eyebrows raised suggestively. When I gathered the courage to make eye contact, he winked at me and blew me a kiss.

I shook my head and started to say, "Sorry, dude, but—"

Elle raised a hand to stop me. "No need to explain. If you need me, I'll be right over here." With that, Elle switched back over to the seat he'd been occupying before, not seeming the least bit bothered by my rejection.

I sighed and turned my attention back to the bartender. "I think I'm going to need something stronger than a beer." Shit, times sure had changed since the last time I was in a bar.

"Hey, Lynn," my new friend said, raising two fingers as she

took the seat next to me. "Get me and the gentleman here a shot of tequila and put it on my tab."

"Oh, no, no," I said, raising my hand in protest. She was getting a little too friendly, and I didn't think I was in a position to be getting to know anyone, seeing as how I was a federal fugitive and all. Of course, she didn't know that, so she assumed I was turning her down for another reason.

"You too good to drink with the only sister in the bar, huh?"

"No, I actually prefer my women dark and lovely. It's just that—" I stopped myself, realizing I had no legitimate excuse to give her. I didn't want to risk pissing her off, so I finally said, "Never mind. I'd love to drink with you."

"Good." She extended her hand. "By the way, I'm Tina."

"I'm J—Johnny," I said, almost making the mistake of giving her my real name.

"So what brings you around these parts this time of year, Johnny?"

I hadn't planned on coming out to converse with anyone, so I wasn't too quick on my feet, but I managed to say the first thing that came to mind. "Uh, construction. I'm working on a house," I said as the bartender slid two shots in front of us.

"So, are you going to drink that or just babysit it all night?" Tina said when I took a little too much time to pick up the shot glass.

I looked over at her. She was smiling and laughing at her own joke. She had a cute laugh, and slight dimples in her round face. She had a few extra pounds on her, probably the result of a kid or two, but she wasn't fat. Most brothers I know would have called her thick, which I liked just fine.

"I haven't had a shot in a long time. I drink this with a pretty lady like you around and I might not know how to act."

Tina stopped laughing and leaned in a little closer. "Honey, a couple more shots and all you need be worried about is where you're going to take me to fuck."

I was stunned—and my dick jumped to attention. I mean, I was horny as shit, but I hadn't expected her to be so forward. *What if all women are this fast now?* I wondered. That was a change a newly freed brother could get used to.

"You're bold, Tina. I like that. And I like the way you think." I picked up my shot of tequila and she did the same, both of us throwing them back at the same time.

Ten minutes and a couple shots later, I was driving Tina's car to the house while she gave me one hell of a blow job. My fear of being discovered as a fugitive was only a distant thought somewhere in the back of my drunken mind at this point. By the time we got to the house, I'd already gotten my first nut of the night, which was good, because with that out of the way, I planned to take my time doing every last thing I'd been dreaming about for the past ten years.

Wil

7

The next morning, I met with Malek, two members of company security, and someone from HR on the executive floor to go over protocol. What they wanted me to do was so impersonal and just wrong on so many levels. Unfortunately, I needed the job just as much as the people I was about to fire, so a half hour later, I was sitting in the conference room with two members of security posted outside the door, about to fire two single mothers, a guy with a pregnant wife and three kids at home, and two people I'd been working with for almost fifteen years.

I stared out at them through the glass partition, wishing that I could magically make things better—or perhaps go on the run with Jay. This was crazy. I was about to devastate the lives of so many people. But like Malek said, it was part of the job.

I hit a button on the conference room table and got my secretary on the intercom. "Barbara, can you ask June, Tom, Kwali, Maria Lopez, Angel, Malachi, and John Monroe to come in here, please?"

"Yes, right away, Mr. Duncan," she replied.

I ended the call and waited for the employees to come to the conference room. The ones I'd chosen weren't bad people or bad employees; they just brought the least to the company.

A few minutes later, they all filed in and took seats around the conference table. Before I even started talking, I could tell that they already knew I didn't have good news. Maybe it was the security guards out front that gave it away, or maybe it was the pained expression on my own face. I didn't want to prolong this tension any longer than I had to, so I stood and cleared my throat.

"I know you're all wondering why I called you in h—"

"No." John Monroe cut me off. "I'm wondering why the hell security is posted outside the door." His comment made everyone turn to the door then back to me.

"Look, I'm sure you all heard about the merger—"

"Cut the bull, Wil, and tell us what's going on." This time I was cut off by Maria Lopez, a feisty single mother who'd been in our department five years.

"Okay." There was no use insulting their intelligence with a bunch of empty platitudes about what wonderful people they were, what valued employees they'd been, and blah, blah, blah. It wouldn't lessen the blow when I let them go, so there was no sense in saying it.

I took a deep breath and said what needed saying. "I have to let all of you go. It's not my call. This decision was made upstairs. I really didn't have a choice."

Angel broke out in tears instantly. June went to rest a reassuring arm around Angel's shoulder, but not before Angel expressed to me how she felt. "I'm in my twenties, but June is fifty-five years old, raising two kids. Where is she going to find another job? Do you know how hard it's going to be for her to start all over again in the workforce with all these kids fresh out of college willing to work for peanuts?"

I tried to explain. "Look, Angel, it's not my fault."

"Fuck you, Wil!" Tom said, jumping up from his seat. "You think we're stupid. They didn't choose who was going to be let go. You did."

"They didn't fire *you*, did they?" John snapped at me, but I declined to respond. "What the fuck am I supposed to tell my wife?"

"I don't know, John. I really don't know," I told him, wishing like hell I hadn't been the one to deliver this news to them.

"Of course you don't know," John replied, pushing his chair away from the table. "You've still got your fucking job."

"I thought you were my friend," Maria chimed in, giving me the finger with both hands.

"I am your friend, Maria, but this is out of my hands," I said, hating how hollow the words sounded as they left my mouth. "Look, I know this is screwed up, but if it's any consolation, each of you will be receiving a three-month severance package."

"Three months!" Malachi said. "My wife has sickle cell anemia. You know that! How the hell am I supposed to pay for her meds and doctor visits after the three months is up?"

I shook my head. I'd completely forgotten his wife was sick. "I can try to push for a six-month severance package," I said, not knowing if the big guys would go for it, but I was at least willing to try. I had to put myself in their place. I would want someone to do all they could on my behalf.

Malachi sucked his teeth. "You just don't get it, man."

He was right. I didn't get it, and I really didn't want to. Still, I wanted to help. "Then there's always unemployment while you look for another job."

I didn't know why I'd said that when it was clear that nothing

I could say would soften the blow. They were looking at me as though I was a white dude who showed up at the Million Man March wearing a white hood.

I allowed them to stew for a couple minutes longer before they eventually filed out of the conference room. An hour later, they'd all been escorted off the property by security, and I was sitting behind my desk. This was too much. It felt as if the four walls of my office were closing in on me. I had to step out for a minute and get some air.

When I walked out of my office, Barbara was sitting there with the phone in her hand. "Hold my calls. I'm going to lunch," I told her. She nodded, and I headed for the elevator.

Outside the building, the first thing I saw was a silver-and-black Rolls-Royce Ghost sitting at the curb. I was about to take a walk to clear my head, until the driver opened the rear door and I recognized the occupant.

"Wil," he shouted. With everything going on at work right now, he was not the person I wanted to see. He shouted my name again. "Wil!"

Knowing that he was not going to let me ignore him, I turned, and we made eye contact. He smiled, waving me over.

Could this day get any worse? I thought.

"Uncle LC, it's . . . good to see you."

Jay

8

I wasn't sure what time it was, but I opened my eyes to complete darkness—with the exception of the blue-and-red lights that were dancing on the walls. I rubbed my eyes, hoping I was just seeing things, but as I focused my vision, the lights were still there. It was like a shock wave surging through my body when it hit me where those lights were coming from.

Cops! Damn! How the fuck did they find me?

I glanced over at the empty space next to me. Tina was gone. *Fuck! Fuck! Fuck! Fuck!* She'd turned me in. After all I'd gone through to get this far, how the hell could I have been so stupid as to bring her to my safe place? I never should have taken those damn shots.

I slid out of bed, then ducked down and crept over to the window. Leaning my back up against the wall, I slowly pushed the curtain aside and peeked out.

"Crap!" I groaned under my breath, counting five cop cars parked out front before quickly letting the curtain go.

I buried my forehead in my palms as I momentarily contemplated the situation I was in. Fuck it, I decided, I was just going to have to make a run for it, because there was no way I was going back to that damn prison.

As I looked around, making a quick mental note of my options, I grabbed my sweatpants and shirt off the floor. Exiting by the front door was definitely out of the question, so I had only one other way out. I dressed in a hurry and headed barefoot out of the room. There was no time to search for my prison-issued sneakers.

Standing at the back door with my hand on the doorknob, I tried to envision the scene I was about to enter. Would they shoot to kill? If I got four warning shots in the back, then so be it, I decided. I'd rather die than go back to prison, unable to accomplish what I needed to out here in the world.

Just as I was about to run out, I heard voices. They had the back door surrounded too, and they were probably going to kick it in at any minute. Four shots in the back was one thing, but looking a bullet in the eye was something totally different. I let go of the doorknob and then backpedaled into the kitchen.

"Think, Jay, think," I said.

Within seconds, another plan had popped into my head. I quickly turned and took off for the basement, creeping down the stairs until I was in front of the heavy metal bulkhead doors that led outside. I listened intently but didn't hear any voices, so I slowly slipped the metal latch open, then pushed the door open an inch to peer outside. There were two cops about fifty feet away, standing on either side of the back door, oblivious to me. I also saw that there was a wooded preserve at the edge of the property.

Gingerly, I pushed open the metal door and slithered through it just as the cops kicked in the back door, yelling, "Police!" as they went into the house. I jumped up and took off toward the woods.

"Hey, you hear that?" I heard someone yell just as I made it to the edge of the woods. "He's on the move!"

I didn't waste time looking back to see where the voices were coming from. I just darted through the woods, ignoring all the sticks and leaves that were poking my bare feet. Keeping my arms out in front of me, I ran aimlessly through the darkness, hoping my hands would hit any obstacles before my face did. Unfortunately, my hands couldn't warn my feet about the trail of stumps and logs I was running up on when I tripped.

"Shit!" I could feel my body falling as if it were all happening in slow motion, but everything was still happening too quickly for me to put my hands out and catch my fall. I closed my eyes and braced myself as I felt my body slam against the ground much harder than expected.

When I opened my eyes, I was lying on the ground, not in the woods, not in someone's random backyard or even a cell, but... next to the bed. I was breathing heavily and sweating profusely. I took a second to look around as I regained consciousness and understood what was happening. I wasn't in the woods; I was still in the bedroom. I hadn't fallen on a mound of rocks or logs and cracked my head open; I'd fallen out of the bed. Hell, it was a dream—or, more accurately, a huge fucking nightmare.

I sat there on the floor and closed my eyes for a moment to clear my mind. I wanted to get rid of all those negative thoughts, but there weren't too many positive thoughts I could muster up to replace them. Then thoughts of last night came to mind, thoughts of mind-blowing sex with Tina. A smile crept on my face. I'd given a pretty amazing performance, if I did say so myself. Just thinking about my rendezvous with Tina made a brotha stiff. And if I was lucky, perhaps I could have an encore.

I slid up off the floor and climbed back into the bed, throwing the covers over myself. Then I rolled over with an extended arm, ready to pull Tina close to me to see if we could start round two. Imagine my shock when all I felt was a cold, empty spot. I sat up and looked at the empty space. In the predawn light I could see that the pillow had an indentation where her head had been, and there was a little makeup on the pillowcase, so at least I knew she had really been there, but where had she gone?

"Tina?" I called out, thinking she was in the bathroom or something, but she didn't answer.

A flickering light in the corner caught my attention, and I realized the TV was on with the sound muted. Then I recalled that Tina had asked if it was okay to turn the TV on because she always fell asleep to the television light. At the time, still half-drunk and 100 percent sexually satisfied, I'd said yes without even thinking about it. Now I realized what a mistake that had been. Was it possible that she'd seen the news, a replay of the story about the fugitive on the run? What if my shaved head wasn't the foolproof disguise I'd thought it was?

"Fuck, fuck, fuck," I scolded myself along with a triple thump to the dome. How could I have been so stupid? Pussy was always a man's downfall. I should have just drunk my damn beer and carried my ass home. Now look at me. Trying to get fucked now had me fucked.

I looked to the nightstand for the TV remote, and that's when I saw the note she'd left. I picked it up and read it: *I really enjoyed last night. Have to work this morning. Sorry I didn't say good-bye, but you were sleeping like a baby. When you get a chance, give me a call.* Her cell phone number was written on the bottom.

I let out a sigh of relief. At least I knew she wasn't off getting the cops and trying to get reward money for my capture. But did that really mean I was safe? Tina knew my face. It was very possible she'd end up seeing the news report, and she might recognize me. No matter how good the sex was, she could still decide to contact the police, and then she'd know exactly where to bring them to find me. That wasn't a chance I was willing to take, especially after the nightmare I'd had.

I hopped out of the bed and gathered my clothes. It was time to move on. But where to?

Wil

9

"Wil," my uncle said, scooting over in the backseat. "Get inside."

That was just like him. There was no asking, just giving orders. He was a very powerful man used to being obeyed. Well, I wasn't one of his family flunkies, nor would I ever be—unlike my father, who had never been able to say no.

"Sorry, Uncle LC," I said as I walked down the steps, "but I was just about to—"

"Get in the car."

"Actually, I—"

"Get in the car, nephew," he said with impatient authority. He patted the seat next to him, then faced front, his way of letting me know that this was not a request. I put my hands on my waist and looked up to the sky in exasperation before I completed the walk to the car and slid in. *Son of a bitch*, I thought, looking over at him just as the driver closed the door behind me.

LC Duncan was my father's brother and probably the most successful African American car dealer in the country, among other things. He and my old man were tight. Maybe if my pops hadn't been glued to his brother at the hip, he would have been around his family more. Seemed like whenever Uncle LC scouted family members to be a part of his business matters, everything else in their lives took a backseat. And now, on what had possibly been my worst day on the job, here came Uncle LC to ruin my mood even more.

Uncle LC looked at the driver and gave him a slight head nod. The driver took off up the block.

I said nothing. He was the one who wanted me to come along for the ride, so clearly he had something he wanted to say. I figured I'd let him do all the talking. We rode for a good half mile before he finally spoke up.

"I know you don't really care for me, nephew. I can't honestly say I know why, but I've guessed over the years that it has something to do with your father, or maybe even perhaps something your mother has said."

"My mother has nothing to do with this," I was quick to say. My mother was a woman with class and grace.

"Nonetheless, I'm your uncle," he continued. "No matter what you think of me, Wil, you are my family. I love you, and I'll always be here for you. There is nothing you can't come to me for and get."

He sounded sincere enough. Besides, if I knew one thing about Uncle LC, it was that he didn't bullshit. If he didn't mean it, he didn't say it. "I appreciate that," I said to him, keeping my tone neutral, "but what is it you really want?" He also didn't like to waste his time, so I figured I might as well help him get to his point quickly.

"I have something very important to tell you, Wil," he said. "Something sad. I needed to tell you face-to-face." He looked out of the dark-tinted window, as if whatever he wanted to say made it hard for him to look me in the face.

"What is it?" I asked, feeling a growing sense of dread.

He turned to look at me but could only maintain eye contact for a split second when he told me, "Trent is dead." He turned his attention back out of the window.

It took a moment for his words to register. "Wha...what do you mean?"

LC faced me again. "He ran into a little trouble out in Los Angeles."

"Los Angeles? I guess that con-man shit finally caught up with him." My brother and I didn't get along too much, but that was because I wanted him to do better, to be better. I wanted him to get an honest job and stop conning women out of their life savings. It was something he'd been doing for the past twenty years—very successfully, I might add.

"Something like that," he said solemnly.

"He was working for you, wasn't he?"

He broke eye contact again, and it was obvious he'd had something to do with my brother being in Los Angeles. As a child, I had heard my mother whispering to her girlfriends a few times that Uncle LC's business was about more than just selling cars. Because of that, I grew up suspicious of him, believing that there was some type of criminal enterprise beneath all his wealth and success. Now I understood that it was highly likely Trent was doing something illegal for my uncle when he died.

I can't describe the depth of the disdain I felt for my uncle all of a sudden. Before, it was a simple case of dislike, but now, with my brother's blood on his hands, it was pure hatred.

"Yes, he was working for me," LC confirmed. "It's what your father wanted. Unlike you, he always saw the wild child in your brother. Your mother saw it too."

"You know nothing about my mother," I spat. He was starting to walk on sacred soil. "My mother was a good woman. She rarely said a bad word against my father or any of his family members," I said, "but a drunken tongue doesn't lie. I thought it was the wine talking when she said you and my father were bad men, but now I think she was being too kind. You're not just bad; you're lowlife scum."

LC caught me off guard when he grabbed my arm. "Speak of me how you wish," he said, glaring into my eyes, "but my brother, your father, was a good man. He would have done anything for you all."

"Yeah," I said, jerking my arm from his grasp. "Anything but be there for us."

My uncle knew he had no comeback to the truth. Nothing justified a man not being there for his family. He of all people knew that.

I looked at my watch. "My lunch is almost over. Your driver can drop me off at this deli on the corner right there. I'll walk back to work."

Uncle LC and the driver made eye contact. LC nodded for the driver to do what I'd asked, and the driver pulled over. I went to open the door once the car stopped.

"What about my brother? Where is he? I've got to start making arrangements." The fact that he was dead had finally hit me. I could feel tears welling up.

"J. Foster Phillips Funeral Home on Linden Boulevard. But you don't have to worry. I've taken care of everything."

"I'm sure you have. That's probably why he's dead."

With that information, I got out and closed the door, holding in my tears for my brother until my uncle's car was out of sight. I didn't know who was worse, Uncle LC or the grim reaper. I was starting to believe they were one and the same.

Allen

10

"So that's it in a nutshell, Al. Trent's dead, and I'm going to need you to be a pallbearer," Wil explained over the phone as I put on my robe, stepped out of my bedroom, and shut the door behind me.

If he'd called two minutes earlier, I wouldn't have answered the phone, because Cassie and I had finally reconciled after our latest fight. After two days of ass-kissing and pleading for her not to go back to work, I'd just been taken off of pussy punishment, and I was making the best of it by leaving my wife naked, thirsty, and thoroughly satisfied. I headed downstairs to get a bottle of wine.

"Whatever you need, you know I'm there for you." I tried my best to comfort him. Wil had always been one of those guys who guarded his feelings, and since he and Trent didn't really get along, I couldn't tell how he felt about his brother's death. I just knew it couldn't be good to find out your little brother had died. He was going to need support from all of his friends.

"You speak to Kyle?" I asked.

"No, not yet. Me and him still aren't seeing eye to eye on Jay's escape. I think he's a little pissed off." Wil sounded more emotional about his disagreement with Kyle than he did his brother's death.

"You should call him. You know he'd want to be there for you. Don't let this thing with Jay tear us apart any more than it has, Wil."

"Yeah, I know. You're right. I'll give him a call." Wil sighed. "Speaking of Jay, you heard anything about his whereabouts?"

"Nah, just what I read online. They did up the reward on him from thirty grand to fifty, and they think he's headed to Texas to confront that g—" I stopped in my tracks as I entered the kitchen. "What the fuck!"

"You all right, Al?" Wil asked.

"Yeah, I'm okay. I almost dropped a bottle of wine. Let me call you back." I hung up the phone without waiting for his response. I didn't want to lie to Wil, but I also didn't feel I had a choice when our other best friend, the fugitive, was sitting at my kitchen table, shushing me with a finger over his lips.

"Hey, Al, long time no see." He looked different with a bald head and twenty pounds of muscle, but there was no mistaking that the voice belonged to Jay Crawford. "Hope you don't mind, I made myself something to eat." Jay lifted a sandwich he'd half devoured.

I was speechless for a minute. All I could do was stare at him with my mouth hanging open.

"What the hell are you doing here?" I hissed. "You've got half the cops in New York and the U.S. Marshals looking for you."

"I know, and I'm sorry." He placed the sandwich back on the plate, wiping his hands on his pants leg as he stood up and took a step toward me. When he was close enough, we did what came natural: We hugged, tight and firm.

"I missed you so much, Al," he said, his voice cracking and his eyes filling up with tears. I have to admit I felt my eyes getting misty too.

We broke the hug, standing two feet apart and staring at one another, until he wiped away his tears and said, "I need your help. I really need your help."

"Sure, sure," I replied. At that moment, I was so emotional he could have asked me to rob a bank and I would have done it.

"Thanks." He sounded relieved, and I saw some of the tension in his face relax.

Then, as if our emotional moment had never happened, he walked back over to the kitchen table and sat down in front of his meal again, taking an enormous bite. "This corned beef is the bomb. Where'd you get it from? Katz's Deli?"

"Yeah, my wife picks it up every Saturday when she teaches yoga in the city," I said, strangely reassured to be making small talk instead of dealing with the elephant in the room.

He reached over and picked up the Corona next to his plate. Two long swigs later, he belched, announcing, "Damn, that was good. You don't mind making a beer run before we go to bed, do you?" Yep, he was starting to sound like the old Jay.

"What do you mean *we*? You planning on spending the night?"

"Yeah, didn't you hear me before? I need your help, Al. Help, like in a place to stay tonight."

I'd heard him now, loud and clearer than I really wanted to. He was asking me to jeopardize my own freedom to protect his. I thought he just needed a hot meal and some cash, but evidently he was expecting to stay. The look on my face must have said it all.

"Look, I'm not trying to jam you up, dawg. I just need a place to crash for a couple of days until I can make some arrangements."

"I don't know, Jay. You're putting me in a really bad position. I got a wife to think about. I help you and we could go to jail."

"I wouldn't be here if I had another choice, Al," he pleaded.

"He's right, Allen." Cassie's voice startled both of us. She appeared in the doorway with her sexy-ass silhouette. The small amount of light was hitting her waist and all her curves. I was thankful she was wearing a teddy, because she had a habit of walking around naked most of the time. Given the way Jay was ogling her, he probably would have lost his mind if she'd been wearing less. After all, he'd been locked up with only dudes for the last ten years.

I was about to say something about the way his eyes were locked on her breasts, but Cassie stepped in and defused the situation.

"Hi. I'm Cassie. Allen's wife." She walked toward me with a seductive stride and pressed her body up against mine. "And why are you two standing here in the dark?" She turned on the light switch, and Jay almost fell backward over his chair. It was one thing to see Cassie half-naked in the shadows, but to truly appreciate her, you had to see her in the light.

"She's your wife?" Jay exclaimed. The look of disbelief on his face was overwhelming. "She's beautiful."

"Yeah, I know, Jay. That's one of the reasons I married her," I said with annoyance, interrupting God only knows what filthy fantasy was occupying Jay's mind. Dude was my friend and everything, but he had a damn tent in his sweatpants at the moment, and part of me wanted to kick the shit out of him for thinking about my wife that way.

"So I take it you're Jay Crawford? I've heard so much about you." Cassie stepped from behind me and offered Jay her hand.

"All good I hope," he said, staring into her eyes.

Cassie smiled and just stood there, allowing her hand to rest in Jay's. "Good enough that he considers you family. And where I come from, we take care of family, no matter what." She turned back to me and said, "Babe, if he's got nowhere to go, I think he should stay with us."

Jay

11

I wasn't sure if I was more hungry or horny when I woke up to the smell of bacon and eggs, and Allen's wife prancing down the stairs in a sheer white robe that left absolutely nothing to the imagination. I had to give it to her, though; she had one of the fiercest bodies I'd ever seen. I still couldn't believe my boy Allen was married to her.

"I hope that sofa wasn't too lumpy. We do have a guest room."

"No, this is fine," I said, sitting up. "I need to be able to see the street. I'm paranoid like that."

"A man in your position should be." She gave me a knowing smile. "Anyway, I hope you slept well."

Aside from the fact that I was on the run, she and Allen also hadn't made it any easier for me to sleep. I'd had to listen to them fucking over my head half the night. I'd known that boy a long time, and I didn't think he had that kind of fucking in him.

"I'm kind of a light sleeper," I said.

"Well, then you must have been quite entertained." Cassie gave me an insightful smirk, then made her way over to the sofa where I'd been sleeping. She picked up the plate and glass I'd left on the floor.

"Very entertained," I said. As she passed by, I got a good whiff of her perfume, which was light and sweet but at the same time intoxicating. "Where's your hubby?"

"He's in the kitchen cooking breakfast." She walked toward the kitchen, and I watched her ass sway rhythmically in her robe. If she was anybody else's wife, I would have been on her like a jockey on a horse. "Come on in the kitchen. Allen usually takes off for work right after he makes my breakfast. I'm sure he wants to talk to you."

Makes her breakfast? I shook my head. That damn Allen was always going beyond the call of duty. "I take it you don't cook?"

She stopped abruptly, turning toward me with a raised eyebrow and a mischievous grin on her face as she placed the plate and glass on a nearby table. She then took hold of the lapels of her robe, yanking them apart to expose her completely naked body. It also allowed me to see her full-body tattoo for the first time. It had to be the most stimulating thing I'd ever seen. Not that he needed much encouragement, but my dick immediately sprang to life. Thank God I was still covered up with the blankets.

"Take a good look. Do you think he married me for my cooking skills?" she asked, letting the sleeves to her robe slide down her arms.

"Great googa-mooga." I swallowed hard, looking every bit like a man who'd been locked away for ten years. "Now that you put it that way, I guess not."

Cassie chuckled, closing her robe and leaving me sitting on that sofa like a little boy who'd just seen his first dirty movie.

It took a while for me to get the image of her nakedness out of my head and lose my erection, but I finally did, walking into the kitchen ten minutes later. Allen was sitting in a chair, dressed for work with his tie flipped over his shoulder, while Cassie sat in his lap, feeding him.

"Good morning, Al," I said, trying not to make eye contact with Cassie.

"Morning, Jay. I made you a plate." Allen pointed to a plate of eggs, grits, and bacon.

I sat down across from them, feeling guilty for wishing that his wife was sitting on my lap instead of his. "Thanks, but what I could really use is a good old-fashioned cup of coffee."

Allen pointed to the counter. "The Keurig's on the counter, and there are some K-Cups in the cabinet next to the fridge. You might wanna try this French roast. It's the only one I'll drink these days."

I looked at him like he was speaking Chinese to me. "K-Cups, Keurig? What the fuck is that? Y'all ain't got a coffeemaker?"

Cassie laughed. "Baby, he doesn't know what a Keurig is."

"Oh, wow, that's right." Allen joined her laughter. "It came out after he went to jail."

"I'll get it for him." Cassie got up and my dick got harder just that fast. I slid my chair as far under the table as it would go.

I shoveled some eggs into my mouth to distract myself. When I felt my hard-on begin to relax a little, I spoke to Allen. "Hey, brother, I wanna thank you again for your hospitality."

"It's cool. I said I would help you, but how long is this gonna last, Jay?"

"I don't know." I shrugged, sitting back in my chair. Cassie placed a cup of coffee in front of me. I gave her a thankful nod but never turned from my friend. "All I know is I have to clear my name, Al. I didn't rape that girl, and I don't want my kids living their lives thinking I'm a rapist."

"What I don't understand is why now? Kyle told me you had

a parole hearing. If you just hung tight, you probably would have been out in the next few weeks."

I couldn't help but laugh. "That parole shit is a joke." I added some sugar and cream to my coffee. "Let me tell you about my parole hearing..."

The clinking sound of the metal was really starting to irritate me as I sat in that room, a closed-in little waiting area that could have stood for the air-conditioning to be pumped up. Sweat beads were rolling down my forehead, and huge damp spots had taken residence under my armpits. Truth be told, no matter how high the air could have been turned up, I still would have been sweating bullets. After all, my life was at stake here. Not just my future, but my present, because if my circumstances didn't change, there was a good chance I would lose my mind. I couldn't stay locked up another five years.

I pressed my hand on my knee to keep it from bouncing up and down. My nerves were eleven on a scale of one to ten, but I knew if I could stop my knee from bouncing, then it would stop the sound of the jingling metal.

"Crawford."

I heard the name being called out, but it really didn't register at first. My thoughts of what could take place in the next few minutes had me paralyzed.

"Crawford!" This time the voice was louder and agitated.

I looked up at Thomas, the CO who had just called my name, twice.

"You just gon' sit there?" Thomas asked me.

I stood, slowly, still trying to gather my bearings.

"Man, bring yo' ass on," Thomas said, frustrated, yanking me by my arm.

It was wise that all inmates were cuffed when being transported. These COs made a nigga wanna go upside their head. My hands being cuffed kept me from doing so, though. Besides, I'd managed to control myself most of the time, and I wasn't about to mess things up now when I was so close to freedom.

My feet were on a two-second delay from my mind, which realized the CO was pulling me and forcing me to walk. I almost tripped. That could have been disastrous, considering my ankles were cuffed and I would have fallen straight on my face. But I caught my balance and was able to regulate my pace.

Thomas led me into a somewhat larger room that had a six-foot table in front of a window. Behind the table were three chairs, each occupied at the moment. One occupant was an older white gentleman, and the other two were middle-aged women, one black and one white.

Across from them was a smaller table, about four feet in length, and two chairs. In one chair there was a white man that I recognized as my attorney. He stood upon my entrance.

"Good afternoon, Jay," he said once the CO escorted me over to the table.

I nodded my greeting. The lump in my throat wouldn't allow me to speak.

"Sit," he said, offering me a chair as the CO made his way over to the door, where he stood like an armed guard, hands straight down and crossed.

I sat, as did my attorney. We both turned our attention to the three people at the table who held my fate right in the palms of their hands.

"I'm sure this has been a long-awaited moment for you, Mr. Crawford," the black woman said, "so let's just get right down to it."

She cleared her throat as she looked down at a paper in front of her. After a few seconds she looked back up at me. "So, Mr. Crawford, it says here that you have been incarcerated for just about ten years."

I nodded, remaining silent. No need for me to confirm. The paper said it all.

"And it also says that you've been a model inmate since the last time you were in front of the parole board five years ago. You've really turned your life around."

Again, I allowed her to speak. I would only speak if asked a question, and even then I'd made up my mind not to elaborate. The best thing to do in order not to say the wrong thing was to say nothing at all. If my experience with the prison system had taught me anything, it was that nugget of wisdom.

"From reading your file, Mr. Crawford," the woman continued, "I would love nothing more than to parole you."

I tried to hide the emotions bubbling up inside of me.

"I agree," the other woman said. "You've set a fine example of an inmate who has truly been rehabilitated. Your work with the younger inmates and gangs has been credited with saving lives."

In my mind, I was yelling out how I actually hadn't been rehabilitated because there was nothing about me that had needed rehabilitation. I should have never been put in jail in the first place. Having been locked up for a decade, it was this place that I would now need to be rehabilitated from. Being behind bars for that long can really fuck with a man's mind.

"I have to agree with these two ladies," the gentleman said. "Your friend Kyle Richmond said some very gracious things about you. He even has a management position lined up for you."

I about jumped out of my skin, but again, my instincts told me to play it cool. From the sounds of things, with all three members of the board in agreement that I no longer belonged locked up, I was going to be out of there before I knew it. I could whoop and holler all I wanted once I was out of that hellhole, but until then, I would remain calm and collected.

"We do, however, have one obstacle," the gentleman added, and I felt my heart drop. "Your victim was here, and she spoke to the board."

"My victim?" I snapped, unable to maintain my calm demeanor at the mention of Ashlee, the lying bitch responsible for putting me behind bars.

I saw one of the women at the table flinch subtly, and I realized I needed to dial it back.

My attorney was poking my leg underneath the table to let me know I was about to blow it if I didn't calm down.

"Listen, Mr. Crawford." The black woman took over again. "As you heard, we are all in agreement of you being paroled, and we are willing to sign the necessary paperwork for that to happen."

I would have gotten excited all over again if I hadn't felt a "but" coming along.

"But we need you to make that happen."

I turned to my attorney for an explanation, but he looked as puzzled as I was.

"We need you now to take responsibility for your crime and admit your remorse." The gentleman picked up where the woman had left off.

I felt my attorney nudge me. I looked over to him, and his expression had changed to a cheerful one. He leaned in and whispered to me, "That's nothing. You can do that."

I shook my head vigorously. "I can't do that."

"Pardon me," one of the women said. "You can't do what?"

I turned to face the parole board. "I can't take responsibility for something I didn't do. Isn't giving up ten years of my life enough?"

The three parole board members looked back and forth at one another. When they all turned their attention toward me, the white woman spoke.

"Then, Mr. Crawford, we have no other option but to deny your parole."

I thought this was all a joke, until she took a stamp and slammed it down on the papers in front of her. She then looked up at me. "Parole denied." She placed the papers on a pile nonchalantly, as if she hadn't just announced that my life was going to be put on hold for at least five more years.

Self-control became a thing of the past. "This is bullshit!" I said, jumping up out of my seat at the table.

"Calm down, Jay." My attorney tried to pull me back down to my seat.

Before I knew it, the CO was over at the table and two more were on their way in.

"Let's go, Crawford," the CO said, pulling on my arm roughly. "Time to go back home," he said with a sinister chuckle. "There's no place like home."

I looked to my attorney as the CO pulled me out of the room. "Fuck you! This is bullshit and you know it," I yelled.

My attorney gave me a sympathetic look, raised his hands, and then allowed them to drop to his side. With no words spoken, he'd told me that his hands were tied and there was nothing he could do about the parole board's decision. I'd made my own bed by not agreeing to do what they'd asked.

I was gritting my teeth so tightly with anger as I exited the room that my jaw muscles began to ache. Tears of anger formed in my eyes, blurring my vision. Even so, when we passed a gated corridor, I was able to make out the person walking down the hall.

"Son of a bitch, that's her," I said under my breath. "That's Ashlee!" I hollered. She must have heard me, because she turned to look at me.

Hell, I'd already received my verdict. Being the model inmate hadn't gotten me anywhere, so screw it. I let my emotions take over. "I'm going to kill you, bitch! Do you hear me? I'm not supposed to be here. I'm not supposed to be here! This is all your fucking fault!"

The CO put me in a bear hug as a couple others joined in his attempt to settle me down. "I don't know what the fuck has gotten into you, Crawford!" the CO growled at me. "But this is gonna get you a month in the hole."

His words made me lose it just that much more. "I don't give a damn. Fuck you! Fuck this place! I'm gonna kill that bitch! You motherfuckers can't keep me here. I don't care what anybody says," I yelled as the three COs tackled me down.

Wil

12

As I rode up the elevator to my office, I was thinking about my brother's funeral. I had taken the day before off to deal with the arrangements despite the assurance from my uncle that everything would be taken care of. To my surprise, I discovered that LC had gone all out for Trent, sparing no expense on anything, from the four carloads of flowers to the $20,000 casket. He'd even rented Antun's catering hall for the repast. Yes, sir, my brother was going out in style on Saturday, and if you knew Trent's pompous ass, you knew it would only be fitting.

I stepped off the elevator on my floor and caught a cold chill from the ghost-town atmosphere. From the looks of things, my department wasn't the only one that had sent folks packing. Damn, what a difference a few days make.

I walked up to my secretary's desk just as she lowered her cell phone. "Ah, Wil, I was just about to text you. I thought you might be staying home again."

"No, I'm here." I reached over and picked up my messages from the slot on her desk. "With all these cuts they're forcing down our throats, I can't afford to stay home. Well, at least we still have jobs." I flashed a grin, but she didn't smile back.

"Malek's in your office," she said. We both turned toward the glass partition of my office. The shades were down, and that's not how I'd left them two days ago.

"Shit. Any idea what he wants?"

She shook her head. "Nope, but I don't trust him. They started laying off secretaries yesterday on the third and fourth floor." She looked up at me with genuine worry in her eyes. "Wil, I need this job."

"I know you do, Barb. And for the record, I don't trust him either." I reached for the door handle, plastering a fake smile on my face as I entered my office.

Malek was sitting behind my desk, talking on my phone. "Yeah, mm-hmm, he just walked in. I'll see you in a few." He hung up the phone.

"Comfortable?" I asked.

"We gotta talk," he said weakly.

"So, talk." I turned my back on him to open the shades. "I hope you're not here to ask me to lay anyone else off, because I'm not doing it."

"That wasn't exactly the plan," Malek said as I pulled up the final shade.

"Then what exactly is the plan?" I approached him and leaned over the desk, getting into his personal space and enjoying the fact that he looked nervous.

"Why don't you have a seat and I'll tell you."

"I think I'll stand." For a moment, I was feeling like the one in control, until I spotted two security guards headed our way. My stomach felt as though it would drop out of my body as I turned around. "You're firing me, aren't you?"

"Wil, I don't have a choice. I'm going to need your work ID and password." He glanced over at the security guards, who were now standing at my office door. They couldn't get in because I'd locked it.

"Bullshit. We all have choices, Malek. I had a choice two days ago not to fire those guys, but I chose to be loyal to the company and save my own neck. Same way you're choosing to save yours. I guess I made the wrong choice. The jury is still out on you." I collapsed into a chair, berating myself inside for having been so stupid. Why did I expect them to be loyal to me after they'd just heartlessly let go half of my department? I had forgotten the number one rule in most businesses: Everyone is expendable.

He tossed a folder to the edge of the desk. "Hey, look. The package they offered is much better than what they were giving out the other day. Smart guy like you will land right on your feet."

I jumped out of my seat, snatching him up by the collar and smashing my fist into his face repeatedly as the security guards rattled the door, trying to get in. "Yeah, right. A smart guy like me."

Kyle

13

It had been nearly a week, and to my astonishment, they still hadn't captured Jay. I guess he'd planned this whole escape-from-prison thing a lot more thoroughly than I'd given him credit for, because you couldn't have paid me to believe he would avoid capture without contacting me for help. Hell, I think a part of me was a little hurt that he hadn't. I just hoped he was safe on some tropical island somewhere, never to be heard from again—however, if you knew Jay Crawford, you'd know things were never gonna be that damn simple.

"Excuse me, Mr. Richmond." One of the assistant managers at the country club approached my golf cart as I drove off the eighteenth green. I'd just finished a round of golf with some political friends of mine.

"Yes, Juan," I replied, stepping off the cart to retrieve my golf bag.

He leaned in, speaking practically in a whisper. "There's a man at the clubhouse bar waiting for you. He gave me the impression it was rather important."

"This man have a name? You ever seen him before?" I

whispered back. This wasn't the kind of place where people came looking for me.

"No, sir, first time. But he did use the name Crawford."

Shit. My body stiffened like I was about to have a colonoscopy.

Once I was over the initial shock, I turned to my friends. "Hey, fellas, I gotta take care of something. Juan here will help you get the bags situated, and I'll meet you in the restaurant in about fifteen minutes."

I didn't get any complaints, so I headed straight over to the clubhouse. Of all the places to attempt to see me, why would he pick a place with so many frigging cameras in every room? My hands were shaking, and I could feel myself beginning to sweat as I went through the door. At the same time, part of me was excited to see him.

I made my way to the bar, where I found U.S. Deputy Marshal Franklin sitting at the bar, laughing his head off. I narrowed my eyes at him to let him know he wasn't funny. Not fucking funny at all.

"You were expecting someone else, weren't you, Mr. Richmond?" The deputy gave me that sarcastic smile of his as I sat on the stool next to him and waved the bartender over to order a beer.

"I suppose I should be glad you showed up in a cheap suit instead of your U.S. Marshal flak jacket," I said flatly. "What is this all about?"

"That was a test," he replied.

I had no idea what he was talking about, but I just played along. "Did I pass or fail?"

"I'm not sure. Your response time was right in the middle. Not that it matters. This time tomorrow I'll be in Texas."

"Texas? Is Jay in Texas?" I asked, grabbing a handful of peanuts from the bowl on the bar. I was trying to keep my composure. Ashlee, the girl who had accused Jay of rape, was from Texas.

"I'm going down there to find out. I just wanted to say good-bye, Mr. Richmond. I know we've been a pain in the ass, but I think under the circumstances, you can appreciate that we're just trying to do our jobs."

"I can." The bartender brought me my drink, and I motioned for him to bring another one for the deputy. "So does this mean that the Con Ed trucks parked in front of my house and business are gonna be gone soon?"

"We pulled the one in front of your house this morning. The Verizon truck in front of your friend Wil's house too."

Shit, I don't even think Wil knew there was a truck in front of his house.

"I don't know anything about your office. That might have been legit." He laughed.

"You're being reassigned, the trucks are being pulled.... Are you saying the investigation of Jay in New York is over?"

"Not on your life. The NYPD is still on the job, and I'll be making periodic visits as long as your friend is at large. We're just not going to waste any more real resources hunting him down here while the trail's cold. Besides, you'd be surprised how many fugitives we've apprehended on simple quality-of-life crimes, like traffic violations." He picked up the beer that the bartender had placed in front of him. "Although the most common recaptures are friends and family turning in their loved one for the reward, which, I might add, has been raised to fifty thousand dollars."

"I'm not sure what you're insinuating, but money is not the motivating factor in my life that you seem to think it is."

He shrugged doubtfully. "If you say so. Then let me ask you in plain terms again, Mr. Richmond: Have you seen, or do you have any idea of the whereabouts of the fugitive Jay Crawford?"

"No, I have no idea."

"Have you helped him in any way?"

"No, I haven't."

The bartender stood nearby, wiping down the bar slowly, and no doubt trying to eavesdrop. I hoped to God he wasn't the type to spread gossip about the members at the club.

"I don't believe you," Franklin said. "You're the only man he knows with resources to make him disappear like this." He stared at me like he was waiting for a denial on my part, but I stayed silent, refusing to help him on his fishing expedition. Finally he got sick of waiting for me to say something and concluded with, "Well, that's neither here nor there. Like I said, I'll be gone in the morning."

"I can't say I'm sorry to see you go. You and your boys have my wife scared of her own shadow. Not to mention the fact that I probably won't get any for the next six months."

"Sorry about that. Like I said, we're just doing our job." He lifted his glass and held it two inches from his smirking lips. "I've got to give it to your friend. He's one elusive son of a bitch not to be having any help." He glanced at me side-eyed, taking a long sip of his beer. "We'll get him. He'll make a mistake or you will."

"What are you trying to say, Deputy?"

"I'm not trying to say anything, Mr. Richmond. I just said it." He finished off his drink, then got up to leave. "Thanks for the beer."

I had to resist the urge to give him the finger.

I joined my golf partners in the main restaurant for dinner, followed by cognac and cigars in the club's smoking lounge—all picked up by me, I might add. I didn't love hanging out with these political types, mainly because they were all cheap and looking for a handout, but these three brothers were the biggest shakers and movers in Queens politics, and since I was the lone Negro in a beauty supply business dominated by Koreans, I was going to need their help to expand.

"Kyle, that was some fine cognac and some superior cigars. If you had been able to rustle up some female entertainment, this would have been a perfect night," Councilman Butch Jones joked as we waited for the valet to return with our cars. Butch was the most influential of the three, so it couldn't have worked out better for me that he was the last to leave.

"I'll tell you what, Butch. If I get this warehouse permit in a timely manner, I might be inclined to send you and your colleagues down to Costa Rica on a poker junket." I gave him a knowing smile. "You ever been on one of those?"

"No, but I've heard of P and P junkets," he said, laughing loudly as his car pulled up front.

"P and P?" That was something I'd never heard of, but the way he was practically salivating over the term, I was sure it was going to cost me a pretty penny.

"Poker and pussy." Butch handed a five to the valet, who was obviously hanging on his every word now. "Let me look into those permits. I'm sure we can find a way to speed things up a bit. What you do is important to the city."

He offered his hand, so I took it. "'Preciate that, Butch."

"No problem."

I watched him get in his Mercedes and speed away.

Mission accomplished.

Not long after Butch pulled off, another valet pulled up in a

2016 candy-apple-red Porsche 911 Turbo that had the other valets losing their minds with jealousy. Being behind the wheel of a car like that, even if only from the parking lot to the club entrance, was every man's dream. I didn't have to dream, because, well, it was my car.

I tipped the valet a twenty, got in my German dream machine, and started driving down long, curvy Country Club Drive doing about eighty. God, did I love driving that car. I only took it out on Thursdays when I went to the club, and on weekends, but whenever I did, I truly enjoyed it.

At the end of Country Club Drive was a strip mall with several stores, including a supermarket, a gas station, and Dunkin' Donuts. Anyone who knew anything about me knew that I was addicted to Dunkin' Donuts coffee, so I pulled in to get a cup to help me knock off the edge from the cognac I'd been drinking.

Five minutes later, coffee cup and a crumb doughnut in hand, I stopped halfway to my car because I could have sworn I'd heard someone call out to me.

"Hey!"

I looked back at the Dunkin' Donuts but didn't see anyone. However, in my peripheral vision I did see a silhouette coming from behind a truck parked halfway across the parking lot. The person began doing a light jog in my direction. This wasn't a bad neighborhood, but I had heard of a few people being mugged late at night near local fast-food places. Not willing to take any chances, I headed for my car, which was still a good fifty feet away because I had been afraid to park next to anyone and get the Porsche scratched.

"Hey, wait up, man," the person called out. From the sound of the approaching footsteps, I knew this person was closing in fast.

Wait up, my ass. I made double time, spilling coffee all over myself as I unlocked the door to the Porsche. Once safely inside my car, I turned toward the passenger's window to see a very shapely woman's silhouette charging toward me. The closer she came, the more apparent it became that this was one big-ass woman, taller than plenty of men I knew. Within seconds she was banging on my window, repeatedly saying my name.

"Kyle! Kyle! Kyle!"

How the fuck did she know who I was? Nothing about this seemed right, but curiosity got the best of me and I rolled down the window halfway. "Can I help you?"

"You don't know how good it is to see you," she panted, out of breath. The bass in the voice confirmed something I had suspected when I noticed her size: This was no woman. "I've been standing outside that Dunkin' Donuts damn near two hours."

"Well, I'm sorry. You may have to wait awhile longer for a customer, because I sure as hell ain't buying what you're trying to sell." I was about to put the car in gear and take off, but in a lightning-fast movement, this drag queen reached into the car, unlocked the door, and jumped into the passenger's seat.

"Drive!" he demanded, still out of breath from the run.

I didn't comply. Instead, I slid my left hand into the little compartment on my door and pulled out a switchblade I'd purchased in Europe. "You need to get out. It's not that type of party," I said, thinking I'd made it very clear I wasn't playing around.

My gender-bending passenger started laughing, not threatened in the least.

"Dammit! Get the fuck out my car!" I waved the knife in his direction, but he grabbed my wrist with a herculean grip.

"Hey, dawg, relax. It's me! It's me! It's me!" He reached up with his free hand and pulled back the wig. "Look. It's me, Jay."

"Jay...What the fuck, yo?" Now that he'd said it, I was able to look past the initial shock and fear that had blinded me to the identity of the she-man chasing me in the parking lot. It all made sense—sort of. "Fuck, that is you, isn't it?"

Allen

14

I was so glad Cassie talked me into letting Jay stay with us for a while. We all knew that eventually he was going to have to move on before some nosy neighbor recognized him, but his presence had brought a warm sense of family to my house, something that hadn't been there since my mother passed away. In fact, the three of us were getting along so well that I'd brought home a Monopoly game, some Chinese food, a six-pack of beer, and a bottle of wine, just so we could have game night together.

"Cassie! Jay! Anybody home?" I walked through the front door, expecting to see at least one of them stretched out on the sofa watching some train-wreck reality TV show like they usually were. Instead, I almost tripped over a pile of shopping bags from practically every damn store at Green Acres Mall.

"Dammit, she's at it again," I mumbled.

"Oh, hey, baby. Is that Chinese from the Jade Inn?" Cassie asked, walking down the stairs. She moved a couple of the bags and sat down on the sofa to watch TV like everything was all cool. I stomped over to the couch, grabbed the remote, turned the television off, and then threw the remote back down.

"Uh, did I do something wrong?" she asked, looking truly bewildered.

"How much?" My eyes went to the shopping bags.

Now that gave me her undivided attention. "How much what?" she asked, batting her eyes and playing dumb.

But I wasn't going for that doe-eyed shit today. Enough was enough. With all those bags, she had to have spent a couple thousand dollars. "It looks like a goddamn swap meet in here." I walked over to the bags and picked up a few, holding them high in the air like Exhibit A. "Seriously, Cassie, how many times do we have to talk about you and your shopping? You've got a closet full of clothes."

"But I didn't shop for myself this time," she said.

This wasn't the first time she'd used that excuse to justify her spending. Sometimes, among several purchases for herself, she'd buy a shirt or a sweater that she'd like to see me in, and then claim that she'd gone shopping for me. She'd pull out the shirt, have me put it on, then gush over how sexy I looked and how hot it made her. We'd end up having sex, and that shit was always so good that her overspending would be all but forgotten. Sex with Cassie was like a drug to me, and sometimes I swear it was killing enough brain cells that I couldn't always think straight around her. I had to learn not to let her trick me so easily or we'd end up bankrupt one day.

"Cassie, you can't keep buying clothes for me. My closet is full, just like yours."

"Don't worry. I didn't shop for you either." She opened the bag of Chinese food that I'd set down on the coffee table. "I bought this stuff for Jay. The man's been wearing that same sweat suit for a week now."

"Well, all right. I guess that makes se—" I opened a bag from Bloomingdale's and pulled out a pair of stilettos in a size I didn't even know they made. Now this definitely did not make sense. "You bought this for Jay?"

"Mm-hmm, and be careful with them. He's very particular about his shoes." She laughed as she opened up the carton of chicken and broccoli, digging in with a pair of chopsticks.

I was so confused I didn't even know how to respond to her comment. "Ummm, where is Jay anyway?"

"He had to go out," she replied, stuffing her face with Chinese food.

"Out? I thought he said he was going to lay low for the next couple weeks. What could possibly be so important that he'd risk getting caught?"

"I don't know." She shrugged her shoulders, then turned on the TV like our conversation was done. Apparently Maury Povich was way more important than keeping track of the fugitive who was living in our house.

I stepped in front of the TV to get her attention. "So he didn't say why or where he was going?"

"No, he just said there was something he had to do, so he had me drop him off at a corner over in Little Neck." She waved her arm at me. "Now can you please move?"

"Are you kidding me?" My face flushed with anger. "You shouldn't be driving him around, and especially not over in Little Neck." I couldn't believe Jay had the nerve to risk my wife getting caught up in his mess, and I couldn't believe my wife was stupid enough to go for that shit.

Then a sobering thought came to mind: Maybe it was me who was getting her all caught up. After all, I was the one who opened my doors to an escaped convict, even if the escaped convict was my best friend.

"I should have never gotten you mixed up in all of this." I sat down next to her.

"Look, babe, I'm a big girl. I know what I'm doing, okay?" Cassie hugged me from the side and rested her cheek against my shoulder. "Besides, didn't you always tell me Jay was family?"

"He is family," I said.

"Then stop bitching. Jay is cool people, and this is what real family does. I'm even more convinced of that after spending time with him. Most of your friends and their wives are full of shit and don't even come around. Jay could have turned to any one of them, but he turned to you for help, because he knows that you trust him and believe in him." She paused for a minute. "I mean, you do believe him, don't you? You told me yourself that the Jay you know would never rape anybody."

"Of course I believe him. And I want to help him, but you're my wife, and I have to think of you first. This whole situation is pretty dangerous, Cassie."

She smiled. "I'm fine, Allen, and Jay really needs us. I know first-hand what it's like to feel as if you don't have anybody in the world, but then there is that one person who proves they're on your side no matter what. That night I showed up on your doorstep, that's exactly how I felt about you. You didn't turn me away. Now it's Jay who needs you. And I know my kind and caring"—she kissed me on the chin—"gentle"—she kissed me on the nose—"husband"—she kissed me on the lips—"is not going to turn his best friend away either." My wife was such a sweetheart. Damn, I was one lucky bastard indeed.

My cell phone rang, interrupting the action that was getting ready to take place. I pulled my phone out and answered the call.

"You have a call from the New York City jail system." It was a recorded voice.

Fuck!

Jay never should have gone out on those streets. The only good news was that he was able to place a call. At least they hadn't killed him.

"Caller, please state your name," the automated voice continued.

"Wil Duncan."

What? I heard the name, but it didn't make any sense. Was this Jay's way of trying to get around something?

"Please press one to accept this call," the automated system stated.

I was so confused that it took a moment before I snapped out of my daze and pressed the button.

"Hello? Hello, Allen?"

Fuck, there was no mistaking that voice.

"Wil? Is that you?"

"Yeah, it's me."

"What the fuck is going on? Why are you calling me from jail?"

Cassie put down the Chinese food and muted the TV, all ears now.

"I got into something stupid at work," Wil said. "I need you to come get me. They set the bail at a thousand dollars."

"What the hell did you do?" I still couldn't believe Wil, of all people, was calling me from jail.

"Dammit, Allen, can you just come get me out of here?" he said in a raised tone. "I'll explain everything when I see you. I'm at Manhattan Central Booking, and whatever you do, don't call my wife."

Jay

15

"You look scared," I said, sliding into the booth across from Kyle. We were at the Landmark Diner on Northern Boulevard, one of our old late-night haunts.

"Shit, I am scared, and you should be too," Kyle replied, scanning the room like some cop was going to pop up out of nowhere at any moment to bust us.

He'd been acting that way since the second he realized it was me in that parking lot and not a deranged transvestite carjacker. You should have seen him pull out of that parking lot like a bat out of hell, driving all crazy, looking in his rearview mirror every five seconds. He must have circled the block ten times before getting on the Grand Central Parkway, only to get off at the next exit and circle the block ten more times. It literally took us forty-five minutes to go eight miles because he took so many damn detours.

"Do you know that a few hours ago a U.S. deputy marshal was at my club warning me not to do exactly what I'm doing now?" He sighed loud and long between gritted teeth. I swear he looked like he was about to shit a pickle. "I shouldn't even be here right now.

Lisa is going to kill me." He placed both hands on the table like he was about to get up.

"Hey, just calm down a sec, okay," I told him in a low and even voice. "Nobody followed us, and if we were going to be busted, we would have never made it into this diner."

He stared across the table, looking me up and down with contempt. "How the fuck am I supposed to be calm when I'm sitting across from the most wanted man in New York?"

"Can I take your order?" A cute waitress, probably in her early twenties, placed two glasses of water in front of us. She glanced at me but looked away quickly. I'd learned that in this day and age, people in New York didn't like to stare at transgender people, because it was rude and politically incorrect. For me it was almost as if I was hiding in plain sight, but then I noticed that she looked more surprised to see Kyle. The way she gawked at him made me wonder if he had screwed her or something. I'd never known Kyle to cheat, but I had been gone a long time, so maybe things had changed.

"Uh, hi, Mr. Richmond," she said, and then I knew he hadn't had sex with her. Nobody you fuck calls you Mister.

Kyle tried to maintain his composure, but I could tell it was a struggle. Can't say I blamed him, considering he would have to figure out how to introduce me now.

"Uh, hi, Tiffany. I didn't know you worked here." He waved weakly.

"Yeah, three days a week. How's Kiki?" Kiki was a nickname for Kyle's daughter Kim.

"She's, uh...good. She's at St. John's, plugging away to finish her senior year. How about you?"

"I'm a senior at C.W. Post." Now she was openly stealing glances at me, and Kyle couldn't avoid introducing us.

"Uh, this is my colleague, uh—"

"I'm Jada," I cut in, using the most feminine voice I could muster. "I'm the wig buyer for his company." I flipped my hair for effect.

"Hi, I'm Tiffany." She offered her hand, looking totally comfortable with my presence. I guess kids nowadays weren't shocked by much.

"Nice to meet you, Tiffany. You think we can get two steaks, medium well, with all the trimmings? And a couple of Cokes?" If I was going to get Kyle to truly calm down so we could talk, I needed her to go away.

Tiffany took the hint and cut short the small talk. "Sure. I'll be right back with your drinks."

She walked away, but Kyle and I just sat there staring at each other. I'm sure he was about as embarrassed as he'd ever been. There we were, in one of our old haunts, sitting across from each other like the good old days—except I was in a dress and full makeup. Aside from worrying that our waitress might somehow recognize me as the fugitive from the TV, I knew that I had less to worry about than Kyle at the moment. Imagine what it would be like as a married man to be sitting across from a cross-dresser and have your daughter's friend roll up on you.

"Is this what ten years in prison does to a man? Turns you into...Jada?" Kyle asked, finally breaking our silence.

I frowned. "It's a disguise, a'ight?"

"Well, you look real comfortable in your disguise." He rolled his eyes, looking like he wanted to throw up.

"Hey, I know this isn't easy, but I needed to see you." I reached over to pat his hand, but he pulled it back abruptly, just as Tiffany brought over our drinks and some coleslaw. I was sure she heard what I'd said, and God only knows how she'd interpret it, but she at least played it cool, setting down our things and walking away without a word.

"Man, as bad as I want to know why Madea is sitting across from me, I'm going to ask you something even more important," he said sternly. He was no longer paranoid or embarrassed; he was starting to look upset. "Why the hell did you break out of prison?"

I sat back in my seat. "Because they denied my parole."

"Bullshit. I'm not Allen or Wil, and you can't fool me. Did you forget I'm the one paying for your lawyer? They would've granted you parole if you just showed remorse and took responsibility for your crime. Why didn't you?"

I shook my head. "Why should I have to admit to something I didn't do?"

"Because those motherfuckers were going to let you out, that's fucking why!" He slammed his hand down on the table, then remembered where we were and lowered his voice so as not to attract any more attention. "Sometimes standing up for principles is overrated when it comes to your freedom. This ain't apartheid or the Civil Rights Movement, and you're not Martin or Mandela. What the fuck is wrong with you, man?" He was really getting worked up now.

"I have to stand for something. If I admitted to raping her, I would have to sign up as a sex offender. I'm no sex offender, Kyle." I sighed. "I got daughters."

"Yeah, you got daughters who haven't seen you in ten years."

Wasn't much I could say to that. I hung my head and listened to him continue his rant.

"You fucked up, bro. Did it ever occur to you that you're a convicted rapist? It doesn't matter if you admit it or not. You were going to have to sign up as a sex offender no matter what."

Once again he was right, but when you've been done wrong by the system, those little wake-up calls never occur to you until it's too late.

"That's why I have to clear my name," I said.

"What I don't understand is, if your principles are so damn high, why the fuck did you escape? You could have just rode out your sentence. Now you're not only a convicted felon, but you're also an escapee."

"Jordan," I said flatly.

"What about him?"

"I did it for him. I did it for my son." My jaw tightened as my mind went somewhere else—a dark somewhere else. I balled my hands into fists. "I can't let that crazy bitch do this to my son. I'll kill her before I let that happen."

My voice must have been a little too loud, because Kyle looked around nervously and said, "Whoa, you need to relax."

I unclenched my fists and took a few deep breaths to try to calm down.

"Who's trying to do something to Jordan?" he questioned. Kyle loved all three of my kids, but he especially loved Jordan, his godson. "Just slow down and tell me what's going on."

I didn't even know where to start. Talking about this was going to be harder than I thought. I dug down into my bra, pulled out a folded piece of paper, and extended it to him.

"Really, Jay." He took the paper with two fingers, looking at it with disgust on his face.

"What?" I said to him. "You'd rather I pulled it out my Victoria's Secret drawers?"

He shuddered like the thought frightened him. "All right, you have a point there." He unfolded the paper and read what was on it. "I don't understand. Who sent this to you?" he asked when he looked up at me.

"It had to be that bitch Ashlee. She's the only one I know who would sign a letter *Love, A.* Plus, the postmark was from Dallas."

"Damn, you sure know how to pick them, don't you? That girl was in love with you. What the fuck did you do to make her hate you so much?"

I gave him a devilish smile. "I put it on her like she'd never had it put on her before. Drove her ass crazy—literally," I joked.

Kyle wasn't laughing, "Or maybe Ashlee was cuckoo for Cocoa Puffs when you met her crazy ass, but you was so enthralled with how fine she was and how good the pussy was that you overlooked all the obvious signs of fatal attraction."

I wasn't laughing now, because he had hit the nail on the head. Ashlee was crazy and it wasn't just because I broke her heart. There was something wrong with her way before I met her. "You're right," I finally said. "I should have seen it coming."

"Hell, I met her a few times. I should have seen it coming too," he said sympathetically. He lifted the letter. "What does this mean? It says the same thing that happened to you is going to happen to your child."

"She's going after my son," I said, feeling the rage, which was constantly bubbling below the surface, threatening to boil over. That happened to me every time I thought of Ashlee. "I won't let that happen. I don't care if I have to spend the rest of my life locked up."

I was fighting back tears now at the thought of my child having to ever go through even one day of what I'd endured for the last ten years. "I know you're mad at me, Kyle, but I need your help. My son needs your help," I said, my voice cracking.

I was able to regain my composure when he reached out and took my hand. "Don't worry, bro. She ain't doing nothing to Jordan, 'cause I got your back."

Wil

16

Come on, man. Hurry your ass up and get me the fuck out of here.

I was sitting on a metal bench in a room filled by about thirty degenerates, wishing that my thoughts would somehow reach Allen and make him get there faster. It had been almost an hour since I'd called, so I didn't know what could be taking him so long. The CO in charge had already made it clear that anyone who didn't get bailed out soon would be shipped off to Rikers Island on the next bus. I still couldn't believe that after all the shit I had talked about Jay, I was the one sitting there like a fool, charged with aggravated assault.

"Nice suit." The sarcastic voice was coming from a man standing up next to me, leaning on the wall. He was giving me the once-over with a slight chuckle.

I sat there on that bench trying not to look intimidated, but who was I kidding? I was afraid. Yeah, I could probably hold my own if I had to go toe to toe with one of these guys, but that wasn't the part that scared me. I was in here with some real suspect-looking dudes. Half of them looked homeless, and the other half looked like card-carrying gangbangers. Shit, I even heard the guy who was eyeing my suit tell another dude that he wasn't to be fucked with because he had AIDS. I wasn't sure if that was true, but it was enough to make me give him a wide berth and a hell of a lot of respect.

I looked down at my suit, noticing the bloodstain on it for the first time. It must have been from when I busted Malek's nose. I still couldn't believe that I had gone off the way I did. How the hell could I have done something so stupid? Then again, that asshole deserved everything he got. After using me to lay off half my staff, that son of a bitch turned around and fired me. He probably knew all along that he was going to let me go. Yeah, he deserved to get his face busted. Too bad for me, the law said that being the one to bust it meant I deserved to be locked up.

"Excuse me!" I jumped up when a female CO opened the door to bring two more people into our cell. "Can you tell me if my friend is here to bail me out?"

"He's going to have to bail you out from Rikers. Paperwork's already been done, and everybody in here has been transferred to Rikers."

Her words devastated me.

"But he's on his way down here! They can't just transfer me when someone is coming to bail me out. That's not fair."

She laughed. "Well, unless your friend is a miracle worker, your ass is going to Rikers. We're about to load y'all on the bus in five minutes." I watched her walk away, shaking her head.

The worst part was that I already knew Allen wasn't persistent enough to ride over to Rikers once they bused me over there. I should have called Kyle. He would have talked shit, but at least he'd make sure I slept in my own bed that night.

"Hey, suit, you got a cigarette?" It was the man posted up on the wall beside me.

"No, I don't smoke," I replied as politely as I could, not looking for any trouble. "They probably don't allow you to smoke in this place anyway."

He snickered. "Oh, so you follow rules but just break the law, huh?"

Even the guy sitting next to me laughed at that one. I wanted to laugh—to keep from crying. God, I hoped Allen would find a way and figure this out, because I didn't know how much longer I could take this. I buried my face in my hands and said a silent prayer.

"Duncan. William Duncan. You're out!" a loud voice boomed.

I snapped my head up and looked to the ceiling as if the voice had come from God.

"You staying here or what, Duncan? Let's move it."

I saw a CO standing at the door, staring at me. He'd already told me twice, and I'd be damned if he was going to have to tell me a third time. I jumped up off the bench and made my way over to the door. "The other CO said all our paperwork was transferred to Rikers."

"Somebody just pulled a rabbit out their hat and got your charge dismissed, and you're complaining?" he asked, rolling his eyes.

"Oh, no, Officer, not at all." I nearly jumped out of my skin when I realized that he had just said my charges were dismissed.

He allowed me to step out of the cell, and then he locked the door behind us, escorting me down the hallway. I didn't know how Allen got my charges dismissed, and the truth was this smelled like Kyle must have had a hand in it, but right now I didn't care who had done what. I was just thankful to be going home. I could only imagine how much someone had to pay to get me out of there, but I was most definitely going to pay him back. He wouldn't have to take me on *Judge Judy*. I would pay him back in full with interest...as soon as my black ass got a job.

The depressing thought of my unemployment slowed my stride just a little. This mistake was going to cost me a fortune in legal fees. How the hell was I going to tell my wife? I swear on everything I love, I thought about asking the officer to just take me back to that cell and lock me up again so I wouldn't have to go home and face Diane. That cell was probably the lesser of two evils compared to the doghouse wifey was going to have me in.

The officer pushed open a door and pointed to the counter. "There's some paperwork you have to fill out to get your property back."

I heard a voice behind me say, "That's all been taken care of, Officer."

I turned around to discover that neither Allen nor Kyle had come to my rescue.

"Uncle LC. You did this?" I should have known. Kyle was definitely successful, but I don't think he had the connections to get my charges dropped.

"Let's just say I have a few friends in the NYPD. The name Duncan comes through the system and they give us a call." He handed me a brown paper bag that I assumed had my watch, cell phone, and wallet in it.

I wasn't surprised in the least that LC Duncan had low friends in high places. But who was I to complain, considering it was all working out to my benefit right about now? I guess this is what they call eating humble pie. "Thank you, Uncle. I appreciate this. Today has been the day from hell. The last thing I needed was to spend the night in this place."

"Yeah, I heard you lost your job."

He sat down and pointed to the seat next to him. As much as I wanted to get the hell out of there, I owed him at least this much, so I sat down. His entire demeanor shifted back to his usual commanding presence as he squared his shoulders and held his head high. My head dropped, knowing I was about to get a lecture of some kind.

"Wil, you're a very smart man. I know we haven't seen eye to eye over the years, but I just want you to know, you always have a place in our family business."

As much as I dreaded the thought of what was to come as Diane and I struggled to survive on unemployment benefits, I couldn't bring myself to accept work from Uncle LC.

"Look, I appreciate what you did today," I said, "but your business destroyed my parents' marriage and ruined my childhood, and now it's killed my brother. I'm not Trent. I promised myself I would never get involved."

"I understand, and I'm not asking you to do anything outside of your comfort zone. I'm looking for a professional to run Duncan Motors' customer service division. It's a position advertised in all the papers and with several headhunters. I've got Ivy League guys interviewing for this job, Wil, but I think you'd be perfect for it, not only because you're a customer service expert, but because you're family."

Although it sounded like a legitimate enough job offer, I still couldn't bring myself to say yes. I shook my head slowly. "Uncle LC, I—"

He lifted a hand to stop me before I could turn him down. "You don't have to give me an answer now. Sleep on it, talk to your wife for a few days. I promise we won't hire anybody until we speak to you."

I nodded, feeling torn. Life was about to get rough without my salary, but considering everything I knew about my uncle and his business, I didn't know if I could take the risk of getting involved with him, even in his legitimate car dealership. I stood up to leave, signaling that as far as I was concerned, our conversation was done.

"Can I drop you off at home?" he asked, sounding surprisingly not insulted.

"No thanks. I called my partner, so I'm gonna go find a bar and have a drink while I wait for him."

He followed me out of the building, and before we parted ways he left me with this: "The job pays two hundred fifty K a year, full benefits, with a matching 401(k) and a California T Ferrari to use as your company car."

Man, this guy sure knew how to tempt a brother. "I'll get back to you after I talk to my wife," I said. Things had changed, and I now had a very tough decision to make. Right now, though, I just wanted a good stiff drink.

Kyle

17

By the time I made my way home, I was stressed the fuck out from all the craziness of seeing Jay. I was also not in the mood to deal with Lisa and her Perry Mason shit. She had this uncanny sixth sense of sniffing things out when something was wrong and then beating me in the head with it. Thankfully, when I pulled in the driveway, all the lights were turned off, which most likely meant she was asleep and I'd be able to sneak in without having to answer fifty million questions. All I wanted to do was get in bed without waking her up and get some sleep. Tomorrow was another day.

I'd made it through the living room and was on my way up the stairs when one of the living room lamps came on. I stopped dead in my tracks, mentally preparing for the verbal beatdown I was about to endure.

"You're home late." My eyes were still adjusting to the light, but there was no mistaking the voice. It was not my wife, but my oldest daughter, Kiki.

I tried to appear nonchalant as I turned around to face her. "Hey, Kiki, why you sitting here in the..." My words trailed off when I saw the look on her face. My daughter and I had always been close, but you wouldn't know it if you saw her expression at that moment.

"Were you at the Landmark Diner having dinner with a transvestite?" She gave me the same hollow stare Lisa would give me whenever she thought I was about to stretch the truth. "And please don't lie, Daddy."

"Don't lie?" I murmured under my breath, having heard that same directive plenty of times from my wife, who often accused me of lying before I could even open my mouth. I didn't like it from Lisa, and I damn sure didn't like it from my child, even if I was about to make up a story to cover for where I'd been.

She turned her phone so that I could see a picture of me with Jay dressed as a woman, my hand over his when I was trying to calm him down. To say it didn't look good was an understatement.

Shit. I knew there was a reason I hated social media. That little traitor Tiffany must have taken a picture and sent it to her.

"Are you cheating on Mommy with a man?"

"No. Hell no!" I came back down the stairs and approached her, uncertain how I could explain this one away without telling her who was in that dress. "It's not what it looks like, princess."

"Oh, no? 'Cause it looks like you're cheating on my mother with a tranny."

If things weren't complicated enough, they got even more complicated when the stairwell light came on and Lisa called out, "Kyle, is that you?"

I sighed. "Yeah, hun, it's me." I wanted to shrivel up and die at that moment.

"Who are you talking to?" she asked as she came down the stairs, tying the belt on her bathrobe. She glanced at our daughter, then at me. "Kiki, what are you doing here? I thought you were staying on campus this weekend."

Kiki didn't say a word. She just stared at me.

Lisa exhaled and dropped her head. She turned around, facing me with her arms folded across her chest. "What's going on, Kyle?" she asked with a knowing tone.

In any other situation I would have tried to skirt the issue, but I couldn't do that with my kid being involved. Lying in front of Kiki when she held the evidence in her hand would put her in a terrible position. So, I told the truth, as bizarre as it was.

"Your daughter thinks I'm having an affair with a transvestite." I tried to laugh it off, but Lisa was not amused.

She turned to Kiki, confused but still in control. "Why would you think that?"

Kiki looked up at her mother with tears in her eyes, then turned to me with a scowl. I'm sure she was torn. Show too much loyalty either way, and the other might just turn on her. Well, I for one wasn't going to let that happen. She may have been twenty, but she was still my baby.

"It's okay, honey. Show the picture to your mother. Like I said, it's not what it seems."

Kiki reluctantly handed her mother the phone, and Lisa studied the picture for a moment, then handed it back, reaching out to hug our daughter tight. "Erase that from your phone and go upstairs. I wanna talk to Daddy for a minute."

"But—" She glanced over at me, the remorseful executioner.

"No buts. Go upstairs, Ki. Your father's right. It's not what it seems."

I should have found some hope in what Lisa had just said, but I knew she was just saying what was necessary to get Kiki out of the room. I didn't think for a minute that I was off the hook.

Damn, damn, damn, I said to myself as Kiki disappeared up the stairs. *Here we go.*

"You got anything to say?" Lisa's voice continued to be low and even, but that didn't mean shit. In a nanosecond, she could be as loud and furious as any black woman.

"What?" I asked with a shrug, trying to look innocent.

"Don't 'what' me, Kyle!" Lisa snapped. "I know you. The minute something is up, you go from acting forty to four. Now what's really going on? Or should I call a lawyer in the morning?"

"You don't actually believe I could be with a transvestite, do you?"

"No, I don't."

I let out a thankful sigh but it was premature, because she was by no means finished berating me.

With hands on hips, she stated, "I'm not stupid. You can dress him up as a girl, but I know Jay Crawford when I see him. You need to tell me what the fuck is going on."

I put my head down, shaking it slowly from side to side. How was my wife always so good at seeing through me? "Was it that obvious? I didn't recognize him at first."

"No, but it just makes sense. Why the fuck else would you be meeting up with a man dressed in drag?" *Angry* was too nice a word to describe Lisa's current mood. She was full-blown pissed the fuck off as she made a beeline to the recliner that had once separated the two of us. "I thought we talked about this. I thought you said you weren't going to meet up with him."

"I didn't go and meet up with him, Lisa. I swear." I had my hand raised like I was in a courtroom. "He showed up at the Dunkin' Donuts when I stopped to buy coffee."

"Oh, so he just randomly showed up at the same Dunkin' Donuts you happened to be in? That's bullshit and you know it, Kyle!"

"It's the Dunkin' Donuts near the club. Everybody knows I go there after a round of golf." I spoke calmly, hoping maybe it would rub off on her, because I could see her ratcheting up for a complete meltdown any minute.

"Do you hear yourself? That doesn't even make any sense. Jay's been in jail. He's never even been to the club." She was still fuming.

"I told him about it when I went to visit him. He liked hearing the stories."

She planted her hands firmly on her hips. "You're going to get yourself in trouble. Hell, you're going to get all of us in trouble. What if someone had recognized him?"

"He was wearing a dress. You couldn't tell it was him."

"I did, and I was only looking at a photo," she said angrily. "You're putting this family in jeopardy, Kyle, and being really fucking selfish while you're at it."

"No, I'm being a friend," I said.

"Friend? Seriously?" She began to pace around the living room. "Look, I've put up with this fantasy of yours for a long time, but it's time you dealt with reality. Jay Crawford is a convicted rapist, Kyle, and now he's an escaped convict. Time to wake up. He's a criminal."

I shook my head adamantly. "You actually think he's guilty? Well, guess what? I don't. He's my best friend, Lisa. I'm not going to abandon him. Not for you or anyone else."

Lisa flinched, stung by my words. "I'm supposed to be your best friend, Kyle."

"Key words, *supposed to be*. If you're my best friend, then why am I just finding out that you thought Jay was guilty this whole time?"

Lisa went to open her mouth but then closed it. For the first time since I could remember, my wife was speechless—but by the way her eyes filled with tears, I could also tell she was hurt.

"Fine, have your little bromance," she said sarcastically, turning away from me. "But one day, I'll be standing there to tell you I told you so. Most likely from the other side of the glass." She stormed up the stairs.

Allen

18

I was half a block away from the courthouse when Wil called and told me he'd been released and that I should meet him at Finnegan's on Broadway. We'd met at Finnegan's before, so finding the place was easy. It was parking that was a pain in my ass. By the time I got into the bar, he already had two empty shot glasses, a half-empty beer, and a grimace on his face that reflected his current state of mind.

"Hey." I sat down next to him.

He gave me a halfhearted greeting. "You want a beer?"

"Yeah, I'll have one."

Wil flagged down the bartender and ordered a beer for me and shots for both of us.

"You all right?" I asked.

"Is that a rhetorical question?" he replied, downing the rest of his beer.

I waited for my drink to arrive without saying another word to Wil. As curious as I was to get the details, I knew my friend pretty well, and until he calmed down, the best thing for both of us was to remain quiet. Twenty minutes later, he'd had another shot and beer, while I was still nursing my first. He still hadn't said a word about why he'd been locked up, but I wasn't planning to leave until I got some answers. It was the least he could do after I'd driven all the way to Manhattan to get him.

"So, you gonna drown yourself in alcohol, or are you going to tell me what's going on?" I broke our silence just as he downed another shot and took a long swig of beer to chase it. "It's pretty obvious you didn't need me to bail you out."

He gave a slight nod, chuckling to himself before slurring this explanation: "I did need you when I called, but then somehow my uncle found a way to get the charges dropped."

I knew about his uncle. He was a very rich and powerful man, perhaps the most powerful black man in Queens, with the exception of Bishop TK Wilson. I also knew Wil hated him, but that was neither here nor there. What I really wanted to know was why he'd been arrested.

"What kind of charges? What did you do?" I lifted my beer to my lips and finally finished it off as I waited for him to answer.

He took his time, but finally admitted, "Aggravated assault." He released a deep belly laugh that was surely fueled by the amount of alcohol he'd consumed. "I beat the crap outta my boss."

"Get the fuck out of here. Like, physically beat the crap outta him?" I asked, wide-eyed. I'd never known Wil to be one to lose his cool like that. Wil was built like a tree trunk and tough as nails for a guy in his early forties, but he was also the most professional guy I knew. In order for him to hit his boss, he had to have been provoked.

"He used me, then turned around and fucked me in my ass." He wasn't laughing now. He was angry, and he delivered his words so convincingly that I wasn't sure if he was being literal.

"Are you serious?" I couldn't imagine a big guy like him being violated like that.

Wil stared at me for a brief moment, giving me that annoyed look I saw from him and Kyle sometimes. I hated that look, because it always made me feel stupid.

"He fired me, Allen," Wil said. "That son of a bitch made me let go some really hardworking people to save my job, then he turned around and fired me to save his own ass. Then the smug bastard had the nerve to act like it was no big deal. I couldn't take it anymore, so I hit him—again and again and again, until security broke down the door and pulled me off him." Wil's fury was so intense that he shook as he spoke. "He's lucky I didn't kill him."

"Damn. Sounds like you really fucked him up."

The bartender brought me another beer, but I declined it. "Nah, I'm driving, man." Then I turned back to Wil and asked, "Is your boss all right?"

"He'll fucking live," Wil slurred, reaching in his pocket. He handed some money to the bartender and we exited the bar.

"Well, I'm glad you're okay. You had me worried there for a minute." I put a hand on his shoulder to guide his drunk ass toward my car.

"Yeah, sorry about that, Al," he said sincerely. "When they locked me up I just panicked. I didn't want to talk. I just wanted to get outta there. It probably came across like I was locked up for murder."

I chuckled, because that's exactly how it had come across. "Hey, no worries. At least you don't have me losing my mind like Jay's stupid ass. That fool had Cassie drive him halfway across town dressed up like Ru—" I hadn't even finished my sentence before I realized I'd fucked up.

Wil swiveled his head in my direction, suddenly sounding close to sober. "What are you talking about? You've seen Jay?"

I clamped my mouth shut, hoping that if I didn't answer, he would forget he'd asked the question. No such luck. He stopped walking and stared me down.

"Al, have you seen Jay?" he repeated.

"Yeah," I said weakly as I arrived at my car and unlocked the door.

I slid into the driver's seat and waited for Wil to catch up and get in the car.

It took a while, but he got in, glaring at me like he was my daddy. "How long has this been going on, and how come you didn't tell me?"

"He's been staying over at the house for a while now," I admitted, knowing it was useless to try to lie now that I'd fucked up and let the cat out of the bag. "We didn't think it wise to tell you or Kyle."

"Why the hell not?"

"Plausible deniability: What you don't know can't hurt you. You guys got kids, man. All me and Cassie have are each other."

"And Cassie's cool with an escaped convict staying at your house?" He gave me that *what are you, stupid?* look again.

"She's the one who thought it was a good idea to have him stay longer than a night."

Wil looked stunned, but that didn't shut him up. "Your wife is one strange bird, Al. But what I really wanna know is what the fuck is wrong with you people? Have you lost your minds? Do you know how much trouble you can get into if they find him at your house?"

"A lot," I replied. I wanted to reassure him that we were being careful, but I couldn't say that now that Jay had taken the risk of going out to Little Neck.

"Five to ten years," he emphasized. "Is helping Jay worth that?"

"No. I mean yes! I can't leave him out there on the street. You may not care about him, but I do, and I'm gonna help him."

"It's not that I don't care about him," Wil said in protest. "I'm just not sure he's innocent."

The look I gave him could have melted steel, but it didn't change his stance.

"Come on, man. You were in that courtroom just like I was, and you mean to tell me you're a hundred percent sure he's innocent? Hell, I'm his best friend, and I would have convicted him."

"That's fucked up, Wil, and you know what? That's the real reason we didn't tell you he was at my house. Jay's our friend, and I know he's innocent."

"Wow, you're more naive than I thought," he snorted, shaking his head. "No wonder he came to you instead of me and Kyle."

"What's that supposed to mean?"

He hesitated briefly, but the alcohol wouldn't let him hold back. "A tiger can't change his stripes, and neither can Jay. What the hell are you thinking about, bringing that man into your house? Forget about him being on the run for a second. You know Jay's history just like I do, and leaving him in your house with Cassie is like giving the fox the keys to the henhouse and telling him how long you'll be gone. What the fuck is wrong with you?"

"Jay wouldn't..." I couldn't bring myself to finish the sentence, because in the back of my mind resided the truth that Jay had in fact slept with my former fiancée, Rose. Wil didn't hesitate to remind me of that fact.

"Jay wouldn't what? He fucked Rose, didn't he? And Cassie's a hell of a lot prettier than Rose."

I had no comeback for that because he was absolutely correct.

"Let me ask you a question," he continued. "What's the first thing you'd want if you spent ten years in prison?" Then he answered his own question. "I don't know about you, but if I'd been locked up that long, I'd want some pussy. You can bet your ass that's exactly what Jay wants, and the way your wife walks around half-naked all the time, well—" He stopped himself from going on any further, but he'd already said enough to plant a poisonous seed in my mind.

Wil

19

"Yeah, Big Daddy, that's it! Put it on me, baby. That's the way Momma likes it!"

My wife, Diane, was on all fours by the edge of the bed, while I stood behind her, pumping away at her sexy, full-figured body. I grabbed her waist and guided her back and forth as her body did a wave. She tightened up around me, and I could feel her juices flowing, which caused me to completely lose it. Now there are a lot of sexy things, but to me, there was nothing sexier than two big people in sync while they were making love. My wife and I were living proof that what everyone said negatively about marriage and sex didn't necessarily hold true. After all these years, I still loved my wife, and even better, I still loved fucking my wife.

"Yeah, come with me, baby." Diane threw her head back, twerking her hips back at me as hard as she could. This was one hell of a way to start off every morning.

"Damn, baby." I placed my hand in the small of her back, pushing down hard as I joined her in orgasm.

"Mmm, I could go to sleep just like this," Diane said as she collapsed onto the bed.

"I know that's right." I spread my arms out to my sides and tried to catch my breath. "Big Daddy still knows how to lay it down, doesn't he?"

I wasn't really expecting an answer, but after getting fired, a little reassurance in the sex department would have been nice. I certainly wasn't expecting what I got.

"It was a'ight. I've had better," she replied.

Her words stung me more than Malek's when he fired my ass.

"Seriously?" I asked, rolling away from her. "How much better?"

"That's not important, is it?" She turned to me with the most serious look ever on her face, but then she burst out laughing and hit me on the arm. "I'm kidding. You know you be laying it down. Can't nobody satisfy me like you." She sat up on her elbow and kissed me on the lips. "I love you, Wil Duncan."

"I love you, Diane. And don't you ever do that again. You damn near gave me a heart attack."

She placed another kiss on my lips and then got out of bed. I watched her, enjoying the look of satisfaction on her face. I hadn't told her about being fired yet, and it made me wonder just how satisfied she would be with an out-of-work loser. It may have been good to her now, but good dick could not keep the lights on in the house.

"I'm going to take a shower. I'd love to remain covered in your scent for the rest of the day, but I can't walk into work smelling like sex, and neither can you." She was at the bathroom door, looking over her shoulder at me. "Aren't you coming?"

"Huh, uh, what?" She had interrupted my pity party when it was just getting started. "Yeah, uh, I'll be right there." I tried my best to return a grin that was sincere, but I couldn't even fake the way I was feeling. I quickly turned to face the flat-screen television on the wall at the end of the bed to avoid her gaze. Diane could always see right through me.

In my peripheral vision, I could see her head turn from me to the television, then back to me again. I guess she was a little confused by the fact that the television wasn't even on, yet I lay there with my eyes glued to the screen as if the latest episode of *Scandal* was showing.

Diane sighed. "Look, I know what's going on here."

"You do?" I snapped my head toward her. How in the world could she have found out that I lost my job? Did she also know about what I did to Malek?

"Of course I do. Your brother just passed. You're grieving." She took a couple steps back over toward me, speaking sympathetically. "It's okay. I can only imagine how hard it must be. Even if you and Trent weren't close, I know how hard funerals can be. But I'm here for you, baby. Now come on. We gotta get ready for work." She held out her hand, waiting for me to get up and walk with her to the bathroom.

I looked up at her and saw the sincerity in her eyes. I could not sit there and let this woman believe the cause for my sudden low mood was the loss of my brother, who I was barely speaking to before he died. Don't get me wrong: I wasn't happy Trent was dead, but it was the loss of my job that had me down.

"Yeah, about work...there's something I need to tell you." I was quite sure Diane would agree that I'd waited long enough to enlighten her on this bit of information. It was better late than— well, even later.

"I lost my job."

She snatched back the hand she had been holding out for me.

"What do you mean you lost your job?" She took her robe from the back of a nearby chair and covered herself. Just like that, I was no longer deserving of viewing her in all her nakedness. "I thought the company had already gotten rid of all the employees they needed to get rid of. Matter of fact, aren't you the one who fired them all?"

"Yes," I said. "Then those bastards turned around and fired my ass."

"They can't do that to you...to us." She began to pace. "We have a mortgage. We have car payments. Car insurance." With every debt she rattled off, she turned to walk in another direction. "We have a kid in college for Christ's sake! How the hell are we supposed to keep a roof over our heads? Clothes on our backs?" She finally stopped pacing and looked to me for an answer to her questions.

If I hadn't already been doubting my manhood and my ability to provide for my family, I certainly was now. I could see myself in her eyes as she stared at me. The reflection of how she saw me was no longer the same. I was no longer the provider who made her feel safe and secure.

"I got a job offer," I blurted out, knowing damn well it was an offer I could definitely refuse and probably would.

She perked up a tad. I now saw a glimmer of hope. I'd always thought that was just some stupid cliché, but I really could see her eyes brighten to the fact that perhaps we weren't totally financially fucked.

"Yeah," I said with more enthusiasm than I'd meant to. But I wanted to match her hope, not destroy it. "Uncle LC offered me a job at Duncan Motors."

And just like that, the glimmer of hope dissolved to a flicker and then burned out. "The family business, huh?" She sat back down on the bed. "And just what would your job description entail?"

I shrugged. "Just working in the customer service department."

She thought for a minute. I could tell by her silence that she was not feeling that idea, so I decided to put her mind at ease. "But you know I can't work for that man anyway. For that family." I stared off again at the flat-screen television. "I have my profit sharing that we can live off of."

"What about severance? Did they at least offer you a package like they did the people they had you fire?" I didn't have the heart to tell her that I doubted it after I beat the shit out of Malek.

"We're better off relying on unemployment than them, Diane."

"Yeah, but how long will that last?" She looked defeated.

"A year if we drain my 401(k) and stick to a tight budget."

Budget was like a curse word to Diane, on par with the word *bitch* as far as she was concerned, but I needed her to understand the reality of the situation. We would need to be extra mindful of every dime spent until I could find another job.

Upon hearing the B-word, she had a change of heart, softening to the idea of me working for my uncle if it meant avoiding restrictions on our spending. "A job working for the Duncans, huh?"

I nodded.

"Well, you are a Duncan," she said.

"I know," I said.

"And we do need the money."

I looked from the black television screen to my wife. "I know," I said. "Believe me, I know."

107

Kyle

20

Two days after seeing Jay, I was still in the doghouse with my wife and with no resolution in sight. The only thing that was going to make her forgive me was to turn Jay in, which I was not about to do. I had to trust that he was doing the right thing, and that eventually, he would find a way to clear his name. I just prayed that my faith in Jay wasn't going to be the end of my marriage.

Hopefully my business in Bridgeport would be a lot less hectic than my marital problems. It had been a while since I'd been up this way, and despite all the other things going on down in New York, I always left Connecticut with a smile on my face.

"Your destination is ahead on the right," my GPS announced as the quaint white house came into view. I pulled over to the curb and parked, staring at the house. It had been almost four months since my last visit, and now that I was here, I began to doubt myself and my motives. What the hell was I doing?

"You should have called," I told myself. I sat in the car for a moment, gathering my thoughts. "You should have called," I kept repeating to myself as I climbed out of the car and made my way to the front door.

I rang the bell, but although I heard movement on the other side of the door, no one opened it.

Yep, I should have called.

In the driveway, I saw the Hyundai Sonata I'd helped purchase a little less than a year ago. If her car was in the driveway, it most likely meant that she was home. I closed my fist and knocked hard the way the police do when they're about to bust down the door. Ghetto, yes, but it was effective.

I heard the sound of the locks clicking and the door opening. A few seconds later, I was greeted by the angry expression of a simply dressed but beautiful cocoa-colored woman. Her long locks hung down to her thick, round hips.

"Kyle, what are you doing here?" The anger on her face dissipated and she self-consciously lifted a hand to check her hair.

I gave her a smile. "Hey, sorry to show up at your door unannounced. I just thought we should talk."

She shrugged nervously. "It's all right. Show up any time you like. I mean, after all, you do own the house."

"Yeah, maybe, but I still should have called," I said apprehensively. We'd known each other for years, but there'd always been an uneasy awkwardness between us. "You look good."

"Thanks. You look nice too. I like the car. Is it new?" Before I could answer, she was being pushed out of the way by a tall, handsome teenage boy. He had an overprotective scowl on his face at first, but then, like his mother, his eyes widened happily when he recognized me.

"Uncle Kyle!" The boy gave me some dap and then I pulled him in for a hug.

"What's up, giant?" I shook my head in awe. He'd grown a good three or four inches since I'd seen him last. I pulled out of the hug, resting my hands on his shoulders and looking into his eyes. "Damn, you've gotten big on me, and you look just like your pops."

"I know. My mom says that all the time. How you doin', Uncle Kyle?" The kid was all smiles.

"I'm doing good. Working hard. You taking care of your mom and keeping your grades up like you supposed to?" He nodded, and I looked past him to his mother. "Is that true, Miss Tracy? Is Jordan doing what he's supposed to do?"

"Yeah, he's been good. He got four A's and four B's on his report card."

"Not bad, but next time I want six A's, you got that?" I reached in my pocket and handed him a hundred-dollar bill. The way he hugged me, you would have thought I'd given him a million bucks. "How about you, Miss Tracy? You doing all right?"

"Yeah, I guess," she said, now more relaxed. "I thought you were the damn marshals again. You know they've been here looking for him."

"Yeah, I figured as much. They been down to my place too," I replied with a nod. "That's part of the reason I'm here. You got a minute?"

She stepped to the side. "Sure. Come on in."

Jordan stepped to the side as well to make room for me to enter the house. I walked in and sat on the love seat, while the two of them sat on the sofa.

"So he really did it, huh? He really..." Her words trailed off.

"Escaped." Jordan finished her sentence, trying to hide a smile. Tracy cut her eyes at him.

"Yeah, he did it," I confirmed, sitting back in my chair. "He escaped."

She twisted her hands nervously in her lap. "What is that man thinking about? They are going to kill him, Kyle. How could you let him do this?"

Why was everyone I knew blaming me for Jay's escape? Sure, I looked out for him while he was locked up, and I kept everyone informed, but we weren't joined at the damn hip.

"First of all," I started, "I didn't let him do anything. Jay's a grown-ass man and he decided to escape on his own. I was just as shocked as everyone else."

Tracy looked skeptical, but I didn't blame her.

"Look, in his defense, everything had been taken from him." I looked at Jordan and then back to Tracy. "So I'm sure he felt like it was the end of his life."

"What about our lives?" Tracy asked. "All he had to do was man up and take responsibility, whether he did it or not. Isn't that what everybody has to do in order to get paroled? Man the fuck up!" Tracy was being a little dramatic, but in this case, she'd called it pretty accurately.

"Look, he's not trying to hurt either of you. He loves you guys."

"So, have you seen him?" she asked.

I looked up and locked eyes with Tracy.

"Well, have you?" Jordan asked eagerly.

"I'd rather not say," I replied.

"He's seen him, Mom." Once again Jordan smirked like he had all the answers.

"Kyle, you're a good friend," Tracy said, "but you're going to get yourself in trouble."

I let out a laugh. "You sound like my wife. She keeps saying the same thing."

"Perhaps you should be listening to her," Tracy replied, her voice filled with frustration. Tracy was hitting pretty close to the bull's-eye. I knew I was jeopardizing my own freedom and thus my family's lifestyle by getting involved, but it was a little too late for that now. I'd already crossed the line. "Then again, you're just like your bullheaded friend, aren't you?"

"Pretty much."

She shook her head. "Kyle, why are you really here?"

My eyes shifted to Jordan. "Him," I told her. "I need to talk to my godson... in private."

"Oh no, you don't!" Tracy was quick to say. "At least not without me being around. You're not going to sneak behind my back and take him to Jay. I know what you and Jay are capable of, and I don't want Jordan involved."

"Come on, Ma," Jordan pleaded.

"No!" she replied firmly.

"Look, Tracy, I'm not here for some scheme to have Jordan and Jay hook up without you, okay?" I said in an attempt to keep her from going off. She was in straight protective lioness mode. "I just need to talk to him on a man-to-man level. It's more of a birds-and-bees thing than anything."

She kept a frown on her face and took her sweet time answering, but finally she sucked her teeth and said, "Go get your coat, Jordan."

He took off toward the back of the house. When he was out of sight, Tracy grabbed my arm as I headed for the front door.

"Kyle, I need to know. Is he all right?"

"I think so."

"That's good." She sounded relieved, but then came the hard question. "He's not mad at me, is he? I mean about Mack and me getting engaged. Part of me thought he might have escaped to confront me. I stopped visiting him without ever giving him an explanation."

"No, he understands. You couldn't wait around for him forever."

"Okay," Jordan said excitedly as he reentered the room. He bent over and kissed his mother. "Be back in a few, Ma." Within seconds, he was out the door and halfway to my car.

"I'll bring him back soon," I said to Tracy as I trailed behind Jordan.

"Oh, man, Uncle Kyle! This car is sick!" Jordan exclaimed as he slid his left hand across the hood of my Porsche 911 Turbo.

"It's all right," I said with a smirk as we got in.

"All right? My butt feels like I'm sitting on a pillow, and the leather feels like butter. I don't think I ever wanna get out of this car again," he said as he sank into the seat and made himself comfortable.

I pulled off and headed toward downtown Bridgeport. "So, has my dad seen this car?"

I hesitated for a second before admitting, "Yeah, he has."

"Be honest with me, Uncle Kyle. Is he okay? Is my dad all right?" Jordan asked. A kid this young should not have to be worrying about his dad like this.

"Yeah, considering he has every cop in the state looking for him, he's doing okay," I said. Then I got to the point. "He wanted me to ask you if anyone has approached you. A woman, perhaps."

Jordan went from serious mode to pimp mode, popping his collar as he spoke. "Well, you know the ladies are always approaching ya boy—"

"Jesus, you are your father's son," I said, lightly slapping his arm so that all the popping ceased. "Will you stop playing and answer my question? Have you been approached by any women?"

Jordan became serious again as he looked at me. "A woman?"

"Yeah . . . older," I said specifically.

"Like old-old, or like my mom old?" Jordan asked.

"You're lucky your mom's not around to hear you say that." I chuckled. "Thirty-five, forty years old. Somewhere in that area."

He thought for a minute and then shook his head. "I talk to a lot of girls, Uncle Kyle, but I never had no old lady come on to me."

"Well, if anyone does approach you, Jordan, I need to know." I put my hand on his shoulder and tightened my grip to let him know I meant business. "You call me right away. You hear me?"

"Yeah, sure." Jordan nodded emphatically, letting me know he understood this was a serious matter. "But what's going on?"

"The woman who set up your pops. We think she's gonna try and set you up too."

He paused for a minute, and I could tell that my words had rattled him. But he pulled it together quickly, straightening his shoulders and trying to convey manly confidence. "Not gonna happen," he said. "We should set her up."

I turned to him sternly. "No, you should stay out of this and let grown folks handle it. You got that?" He didn't answer, so I raised my voice and repeated, "You got that, Jordan?"

"Yeah, Uncle Kyle, I got it."

I glanced out the window. I couldn't even look the boy in the eyes when I said, "Look, I gotta get back to New York for a funeral, but you need to know. Your pops is in more trouble than ever before. He don't need to be worried about you too."

Wil

21

Unlike my sister, Melanie, and my wife, I was able to make it through my brother's funeral without shedding a tear. I don't mean to sound insensitive, but I was more bothered by my sister's distress than I was by the loss of my brother. Truth was, Trent was a real fuckup who duped a lot of women. Perhaps somewhere in the midst of all that I should have found the time to be my brother's keeper, but we were two grown men living by very different moral codes, and I found it almost impossible to be around him. Even if I had tried to steer him straight, Trent would not have listened to me. Still, I felt like maybe me losing my job and everything going on with Jay was my punishment for not doing more.

"Hey, man, condolences. How you holding up?" I turned around and saw Kyle. We hadn't spoken since our disagreement concerning Jay, but I was glad he'd come to the funeral and the repast. "You hanging in there?"

I took a sip of the punch I was holding. "Yeah, you know, as well as can be expected."

"I feel you." He looked down, as if searching the floor for his next words. He must have found them, because he looked back up at me and said, "I know we haven't been seeing things eye to eye lately, but I just wanted you to know that I'm here for you. Always have been, always will be. Love you, man." He gave me a sincere smile that told me he was not just saying words he thought I wanted to hear. He was speaking from the heart.

"I appreciate that, man. And I love you too." I finished my punch and pitched the empty cup into a garbage bag, then gave him a brotherly hug.

"So what is this crap Lisa tells me about you, uh, losing your job?" He spoke as if he was embarrassed for me, which he didn't need to be, because I was embarrassed enough for myself. I looked away toward the food buffet. "Hey," he said. "You know you can talk to me about anything, bro."

"Yeah, I know, and I appreciate your concern, but I got things under control. Matter of fact, there's someone I need to go talk to about this very subject. Excuse me." I didn't even wait for a response before walking over to the food spread.

I walked up behind my uncle. "Hey, Uncle LC."

With a full plate in his hand, my uncle turned to face me. "How's it going, Wil? That was a nice little eulogy you gave your brother."

As Trent's older brother, I felt obligated to say a few words at his funeral. Either I had done a really good job of convincing everyone I was sad to see him go, or Uncle LC was just offering empty praise. Either way, I didn't think it was necessary to respond to his comment.

I looked around at the catering hall. "Thank you for this. Melanie and I appreciate you making sure my brother had a nice homegoing."

"No need to thank me. We're family," LC said.

"Yeah, I guess we are," I said halfheartedly, still harboring very mixed feelings about what I was about to do. "So...I've been thinking about that offer you made me, the one for a job."

He gave me an intense look. "And you know the offer still stands. The doors to Duncan Motors are always open to you. You just have to walk through them."

"Yeah, well, I think I'm ready to do that. Walk through that door, that is. I want to take you up on that offer." I suppressed a sigh, hoping to appear genuinely interested in working for him, rather than just desperate enough to sell my soul.

My uncle's eyes lit up. Behind them I could even see a shadow of pride. It was a family business, and I couldn't deny that my uncle was all about family.

"We'd be glad to have you." A huge smile covered his face. On the outside looking in, one would never know he'd just attended the funeral of his nephew. "I have the perfect position. You can work with—"

Before my uncle planned out my entire career, I had to stop him. "I don't want some fancy position. What we talked about will suffice."

"Customer service manager. So be it." He let out an amused chuckle.

I nodded. I certainly wasn't anywhere near as excited as my uncle, but I was grateful nonetheless. At least I wouldn't have to worry about money for a minute. I wasn't looking to make a career with Duncan Motors, but I would at least stay until I found something that suited me better.

"If you'll excuse me, I'm going to go tell Orlando the good news."

"Sure, and thanks again, Uncle LC."

He walked away to search for my cousin Orlando, who was his second in command. Uncle LC kept all his kids involved in the family business.

As LC was walking away, Kyle and his wife were making their way over toward me. At least now I had an answer for him if he asked about my employment status.

"Hey, bro, I'm gonna get ready to head on out." Kyle offered up his hand and we gave each other some dap.

"All right. Well, thanks for coming." I released him, then bent over and gave his wife a kiss.

"No doubt, but before we leave, I wanted to let you know that you can always come work for me. I could use someone with your talent."

"I appreciate that offer," I said, "and if you'd caught me five minutes ago, I may have taken you up on it. But I just accepted a job from my uncle."

Kyle took a step back, looking shocked. "I thought you said you'd never work for that guy."

"I did, but he gave me two hundred and fifty thousand reasons why I should."

"Well, then I ain't mad at ya." Kyle wrapped his arm around his wife. "Congratulations, bro. I hope this is the start of something great for you."

Jay
22

I left Allen and Cassie's place while they were at Trent Duncan's funeral and headed to the city to take care of some unfinished business. In my transvestite gear, I felt relatively safe taking public transportation without being recognized. That didn't mean I wasn't nervous, but this was important enough for me to take the risk.

It took about half an hour to find the address, but it was worth it the moment I saw her step out of the building. I thought my heart was going to jump out of my chest. It had been so long since the last time I'd seen her, but she was still just as lovely as I remembered. Her beauty made me breathless. Forget about boys to men: This one right here had definitely gone from girl to woman in the blink of an eye.

As she stood at the crosswalk, I fell back, pretending to be reading a window sign. I couldn't just walk up and stand next to her. Not yet. I had to get myself together first. Besides, she was far too engaged in whatever it was on her cell phone that had her tap, tap, tapping away at the screen. Even doing that, she looked so sophisticated, well put together, and about her business. That made me smile. There was nothing I loved more than a woman who had her shit together, or could at least pull off looking like she did.

The light turned, and she went strutting across the street. I followed several feet behind, so amazed by the way she carried herself that I actually stopped in my tracks to watch her. She was like a tall, dark gazelle in her stilettos—such grace and poise.

She was almost a quarter of a block away before I was finally able to get my feet moving to follow after her. Every now and then she'd look up from her phone and check out her surroundings. If I didn't know any better, I'd think she knew I was watching...or at least that someone was watching. I looked around. Shit, every man in the vicinity was watching. With the certainty and confidence that made up her aura, I'd say she knew exactly what she was doing when she'd walked out of that house.

Trying to be discreet while following her had its challenges. Keeping up with a woman on a mission was no easy feat in itself, but doing it in an uncomfortable pair of women's flats brought the difficulty to a whole new level. I tried my hardest not to draw attention to myself and to remain incognito. I guess one might say that being six feet tall dressed like a woman wasn't the route to go. Hell, I felt like once she passed by, everyone's attention shifted to me, which made me pretty damn uneasy. It was possible those sneaky-ass feds were somewhere in the cut, which was why I couldn't get close to her, not just yet. I had to make sure everything was safe first.

After a few blocks, I was elated when she finally went inside a café. I didn't know how much longer I could have walked down that street. Trying to be light on my feet and not walk like a man had actually taken some leg strength. My calf muscles were on fire.

I entered the café a few seconds after she did. I watched the hostess escort her over to a little table for two.

"How many today?" A second hostess came out of nowhere and startled me. I'd had my eyes glued on the prize.

I cleared my throat nervously. "Just one. Over there, please." I pointed at a booth across the café from where she'd been seated.

The hostess gave me a peculiar look but didn't comment as she led me to the booth I'd requested. I had tried to lighten the pitch of my voice, but I could tell by the expression on her face that my baritone voice had given her pause.

"Here you are," the hostess said as she handed me a menu.

I nodded and smiled. The less I said, the better.

"The soup of the day is chicken noodle," she told me. "It'll do that throat of yours some good."

If I were a woman, I'd say she was throwing shade, but since I wasn't a woman, just wearing women's clothing, I let it go.

"Julie, your server, will be right with you," the hostess said, then went to assist some other customers that had entered the café.

I was able to turn my attention back to the woman I'd come to see. I had waited outside her apartment building all day for her to come out, and she was finally in a circumstance where I could approach her, but now my nerves were getting the best of me. I mean, even if I weren't wearing a dress, I wouldn't be worthy of stepping to her. But I had no choice. I had to do it now before the opportunity escaped me.

As soon as I gathered my nerves and stood up from the booth, I saw a man join her at the table.

"Damn," I muttered, sitting back down.

Playboy had no problem at all stepping to her. The brotha, wearing creased khakis and a fitted sweater that proved he worked out every day, took the other chair at the table and dragged it over next to her. I watched her eyes light up.

"Hi, I'm Julie." My server approached my table. "Can I start you off with something to drink? Some water or—"

I quickly nodded and let out a cough.

Julie tried not to look disgusted, although she backed up subtly to put some distance between us. "Water?"

"Mm-hmm," I said in a singsongy tone, hoping that would conceal my manly voice.

"Would you like some lemon with that?"

Again, I nodded.

"Okay, I'll be right back. You just take your time in looking over the menu." Julie walked away.

I turned my attention back to the couple, who were now engaging in a public display of affection. He was rubbing his nose on her ear as he whispered something to her. Her cheeks got all rosy as she giggled. I felt my blood pressure rise when I saw her playfully swatting his hand away, underneath the table.

I watched as her server brought her a soda. It looked like she was maybe asking playboy if he wanted something. He shook his head, and the server walked away. He stood up and said a couple more words that made her blush. He then kissed her on the cheek, returned the chair to its original position, and left the café. I was glad to see him go.

I wasted no time going over to her table and sitting in the now-vacant chair. "Hi, Kiana."

She looked up at me, her eyes spooked. "Excuse me, do I know you?" She was clutching her purse, and I hoped to God she wasn't about to pull out a can of Mace.

"You mean to tell me that you don't know your own father?" I said bluntly, no longer trying to conceal my deep voice.

Kiana squinted her eyes, focusing in on me. All of a sudden they widened. "Dad!" She practically jumped up out of her seat.

"Shhhh. Shhh." I lowered my hands, signaling her to stay seated. "Keep it down," I whispered.

"Oh my God, Daddy. I can't believe it's you." She struggled to contain her excitement. "I'm sorry, but I gotta hug you."

I could tell there was no stopping Kiana, so I just let her get it over with. Besides, there was nothing I needed more right about now than a hug from my youngest daughter.

"Oh, Daddy," Kiana said as she wrapped her arms around my neck.

I allowed her the moment, but then, afraid she would draw too much attention to us, I patted her arm, signaling to her that it was enough. Kiana sat back down.

"Thanks, baby girl," I said to her. "You don't know how much I needed that hug." Then I tried to put on my best "disapproving daddy" face. "Speaking of hugs, who was ol' boy all hugged up on you just a moment ago?"

Kiana blushed. "He's just a friend." She began playing with her straw, swirling it around her drink, suddenly fascinated by the ice cubes clinking in her glass. Anything to avoid eye contact.

"Friend, huh? Well, your friend needs to learn to keep his hands to himself," I snapped.

Kiana laughed, and I couldn't help but join her.

With some of the tension now gone, I asked, "So, how's your mom?"

"She hates you." There was no hesitation in her answer. "Even more now that the police have been by the house three times. They left a card telling us to call them if you came around, but I threw it out."

"They say anything else?"

"Not really, but everybody's saying you're in Texas."

"Good." I stared out the window and briefly watched the people passing by. "You really are something, you know that?"

"Daddy, I'm sorry I didn't see you as much as I wanted to for all those years. But as soon as I turned eighteen, who was on the first thing smoking to go see her dad?" Kiana said proudly. Not many eighteen-year-olds looked forward to going to jail on their birthday, but that's what my daughter had done. Her loyalty was second to none.

"You don't have to apologize. I know your mother wouldn't bring you to see me." I took her hand and caressed it between my fingers, changing the subject. "How's your sister?"

"A bitch like always." She rolled her eyes for emphasis.

"Hey, hey, that's your sister. Don't talk about her like that. One day—"

"All we're going to have is each other," she said, finishing my sentence. "That doesn't change the fact that she's a bitch, Dad. She hates you more than Mom does."

Her words stung, but they were the truth. "Well, she takes after your mother."

Kiana laughed.

"What about your brother? Have you talked to him?"

Kiana shook her head. I hadn't expected her to speak to Jordan, considering my relationship with his mother. Tracy was the reason Kiana's mother and I broke up.

"I've been keeping an eye on his social media and he seems all right," she said.

"Does he have a girlfriend?"

"He's got some interest, but he's a little awkward." She laughed. "He's a cute kid, Dad."

I wish I could have sat there and listened to the sound of her laughter all day long, but that wasn't in the cards. I'd already sat there a minute too long. "Look, I have to go, but give me your cell phone number." It would be much easier to reach out to her via phone than to have to follow her in drag and try to find a spot to talk to her.

Kiana dug into her purse, retrieved a piece of paper, then dug around some more. "Dang, I thought I had a pen in here. This will just have to do." She pulled out what looked like a makeup stick, eyeliner or something. She wrote her number on the paper and slid it to me.

I put it in a place that I'd recently discovered to have more than one use: my bra. "I wish I had some money or something to give you," I said. Before I got locked up, I always had something for my baby girl, whether it was a little change or some candy. I loved letting her feel spoiled by her daddy back then. It hurt me knowing that I hadn't been able to take care of my children for all these years. I had nothing to offer any of them.

"The fact that you're here is enough," she said, and I could tell she genuinely meant it.

I stood up to leave. "That's why I love you, baby girl."

"I love you too, Dad."

I kissed her on the forehead. "And by the way, if by chance the police come back to the house..."

"I never saw you," she said.

"That's my girl," I said with a smile, exiting the café a hell of a lot happier than I'd come in.

Wil

23

"Big Wil. How's it going, cuz?" Orlando greeted me at the front door of Duncan Motors as if he'd been standing there waiting for me to arrive. Maybe he had. He couldn't have been standing there too long, though, because I arrived at nine a.m. sharp. "Hey, man, again, I'm sorry about Trent."

We joined our hands into a fist and pulled one another in for a hug.

"It's all right, O. I appreciate the kind words you said at the funeral. I know you and him were close." He lowered his head in acknowledgment. "So how you doing?" I asked.

"I can't complain," Orlando said. "Business is great, and it's about to be better now that you're here." He rested his hand on my back. "Come on. Let me give you a little tour and introduce you to the team."

I followed Orlando as he walked toward the double glass doors. "I'll be in charge of customer service, right? Not just a supervisor on a team, but the—"

"Head nigga in charge." Orlando finished my sentence with a laugh. "You are the only one anyone in customer service can and will report to. After you, there is only me and Pop."

face. Finally, he spoke. "Why are you sitting there?" He nodded toward the large ergonomic chair on the opposite side from where I'd settled in. "Get comfortable behind your desk."

"My desk?" I questioned. He'd just introduced me to every member of the Customer Service Department, and every last one of them worked out of a cubicle. How could I have possibly known that I was working in anything other than a cubicle as well?

"I'm sorry," I said. "I thought this was your office."

Orlando laughed. "Oh, no. It's all you, cousin." He looked around. "Besides, do you think I'd work out of a dump like this?"

I laughed with him, even though his arrogance reminded me a little too much of my brother. No wonder Trent had joined their team.

"Anyway..." He walked over to the credenza behind my desk and powered up the computer. "You might want to spend some time getting a feel for how things have been run in the past, and then forget all about how things were run in the past and make it ten times better for the present." He looked at me. "Pop wants Duncan customer service as efficient as possible. He wants every customer happy. These people are paying a lot of money on these high-end cars. That may mean you have to tear into some people...even firing them if need be." Orlando stood up straight and looked at me. "Think you can handle that?"

"Oh, yeah," I said with a sigh. Unfortunately, I knew more about getting rid of employees than I wanted to.

"Fine. Well, I'll leave you here to get started. I've got business outside the office, but like I said, if you need anything—"

"Clyde," I said.

"Yes, Clyde." Orlando looked around. He pointed to a door. "Bathroom." He turned and pointed to the back wall over by the sitting area. "Fridge and coffee station. You should be good to go." He walked to the door and then turned to face me. "Can you think of anything else you might need?"

I shook my head. "No, for the moment, I'm good."

"Great," he said. "I'll try to stop back in later this afternoon. Maybe we can grab lunch. If not, if you have any trouble, just hit me on my cell."

Orlando exited the office, and I took a moment to soak in the reality surrounding me, thinking, *This might work out after all.*

Allen

24

I pulled into the garage next to Cassie's car at about two in the afternoon. I'd be lying if I didn't admit that Wil's drunken tirade had planted a seed of paranoia in me. Not that she'd been giving me any less attention, but Cassie had also been bending over backward to make sure Jay was happy and well cared for since his arrival. He was my friend, for sure, but I couldn't help but feel jealous and a little insecure about the idea that they were spending so much time together every day while I was at work. I decided it wouldn't be a bad idea to make an unannounced trip home in the middle of the day, if only to allay my paranoia. Best-case scenario, I would discover that nothing was going on, and then I would take my wife out shopping, then for a romantic dinner and some alone time in a local hotel.

I placed my hand on the hood of Cassie's car to check the temperature. It was cold, which meant she hadn't gone anywhere in the last couple of hours. That concerned me, since she was supposed to be at school.

I entered the kitchen through the garage, calling out her name. There was no response. My mind immediately went to a dark place, filled with thoughts no man should ever have to have about a friend.

Stop it. Stop it, Allen, I kept telling myself, trying to banish the image of Cassie and Jay together from my mind. *Jay would never do that to you, and neither would Cassie. You have to trust them.*

Of course I knew that was the right thing to do, but I couldn't shake the uneasy feeling that Jay was going to try to screw my wife—just like he'd done with my fiancée back in the day. I mean, they do say that history repeats itself.

"Cassie! Jay!" I called out both names this time.

Not getting a response, I headed into the kitchen, which I was shocked to find in total disarray. There was a half-eaten bag of chips, an open box of Entenmann's doughnuts, an empty milk carton, and a dirty cookie sheet covered in the crumbs of what must have been chocolate chip cookies. The oven door was still wide open, filling the room with heat because it had not been shut off after someone baked the cookies. I closed the door and shut off the oven, then turned around to clean up some of the mess. That was when I heard a rhythmic thumping noise above me. I looked up to the ceiling just as the moaning sounds started. There was no mistaking the sound of sex.

Fuck friendship, I went into straight protective mode, heading for the foyer closet to get the hammer from the small set of tools I kept in there. Then I hustled up the steps two at a time.

At the top of the stairs, I stopped to listen, halfway hoping that I had just hallucinated the sexual noises. Unfortunately, as I stepped closer, the moaning and groaning became even more obvious. I'd be a fool to deny what was going on under my roof. I could try to think good thoughts all I wanted, but the fact remained that my best friend and my wife were getting it on.

"Damn, girl, that shit feels good," I heard Jay growl.

For a second I thought I might puke right there as I stood outside the bedroom door. I had so many emotions rolling around inside of me at the moment: rage, jealousy, pain, disappointment, and confusion. They took over my being until I became someone I couldn't even recognize. Part of me wanted to curl up in a corner and die, but first I wanted to take someone out with me. Oh, yes, there might just be a murder-suicide up in this bitch!

Jay was yelling, "Whose pussy is this? I said, whose pussy is this?" The headboard was crashing against the wall like he was trying to drill right through my wife.

I had heard more than enough. I took four steps back, then with all my weight, slammed into the door, almost tearing it off of its hinges.

"It's my pussy!" I yelled out as I stood in the doorway with my chest heaving up and down.

"What the fuck?" Jay said.

I barely saw Cassie, who went scrambling under the covers. Who could blame her? Who wanted to be caught on all fours with her husband's best friend's dick inside of her?

"Al, what the fuck is wrong with you?" Jay shouted.

"What do you think is wrong with me? You're fucking my wife, and I'm gon' kill you and her!" I raised the hammer over my head, about to rush at him, until the woman—who I now clearly saw was not my wife—popped her head out from under the sheets. She screamed, and I froze in my tracks.

"You're not Cassie," I mumbled, feeling disoriented.

"No, that's not Cassie," Jay yelled at me as I backed out of the room. "That's my friend Tina. Or at least she used to be my friend." And with that, he got up and slammed the broken door in my face.

Wil

25

"I have to admit, Mr. Duncan, I was skeptical at first, but offering all our high-end customers free oil changes was a stroke of genius. Service tickets are up almost fifty-five percent this week, and both sales and merchandising are on pace to break weekly records," Clyde said as he stood in the doorway to my office.

The chip he'd had on his shoulder the first day was pretty much gone now. Thank God he'd gotten over the fact that he was no longer the big man on campus. I'd worked hard over the last two weeks to make sure people understood I was more than a seat warmer with the last name Duncan, and it was paying off. If I had to say so myself, I was fitting in pretty well around this place—and no one was more surprised about that than me.

"Thanks, Clyde. Sure, the oil change on a Porsche or Lamborghini is no cheap nut to absorb, but that kind of good service keeps our customers coming back. We want people to feel good about the Duncan brand so they continue to buy from us."

"Makes sense," he said.

"It'll make even more sense once we get that new computer system I talked Orlando into buying. Then we'll be able to profile each customer, give them a call just to chat and see how the car is running."

"The gearheads and yuppies will lose their minds. Someone calling just to give them a chance to talk about their precious cars."

"Exactly," I said.

Clyde stood there staring at me for a minute, and then he said, "You know, I can see why they brought you in. It's gonna be good working with you, Wil." He shot me a slight smile, tapped the frame of the door, and then walked away.

That was the first time he'd called me Wil. I took that as his sign of approval, and I found myself smiling too as I got back to work on the invoices in front of me.

"Mr. Duncan." My receptionist's voice came through the intercom.

"Yes, Allie."

"Someone is here to see you," she said, and I thought I detected a hint of uneasiness in her voice.

"Can you ask Clyde to deal with them, please, Allie? I'm just finishing up something."

"I already tried that, but she's insisting she has to talk to you."

I assumed it was a disgruntled customer who had probably already cussed out someone else and now wanted to speak with the head of customer service. This would be my first interaction with a dissatisfied customer. I had to make sure I handled things appropriately.

"Okay, send her back."

I straightened my tie and pulled a breath mint out of the drawer, preparing to charm this customer out of whatever mood she was in. When she walked in the door, I realized this was going to be a little more complicated than I had imagined.

"Wil." She said only my name, but there was an intensity to her voice that let me know this was not a social call. She was clutching her large purse as if she had a million dollars in it and was worried someone might snatch it off her arm. Her face was tense and uptight, certainly not the face of a woman to be played with.

"Kenya, what are you doing here? I wasn't expecting to see you," I said, unable to conceal my surprise. It wasn't every day Jay's ex-wife stopped by unannounced.

She dove right in. "I need your help." There was no "How have you been? How's the wife? The kids?" She sounded desperate.

I stood, and we hugged briefly. "Have a seat." I extended my hand toward the chair in front of my desk. "So, how'd you even know I worked here?"

She shrugged. "Facebook. Diane congratulated you on your first day here last week."

My wife and I were going to have to talk about this social media thing.

Kenya sat down in the chair and took off her sunglasses. "Wil, have you seen Jay?"

My back stiffened. I was pretty sure this conversation was going to come down to Jay at some point, especially since Kenya hated him more than anyone in the world, but I didn't think she'd go in this quick. I guess she was still pissed about him leaving her for Tracy, who was half her age. My first thought was that she might be working with the police to apprehend Jay.

I sat back in my chair and then looked to my open office door, letting out a sigh. "Look, if you came here to talk about Jay, this is not the time or the place."

"You're right, Wil." She reached into her purse and pulled out a brown envelope, which she flung across my desk. "I'm here for something a lot more important than Jay's sorry ass. This is what I got in the mail the other day."

I could tell she meant business and that she was scared. I picked up the envelope and opened it, pouring out its contents onto my desk.

"What's this?" I asked, staring at a pile of photos.

"Look at them," she said.

I picked up one, a picture of two women having sex. I was already uncomfortable looking at dirty pictures in front of Kenya, but then shit got way more uncomfortable when I realized I knew one of the women. "What the fuck! Oh my God!" I blurted out. "Is that—"

"Yes!" Kenya exhaled loudly. "And they want a hundred thousand dollars or they're going to put them all over the Internet."

"Fuck." I looked from Kenya back at the pictures. "Where the hell do they expect us to get that kind of money?"

Kenya leaned back in her chair and crossed her arms over her chest. Her voice was deadly calm when she said, "Well, for a start, we can turn Jay in for the reward."

Jay

26

After slamming what was left of the door in Allen's face, I tried to apologize to Tina and pick up where we'd left off, but she wasn't having it. She was totally freaked out and probably a little creeped out, so she started getting dressed right away. Not that I could blame her. Having a deranged hammer-wielding dude break the door down while you're in the middle of sex would freak out anyone. Shit, I was completely unnerved by Allen's actions, and I'd known him most of my life.

"You okay?" I asked.

She nodded timidly, but she was still trembling as she sat down on the bed to put on her shoes.

"I'm gonna go talk to him. Stay right here. I'll be back." I left the room to find Allen and get some answers. I found him locked in the bathroom downstairs.

I started pounding on the door. "Yo, Al! Bring your sorry ass out of there. What the fuck was that shit about?"

He spoke to me through the locked door. "Look, Jay, I know you're mad and all, but—"

"But what? You was the one acting all Billy Badass a minute ago. Don't be a pussy now. Bring your ass out here!"

I kept pounding until I heard him unlock the door and I saw the knob turning slowly. He stepped out with his hands up in surrender, although he still clutched the hammer in one hand. I almost wanted to laugh. Did he really think that hammer could protect him now? I had learned at least ten ways in jail that I could have taken that shit from him.

"I'm sorry, Jay, but you have to understand how that looked to me. Usually I come home and Cassie's right there on the couch."

He wasn't lying about that. I'd never seen anyone lie around and watch as much daytime TV as Al's wife. For someone who was supposedly a full-time student, I never saw her go to class.

"So she wasn't on the couch and that automatically means I'm fucking her?" I asked. "That's foul, Al. We're supposed to be tighter than that. How could you think I would do that?"

Al raised his eyebrows in disbelief. "Does the name Rose ring any bells?" he asked, reminding me of one of the biggest fuckups of my younger years. The sad thing was, Rose meant nothing to me, and I had kind of forgotten about that whole thing.

My shoulders slumped a little, and all the fight went out of me. "Oh. Yeah. Sorry about that. Listen, man, I hope you know I wouldn't do something like that again. That was a long time ago. We were damn near kids."

He also relaxed a little, lowering the hammer and placing it down on a nearby table. "I sure hope not," he said. "Cassie means a lot to me, man, and I don't want to lose her—or you—over some stupid shit."

Just then, Cassie walked into the house carrying several shopping bags. Allen started frowning immediately.

"Where the hell have you been? I thought you were supposed to be going to school today," he said, gesturing to her shopping haul. "I guess you decided to go spend some money instead, huh?"

She rolled her eyes as she set the bags down on the floor. "Oh, give it a rest, Allen. You are like a broken record with your anti-shopping speech. Besides, I saved money by taking the bus instead of wasting gas and driving. I just went to buy Jay a few more sweat suits."

Allen shot an angry glance in my direction. "Yeah, well, he's got enough shit now, so stop shopping for him."

I was starting to understand his insecurity a little better now that I saw the way she talked to him. It was pretty damn obvious who held all the strings in this relationship. If only she hadn't put me in the middle of it. I hadn't asked her to go buy me no damn clothes, this time or the last time she did it.

Cassie rolled her eyes yet again. This woman had attitude for days. It was a good thing she was so hot, or even a man as docile as Allen wouldn't have put up with her.

"Yeah, well, whatever. What is wrong with you two anyway?" she said, looking at Allen and then at me. Suddenly she realized what I was wearing. Her eyes roamed up and down my half-naked body, and I could have sworn she paused a little on my package.

"Uh, Jay, why are you in your underwear?" she asked.

Allen answered for me. "Jay has a lady friend upstairs."

Cassie's eyes narrowed. "A lady friend? In our house?"

I tried to make light of the situation. "Uh, yeah. You know, a brotha's been away for a long time, and I was feelin' a little backed up. You can't blame me for needing a little companionship, can you?"

She did not look amused, and neither did Allen when he said,

"You know, Jay, now that I think about it, what the hell made you bring her here? What if she recognizes you? You can be one selfish bastard sometimes. Did you even think about what could happen to me and Cassie?"

"Yo!" I said, waving my hand at him. "Keep your voice down, man. She don't know anything. I met her out in the Hamptons when I first came home. She's cool, but if you keep running your mouth like that, things could change real fast."

"Well, you never should have brought her here, Jay," he said.

"No worries." Tina's voice came from the top of the stairs. "I'm leaving anyway."

My heart started pounding. I had no idea how much of that conversation she had heard.

She came down the stairs and kissed me on the cheek. "It was real good seeing you again, Johnny." She sounded calm, and I decided she hadn't heard much, which made me feel better. "But next time, you can come out and see me. I think it's safer at my place." She glanced over at Allen and brushed past him, and then past Cassie, who glared at her.

I watched her switch her ass as she walked to the door. "I'm looking forward to seeing you again," I said as she left.

"Humph." Cassie's exasperated sigh made me look in her direction.

The expression on her face took me by surprise. She said no words, but I read the message loud and clear: "Harpo, who dis woman?"

Kyle

27

As I sat out on the deck at the marina, enjoying the evening breeze, I saw a male figure headed my way. It had to be one of the boys, most likely Wil from the size of the silhouette. He'd called earlier saying that he wanted to get together, and more importantly, that he wanted to see Jay. I was happy about that, and I knew just the right way to make it a memorable night for all of us. There was no doubt there was a need for an icebreaker, so I figured this was as good a time as any to introduce the fellas to the new lady in my life.

I stood as Wil approached, ready to make the introduction.

"Holy shit, she's for real," Wil muttered.

"You think I'd lie about something like this? Wil, old buddy, I'd like to introduce you to my new lady." I watched proudly as his eyes took in her beauty. I'd been talking about her for quite a while, but I think they figured she was a figment of my imagination the same way we thought Cassie was a fairy tale until Allen brought her around.

"Oh my God, she's beautiful, Kyle."

"Bro, *Vanessa* is more than beautiful." I rubbed my hand along her side. "She's every man's fantasy. From the moment I saw her, I knew I had to have her. I didn't care what I had to do or how much it cost. I was determined to make her mine."

"*Vanessa?* You done named her already?" He chuckled.

"I named her the first time I laid eyes on her," I said.

"Man, you crazy," Wil said. "Talking about a damn boat like it's your woman or something."

"Well, in a way she is. She's my side chick. Come on board," I said, and he stepped onto my brand-new hundred-foot yacht. I'd always loved the water and had owned a few boats in my life, but purchasing this beauty made me feel like a real success.

"Side chick, huh? You know what, Kyle? You need help." Wil walked over to the fully stocked bar and began making a drink. "So you think Jay is coming?"

"He better." I held out my glass and Wil refreshed my drink. "You should see the spread I ordered from the caterer."

"Look, Kyle, I'm sure the food is off the chain, but I don't think anyone is going to have much of an appetite once I say what I have to say."

I didn't like the sound of that. "What's going on?"

"Let's just wait for Jay and Al to get here." He took a long swig of his drink. "Y'all are not going to believe this shit."

When I heard a noise, I exited the galley with Wil right behind me. Allen was standing on the deck, wearing a fishing hat, vest, and boots. His pole was flung over his shoulder. This dude looked like he was about to star in an episode of *Wicked Tuna.*

"Hey, I thought we were going fishing tonight. You guys aren't dressed for a fishing trip—and this is not a fishing boat."

He looked so excited I hated to break the news to him. "We're not going fishing, Allen. Wil wanted us all to meet up because he has to talk to Jay. I just didn't want to say any of that over the phone."

My news wiped the excitement right off his face. "Why? What's going on?"

"Jay is meeting us, right?" Wil asked.

"I guess," Allen said with a shrug. "I left a note for him this morning after I got Kyle's text, but Jay and me haven't been seeing eye to eye lately."

"What's that about?" I asked.

Allen shook his head. "Nothing. Just a little misunderstanding," he said. Then, obviously not wanting to talk about it, he turned to Wil and changed the subject. "What do you need to talk to Jay for?"

Wil sighed uneasily. "Come on and have a seat, because what I'm about to show you will knock you off your feet."

Allen set down his fishing pole, and we all got situated around the small table in the stern. Wil pulled an envelope out of his jacket, took some pictures out of the envelope, and then threw them on the table. "Take a look at these."

I picked up one of the pictures, totally unprepared for what I was about to see. "Holy shit! Where did you get these?" I shuffled through some of the other pictures with my heart pounding. Allen couldn't even look at another picture after his initial glance.

"I had a visit from Kenya at my office," Wil explained.

"Kenya gave these to you?" I asked in disbelief. "Why the hell would she do that?"

Wil let out a halfhearted laugh. "Kyle, my man, that's the million-dollar question."

Wil

28

"What's the question?"

I turned around when I heard Jay's voice, but what I saw certainly wasn't what I had expected.

"What the fuck is he wearing? Has he lost his fucking mind?" I blurted when I finally regained my composure. It took my brain a second to realize that the tall, homely woman standing in front of me was actually Jay. I'd heard he was running around in a dress to disguise himself, but seeing him standing there all dolled up was almost more than I could bear. It was bad enough that he was an escaped convict, but now he was an escaped convict in drag. And to think I used to look up to this guy.

"Damn, Wil, lighten up. You ain't never seen a man in a dress before? Where's the love?" Jay joked.

Allen and Kyle just looked on in silence. I wanted to rip that stupid dress off of him, but we had more important things to discuss at the moment. I took a deep breath, walked over to him, and shoved the pictures into Jay's hand. "We ain't got time to be joking around, man. We have serious things to discuss."

He nonchalantly looked through the stack of pictures, then

looked back up at me. "What the fuck is this? You act like you've never seen naked women."

"Look at them closer, Jay," Kyle said, stepping up. "What do you see?"

Jay thumbed through the pictures again, a little more slowly this time. "What do I see? I see a party that got started without me."

"Aw, hell no! He did not just say that," I heard Allen groan.

I shot Kyle a look that said, *Is this guy for real?* Clearly Jay was not seeing what we were seeing, which was mind-boggling. Finally, Allen walked up and snatched one of the pictures out of Jay's hand and waved it in front of his face. "Don't you recognize your own fucking daughter?"

Jay looked at the picture again but shook his head. "That woman looks nothing like Kiana. She's way too dark," he said confidently.

"Last time I checked you had two daughters, one of them being my goddaughter," I said, wondering how much longer it was going to take for him to put all the pieces together.

Jay's face fell as recognition finally settled in. "Stephanie?" he muttered under his breath, looking at Kyle like he wanted to hear him say it wasn't really her in the pictures. Kyle nodded, and Jay flinched as if he'd been punched in the gut. He covered his mouth, and I could see he was trying to hold back tears. "Fuck. That's my baby, Kyle."

Kyle placed a hand on his shoulder and said sadly, "I know, bro. I know."

"Al's right. I didn't even recognize my own kid," Jay said, lowering his head.

Kyle tried to comfort him. "It's been a long time since you've seen her. She's grown up a lot in ten years. Become a young woman."

"Where'd you get them from?" he asked, still hunched over.

"Kenya," I replied.

"Why did Kenya give you naked pictures of my daughter?" Jay asked, anger simmering just below the surface.

"Because I'm Steph's godfather and someone is blackmailing her. The photos are going to be posted online if she doesn't pay a hundred thousand dollars. She's studying to be an elementary school teacher, Jay. What school district is going to hire her with these pictures of her online?"

Jay threw the pictures down on the table. "This shit is crazy! Who would do something like this to a nineteen-year-old kid? And who's the other chick in the pictures?"

"I don't know," I said. In every photo, the other woman's face was either turned away from the camera or her head was cropped out of the picture. "To tell you the truth, I didn't even think to ask Kenya if she knew who it was. I was too damn shocked to even think straight."

"Oh my God, Kyle!" Jay said frantically. "What if it's Ashlee?"

Kyle considered it for a moment, then said, "I doubt it. During both your trial and your appeal, my investigators went over her life with a fine-tooth comb. They found plenty of evidence that she's more than a little crazy, but she's not a lesbian."

"Fuck!" Jay punched his fist into the air like he wanted to hurt someone.

"Calm down. We'll figure this out," Allen said.

"Fuck calming down!" Jay yelled back at him, pacing nervously in those stupid high-heeled shoes. "I am not going to let this shit happen to my daughter."

We all watched him helplessly for a minute while he paced around and ranted. There was really nothing we could say to a man whose child was being threatened. Nothing could make that better.

"What am I going to do?" Jay buried his head in his hands.

"We'll give them the money," I said.

"And where the fuck am I supposed to get a hundred grand?"

On that note, all eyes turned to Kyle.

Kyle

29

So much for me and the boys enjoying my boat. I'd spent over five hundred dollars on food, and most of it ended up in the backseat of my car to become breakroom snacks for my office the next day. Not that the food was even remotely important compared to everything else. During the entire drive home, I couldn't get those images of Stephanie out of my mind. Seeing her in such an intimate moment— or, more accurately, a pornographic moment—after watching her grow up felt like a violation, even though I hadn't seen them by choice. I know she was nineteen, but as a father of two daughters and as her uncle, I didn't want to see her as anything but a little girl. So I could imagine what Jay must have been going through. If that were my daughter, I would want to kill someone.

I had a feeling that things were about to go from bad to worse. Of course, this situation was complicated by the fact that Jay was still on the run and had to also focus on his own mess. We would all need to pull together to help Jay and Kenya figure this shit out. But for now, I needed to go in my house, shower, and pray to God those images washed down the drain as well.

I closed the front door and turned around, almost running right into Lisa, who stood with her arms crossed and her weight on one leg as she tapped the other foot impatiently. She looked like she'd been waiting there a long time to drill into me. She'd probably been rehearsing a speech all night.

She started with "You saw Jay tonight, didn't you?"

I stood there for a moment as she glared at me, waiting on a response. I wasn't trying to think of what to say, but what not to say. I hated straight-out lying to her, but lying by omission, now that was another story. But as I stared back at Lisa, I could tell she already knew the answer. She had this look in her eyes that dared me to lie—which made me wonder why the hell she even bothered asking the question in the first place.

Now on to my next question: How the fuck did she know?

"I knew it!" Lisa said. "The moment you sent me a text that you were having a drink with the guys, I knew something was up." She waved an accusatory finger in my face. "Ordinarily you would have just called, but this time you sent a text." She began walking back and forth, pacing like a younger version of Angela Lansbury from *Murder, She Wrote*. "You were afraid if you talked to me on the phone that I'd start asking questions."

She'd hit the nail right on the head. I could hear her drilling me over the phone now.

"Look, babe," I said, holding my hands up to try to relax her or to defend myself if she suddenly flew off the handle. "I did see Jay tonight, but it was for a good reason."

"Ooooh, I knew it!" She clenched her fists down at her sides and stomped her foot. "There is no such thing as a good reason when it comes to that man."

I was starting to get agitated because she was standing there looking like a three-year-old throwing a tantrum. What was the fucking big deal? Jay was my best friend, he was family, and I shouldn't have to defend myself for being loyal to him. "I don't get it. Why do we always have to talk about Jay?"

"Because he's ruining our marriage, that's why. I mean, this is ridiculous. I could see if we had issues with bitches trying to come between us, but a dude? This is crazy."

"I agree. It is crazy, which is why I don't understand why you don't just let the shit go!"

"I can't let the shit go, Kyle!" She paused briefly. "Because I'm scared." Lisa had a serious look on her face as her eyes moistened. "Every time you walk out that goddamn door I'm scared. Do you not see the danger you're putting yourself in, let alone our family?" She sniffed.

It softened my position to see her like this. I walked over to her and placed my hands on her shoulders. "You don't have to be scared, and I'm sorry if I'm coming off harsh. It's just that I don't need you acting like Wil."

"And how does Wil act?" she asked.

"Like he's going to call the police on Jay or something."

"Well, wow!" she said sarcastically. "At least one of you fools has some sense. Good for Wil. He ought to call the police. Hell, *I* ought to call the police."

She went to pull away, but I tightened my grip on her shoulders. "Don't you even think about it." I shook her slightly. "Do you hear me? I'm Jay's friend. Friends help one another, and we're trying to figure things out. So I swear to God, Lisa, don't you even think about sending that man back to prison. I'm serious." I released her and then stormed off.

"Fine, Kyle," I heard her yell as I kept walking. "But mark my words, you're going to end up sharing a cell with your best friend if you keep it up."

I hated to say it, but Lisa had a point. What I was doing could be considered aiding and abetting. I just hoped it never did get to the point where I had to choose between Jay's freedom and my own.

JAY

30

"Hey, no dress," Cassie said as I came down the stairs in a pair of sweats and a T-shirt. "Guess you're not planning on going out today, huh?"

She was half-naked as usual, spread out on the sofa like she was about to do a photo shoot. If I was a betting man, I would have laid money on the fact that she had been waiting for me to notice her. Ever since the day I had Tina at the house, Cassie's behavior toward me had been borderline flirtatious—whenever Allen wasn't around, of course.

I glanced toward the kitchen, noticing that there was no smell of bacon frying like most mornings. "Al left already?"

"Yeah, he's gone. He had an early meeting." She delicately patted the cushion next to her. "Come, sit down. I've got a present for you."

I stayed where I was. "Listen, Cassie, you gotta stop giving me presents. I don't think Al appreciates you spending his hard-earned money on me."

"Oh, please, I'm not worried about Allen, and neither should you." She waved her hand dismissively. "So are you gonna come

over and get this or what?" she asked. I was nervous for a second when she reached into her robe. I swear to God I thought she was going to expose herself to me, but instead, she pulled out a blunt. "It's about to be on and poppin', Mr. Jay."

She placed it between her lips, picked up a lighter from the coffee table, and lit the blunt. "You said last week you wanted to get high, didn't you? I figured with everything going on with your daughter, this was as good a time as any."

I couldn't argue with her logic . . . plus the smell of the weed was driving me insane. I had missed that so much when I was locked up. She held the blunt in my direction, and I wasted no time going over to the couch and taking it from her.

It had been so long since I'd smoked weed that I went into a coughing fit immediately. Cassie thought that shit was the funniest thing she'd ever seen. She was laughing so hard I thought she was going to pass out. I ignored her and stopped coughing just long enough to take another drag.

"Hey, it's puff puff pass. And if I'm not mistaken, that was three puffs," Cassie said jokingly, rolling her eyes as she snatched the blunt from my hand. "You know I'm just messing with you, right?" she said with a giggle, then took a deep pull. "Mmmm," she moaned as she exhaled and then leaned back against the sofa.

I sat there, feeling a buzz wash over me, mesmerized by the way she handled the blunt. I'd never seen someone make smoking a blunt look so much like sucking a dick. After a few seconds watching her, I settled into the couch cushions and leaned my head back.

"Fuck, that's some good shit. I'm high already," I said.

"Yeah, I got this shit from my girl Destiny. Them Dominicans always have the best shit."

the truth, because she tried to clean it up a little by adding, "But he's your friend and he's going to stick by you."

My mind started racing as I imagined all the possible scenarios. Should I pack up and get out of there immediately? Should I stay put and confront Allen and Wil, and try to work things out with them? As I became lost in my thoughts, Cassie's hands started wandering. They slid up my arms and then across my chest.

"Jay, I don't want you to leave. But I know you don't want to go back to jail either. You don't belong there. I don't care what Allen or Wil or anybody says."

"I gotta figure out some way to clear my name, but I can't do it from here. Especially not if my boys don't have my back. Maybe I should leave the country."

She started massaging my shoulders as she talked. "I know, but if you have to go, you're going to need someone to have your back. You know, like that woman who helped Whitey Bulger. He stayed on the run for like thirty years." Her lips gently pressed against my neck. "I could help you like that."

I knew we were treading into dangerous territory, but between the weed and her soft kisses, I felt so good that I didn't want it to stop. Besides, at the moment, I was a little pissed at Allen now that I knew he had been talking to Wil about me behind my back. If he thought I was being selfish, then I might as well go ahead and be that way.

I felt Cassie's hand caressing my dick, and I did nothing to stop it. I laid my head back and enjoyed the sensation as she pulled down my sweat pants and then lowered her head to my waist. For a quick second I was overcome by how good her warm, wet tongue felt, but then something in the back of my drug-addled brain broke through the haze, and I realized what the fuck was about to go down, where it was about to go down, and with whom.

"Whoa, whoa, hold up. This can't happen." I grabbed her wrists and pushed her away from me.

"Why not?" she asked. From the look on her face I could tell she wasn't used to being turned down. "If it's protection, I have—"

"It's not protection," I said, flinging her arms as I released her wrists. "It's you. You're my best friend's wife."

"Your best friend's wife who can help you. In more ways than one." She went for my private parts again. Call me weak, but I let her get back to work, pushing any feelings of guilt out of my head. Her skills were that good.

"You'd do that? You'd leave your husband and all this to run away with me?" I asked, allowing myself to imagine what it would be like to have her by my side as I went on the run again.

"Yes," she said, taking a break to answer me. "I'd do that and leave all this."

"What about money? It's going to be hard enough taking care of myself, but taking care of two? What would we do about money? I can't exactly work."

"You don't have to. I can work."

I made a face. "Yeah, right. Doing what?" As far as I knew, the only thing she was good at was spending Allen's money and watching trash TV. She damn sure didn't have a degree, and maybe not even a high school diploma.

"I do have skills," she said confidently. "You mean Allen never told you about what I was doing when he met me?"

She sat up, and I instantly regretted getting into this conversation. I wanted her to shut up and put her head in my lap again.

"Yeah, he told me you were working at the library," I said.

She laughed. "The place I worked at wasn't exactly a real library, silly. It was a strip club in an old library building."

Well, I'll be damned. She was a stripper. That made a hell of a lot more sense than her being a librarian. "Yeah, I could see you as a stripper," I said.

"I wasn't just a stripper," she bragged. "I was the best exotic dancer that place had ever seen. My old boss calls me almost every day asking me to come back to work." She stood up and showed me some of her moves. I could definitely see why her boss wanted her back. She could shake that ass and have a brother hypnotized in no time.

She sat back down on the couch and continued her fantasy about us running away together. "And the beauty of it is I can dance anywhere, Jay. Not only that, but I can take care of us both. I make at least five hundred a day. What do you say? All you have to do is sit back and collect the money."

"Like a pimp?"

"Call it whatever you want. Just take me with you."

"Why the hell would you wanna go on the run? Hell, I don't even wanna be on the run."

"Because I like you, and it would take me away from the boredom of this house and Allen's corny ass. We could be like Bonnie and Clyde traveling the world."

I'm not gonna lie; it was tempting. Part of me loved the idea of having this incredibly hot stripper by my side. It sure would make my time less lonely while I figured out how to clear my name and stay out of jail. But the more I thought about it, the more images of Allen kept flashing in my head. Finally, the thoughts of my friend overpowered the seductive nature of her fantasy.

Fuck! You can't let this happen, Jay, I told myself, although a large part of me still wanted to ask her to stand up and give me another lap dance. I had to repeat my warning to myself...in less diplomatic terms. *Quit thinking with your dick, man. This is your man Al's woman, and you're a grown-ass man now. Don't repeat what happened with Rose.* That last little scolding did the trick.

"No!" I shook my head adamantly. "If this was twenty years ago, I'd be on your ass like white on rice, but I will not betray my friend."

She stared at me for a moment like she was having trouble processing the word *no*. I was sure she didn't hear it often.

"You're fucking serious, aren't you?" she asked.

"Yeah, serious as a heart attack," I replied with my head held high. My resolve was growing stronger. I felt like I was out of the danger zone now.

"First you pull that little stunt with that bitch the other day, and now this."

"Wait a minute. What the hell are you talking about?"

"Don't try to play stupid, Jay. You bring another woman into this house and fuck her in my house knowing how I feel about you."

I had to wonder what the hell was in the weed we had smoked, because this chick was straight trippin' now. "First off, I have no idea what the hell you mean by I know how you feel about me. You shouldn't be feeling shit about me. All your feelings should be for your husband, my best friend."

She sucked her teeth. "Negro, please. You know damn well a woman like myself can only be with a weak man like Allen for so long. I was already getting bored with his ass before you showed up."

This was blowing my mind. Al and I might not have been on the best of terms at the moment, but this shit was over the top. I had never heard a woman dog her man so completely before.

"Well, damn, Cassie. If you felt that way about Al, then why'd you marry him?" I asked.

"Because I had nowhere else to go. It was either Allen or the streets. And you of all people should know how mean the streets are, considering you've had to spend a few nights on them. That's why you can't go back out there." This crazy bitch was still trying to talk me into letting her go on the run with me.

"I can't go back out there? Are you kidding? I have no other choice. Especially after"—I gestured to my still-naked crotch where her mouth had just been—"this." I stood up and pulled up my sweats, making sure she understood that there would be no more action between us.

She stood up next to me, and once again her hands were all over my chest and arms. "You don't have to go out there alone." She had this passion in her eyes, like we were characters in some corny-ass romance flick. I mean, this chick was on the stage.

I stepped back to put some distance between us because this was too damn much. I had to get out of there quickly.

"You got me fucked up right about now. Look, I have to get out of here. I need some fresh air. I need to think." I walked toward the stairs. "Tell Al I'll talk to him later."

"What do you mean, talk to him?" She raced after me, attempting to block the way. "Are you going to tell him about what just happened?"

"You mean that you admitted you're only with him because you didn't want to have to be on the streets, yet you're willing to leave him to be on the streets with his best friend?" I asked, hoping it made her feel real stupid. "I don't know. I'll have to think about that." On that note, I pushed her out of the way and headed upstairs to pack my shit.

Kyle

31

My new boat was probably the safest place for us to meet, but with Lisa on the rampage, I didn't want to push my luck. She'd made it clear she didn't want Jay anywhere near our properties. Technically the boat wasn't a property, but wives can get touchy when it comes to semantics. So I reserved a small conference room in a library out in Amityville, Long Island. I imagined the last place cops would be looking for Jay was at a library. Jay wasn't exactly an intellectual giant, but he had actually been spending a lot of time at libraries lately, doing Internet research on Ashlee. He was afraid to use the computer in Allen's house, in case the feds were monitoring our phones and computers. Unfortunately, none of his searching had turned up any useful information yet.

"Did you get the money?" Jay asked when he entered the conference room where Wil and I had been waiting for nearly forty minutes. Unlike the last few times I'd seen him, he was no longer wearing a dress. Thank you, Jesus. Ever since the authorities had moved their search to Texas, his face had dropped off the evening news, so he was feeling a little safer going out of the house without his ugly-woman disguise.

He closed the door behind him, looking like he had the weight of the world on his shoulders.

"We were starting to think you weren't gonna show up." I could hear the aggravation in Wil's voice.

"Calm down, big man. You know the Long Island Rail Road is never on time. Besides, I had to check the place out before I came in. You never know when someone might turn you in for the reward on your head," Jay said sardonically, staring Wil dead in the face like he was accusing him of something.

"What you trying to say?" Wil questioned, taking a few steps closer to Jay.

Jay puffed out his chest. "I'm not trying to say nothing, but you sure sound mighty guilty. You got anything to tell me, friend?" Jay's voice was full of contempt. Despite our lifelong friendship, these two were closer to blows than ever before.

Trying to stop any violence before it started, I stepped in between them. "Look, we're not here for y'all's petty bullshit. We're here for Steph, remember?" I pushed them apart. Wil seemed to relent, but Jay stood his ground. "Steph, Jay. We're here for Steph, all right?"

"Yeah, a'ight." He finally relaxed. "But understand something: My freedom's not a game, and any person thinking about turning me in better pray the cops get me before I get them, 'cause I will damn sure make any rat pay."

"Is that a threat?" Wil asked.

"No, that's a fucking promise." Jay turned to me, ending their standoff, even though I could tell Wil was still vibrating with anger.

"Now, did you get the money to get my baby's pictures back?" Jay asked me.

I reached under the table and pulled out a briefcase. "I could only get twenty-five thousand. I'm sorry, bro, but with the purchase of the boat, I'm cash-strapped." None of my boys had ever asked me for this type of money, but I was embarrassed that I'd let them down. Their reactions didn't make me feel any better about it. Jay hung his head, and Wil cursed under his breath.

Wil stared into the open briefcase, looking totally disappointed. If I didn't know better, I would have thought it was his kid.

"I can probably come up with twenty-five thousand, but when Diane sees it's missing, I'm going to need it back," he offered.

"I'll get it back to you. I just need a little time," I said, trying to reassure him. "The real question is where are we going to get the other fifty K in the next couple of days?"

Jay's reaction surprised me. "I don't think we should give them a dime."

I turned to him, my eyes wide with confusion. "So you're okay with those pictures being released?" I asked.

"No. But you can't trust people like this. Even if you do stop them this time, whenever they need more money, they're going to threaten to release the pictures again," Jay said, surprisingly calm.

"Fuck that! We gotta try," Wil said, having none of Jay's resistance. "You wasn't around, but she spent every weekend at my house up until last year when she graduated. She's a good kid, and she doesn't deserve to be exploited. I don't care if it's a million dollars. We need to do whatever it takes."

"It's a moot point anyway if we can't get that other fifty grand," I explained.

"There's gotta be someone we can get the money from." Wil sounded desperate.

We had all come from modest backgrounds, so there weren't

many people we knew—if any—who had that kind of cash lying around. Then it hit me: There was one person who had plenty.

"Why don't you ask your uncle for it, Wil?" I closed up the briefcase and sat down at the table.

"Yeah," Jay agreed. "That brother's got more money than a bank."

Wil shook his head. "Listen, I don't want my uncle involved. You guys don't know how ugly this could get. My uncle doesn't just give money away. It comes with a price. Do we really want that?"

"You're the one pushing for us to get the pictures," Jay snapped. The tension between these two lately was off the charts. "Where else are we going to get the money?"

"He's right, Wil. Your uncle is the only person who might be able to help us. Could you really live with yourself if you didn't ask him and then Steph's pictures get released online?" I asked.

Wil stayed silent for a minute, obviously arguing with himself about whether it was more important to help Steph or to avoid getting tangled up with a loan from his uncle. Finally, he broke down and decided in favor of his godchild.

"Okay, I'll call him," he said with a frustrated sigh. "But you guys have no idea what road you're taking us all down."

"Stop being so damn dramatic," Jay said.

"It's not dramatic, Jay; it's fact. Because when I tell him what I need the money for, it's not just me he's going to hold responsible for paying it back. I'm a Duncan, so I'll be all right, but if that money's not paid back…" He looked at me. "Kyle, you could lose your business or wind up dead alongside our resident fugitive."

"We'll be all right." Jay sounded confident, but I was starting to understand Wil's hesitation. Owing LC Duncan money was something we didn't want to take lightly.

"I sure hope so," he said, shooting Jay an irritated look as he headed for the exit. "Kyle, I'll hit you up once I talk to my uncle."

"What's his problem?" Jay asked after Wil was gone. "I thought it was one for all and all for one."

"Think about it. Wil always said there were rumors about his uncle's business. Now his brother starts working for the guy, and he ends up dead," I explained. "Wil's uncle is no joke."

"Hell, if he's so bad, then why is Wil working for him?"

I had asked myself the same question when I first heard that Wil accepted LC's job offer, but unemployment will cause a man to make decisions he might not otherwise make, I guess. "Look, man, you know he'll do anything to keep his wife happy. He was out of a job, and his uncle offered him some serious money to take over the Customer Service Department at the dealership. It sounds legit from what Wil has told me."

Jay slumped down into the chair next to me. "If you say so. I just hope he comes through with the money. I don't know if I can take much more stress." Despite his sometimes nonchalant attitude, Jay had a lot on his shoulders, between worrying about his kids and trying to clear his name.

"I hear you. I know you're carrying a lot these days," I said. "How's it going with your Internet searches anyway? Anything turn up that might help you?"

He shook his head. "Nah. It's like she don't even exist on the Internet. I can't even find a Facebook page."

"So where do you go from here?" I asked.

"I was hoping you could call that private investigator you know. Maybe he can find something for me."

"You mean the same one we used when you went to trial? He

didn't exactly find anything that helped you win your case last time," I said doubtfully.

"What other choice do I have?" Jay asked. "Besides, it's ten years later. Maybe he'll find something new."

"You're right. I'll give him a call." This particular investigator was discreet, so I wasn't worried he would call the feds and turn Jay in, but he wasn't cheap either. I sure hoped he accepted credit cards, otherwise I didn't know how the hell I was going to pay him. Still, I couldn't let my friend down. He needed me, and I would do whatever I could to help him.

I stood up to leave. "In the meantime, try to keep your head up, man, and stay off the streets as much as possible. No need to be taking any chances out here."

Jay

32

"Hello?"

My back stiffened and I froze up like a little bitch when I heard Kenya's voice on the phone. My ex-wife had this way of making me feel like the bad kid who was always being punished when he did nothing wrong, because eventually he was going to do something wrong.

"Hello?" she repeated.

It took me another moment to regain my composure, but one look at the pictures of Steph that I was holding jolted me back to reality.

"Hey, Kenya, it's me." There was silence on her end now. I guess she had to get her shit together too. It had been a long time since we'd talked.

She finally spoke, and her voice was full of venom. "What do you want, Jay? Don't you have better things to do, like trying not to be captured?"

"Look, I didn't call to argue with you." I glanced down at the pictures again. "I called to check on Steph and see if there is anything I can do to help with this situation."

"My daughter is fine, and what situation are we talking about? The fact that she's gay, or that she's gay and you didn't know about it?"

"*Our* daughter, and I don't give a damn if she's gay," I shot back. "What I care about is that she's being exploited for a hundred thousand dollars. Did Steph give you a name? Maybe we could track down the other woman in the picture."

I could hear Kenya suck her teeth. "The other woman is a ghost. Steph said she was just a hookup. Some woman she met in a club."

"How could she be so reckless?" I blurted, then immediately wished I could take it back.

"I don't know, Jay. Maybe she takes after you?"

I closed my eyes and counted to ten. God, she still knew how to pluck my nerves. "Kenya, it's been almost fifteen years since we've been divorced, and it's time to let it go," I said. "I know I cheated on you and did a whole bunch of fucked-up shit, but that was a long time ago."

"That's funny. It seems like yesterday to me." She was getting choked up. Kenya had always been a crier. "You destroyed our family and then left me with two kids for Tracy, a woman half my age, so excuse me if I have a hard time forgetting that you ruined my life." That was when I heard the waterworks begin.

I softened my tone, trying to be sympathetic. "Kenya, listen, baby. I'm sorry—"

"No, Jay!" She cut me off. "You don't get to sweet-talk and charm your way out of this. Not anymore." She stopped crying and hardened her voice. "Now, if you wanna do something for our daughter, let Wil or Kyle turn you in. We could use the reward money to help stop those pictures from going viral."

"Wil and Kyle are both putting up twenty-five thousand."

"They're very generous, but we still need another fifty thousand."

"Wil's asking his uncle for the rest," I said.

"But this isn't their problem, Jay," she argued. "It's ours, and you should be man enough to do whatever it takes to help our daughter. Eventually you're going to get caught—nobody runs from the U.S. government forever—so just let one of us turn you in. Last I checked, the reward is up to fifty thousand."

I didn't like the idea that she was checking my reward. "Do you realize what you're asking?"

"I'm asking you to do the right thing. Steph is only nineteen. She has her whole life in front of her, and she wants to be a teacher like me. No school would ever hire her with pictures like that out there on the Internet."

"I'm not going back to prison, Kenya."

"You selfish bastard! I hate you!"

"Look, just let me and the fellas—"

She hung up before I could finish my sentence.

I didn't bother to call her back, but her words were still ringing in my ears. I exhaled, wishing I could drown out the sound of her voice and also erase the images of Steph and the other woman from my mind. I knew I needed to put the pictures down and go back to bed, but I just couldn't. I shuffled through the photos, trying to figure out what it was that was nagging at the back of my mind.

"You okay out here?"

I heard Tina's voice and quickly put the pile of photos facedown on the coffee table. I'd been so wrapped up in all my drama that I'd almost forgotten I was at her house. She'd been knocked out ever since I put it on her after dinner.

"Yeah, I'm good," I said as she sat down beside me on the couch.

"What's that?" she asked, pointing to the pictures.

"Nothin' important," I said, then rushed to change the subject. "I'm surprised you're up. Don't you have to get up early in the morning?"

"Yeah, but I couldn't sleep. I've been worried about you."

"Why you worried about me?" I asked as I picked up the pictures and slid them back into the overnight bag I'd brought with me.

"'Cause your name is Jay Crawford and not Johnny Graves."

Her words paralyzed me for a minute. When I felt my heart start beating again, I slowly turned and looked at her. "How long have you known?" God, did I feel stupid.

She shrugged. "I had an idea when your crazy friend started calling you Jay. Not to mention the fact that your mug shot is all over the Internet. I mean, your shaved head might fool some people, but they haven't been up close and personal with that face like I have." She let out a chuckle.

"Tina, I can explain."

She held up a hand to stop me. "I'm not looking for an explanation. I just want one question answered." She waited until I made eye contact before she asked, "Did you rape that woman?"

I shook my head adamantly. "No, I didn't. I swear to God. We used to date and she took 'if I can't have you, nobody will' to the extreme."

She kept her eyes locked on mine, like she was searching in there to determine whether I was being honest. Finally, she said, "I believe you. Don't ask me why, but I believe you."

"Thanks," I said, keeping it short and sweet. I didn't want to say the wrong thing and make her change her mind. If she felt threatened in any way, she only had to make one phone call, and the cops would be waiting for me as soon as the bus pulled back into Queens.

"So now that you know, what do you plan on doing about it?" I asked cautiously.

She looked away and thought for a minute. "Nothing," she replied, turning her attention back to me. "I like you, Jay. I would never turn you in."

I looked into her eyes and saw a sincerity that matched her tone of voice. "I appreciate that, but I don't want to bring trouble your way. I'm out of here in the morning. You never saw me. That's our story, and we should stick to it ... for both our sakes."

"You don't have to leave."

"Yeah, I do. You've been really kind, but you don't want this type of heat. Besides, I got things I need to take care of up the island."

She placed her hand on my back. I closed my eyes and enjoyed the gentle pressure she applied as she rubbed in a circle, comforting me. God, how I had missed this type of simple human contact. I wished I could stay there forever.

"Well, you always have a place to stay if you need it."

Allen

33

"Hey, babe," I said, entering the living room. I'd just gotten home from work, and even more than seeing my wife, I was hoping to see Jay. For the third straight night, he wasn't anywhere to be found. "You heard anything from Jay? I'm starting to get a little worried about him."

"Fuck Jay. Do I look like his keeper?" I could almost feel the venom in Cassie's voice, which was strange, because up until the night Jay and I had a fight, they had been thick as thieves.

"You think he's still mad about that shit with the hammer?" I asked. I thought we had cleared the air that night on Kyle's boat, but he'd barely been at the house since then.

"Who knows what that motherfucker is thinking? Far as I'm concerned, he can stay gone. We don't need his ass around here anyway," she ranted.

I walked over to the couch and sat down next to her. Cassie had been Jay's biggest cheerleader, so her new attitude took me by surprise. "What's wrong? I thought you and Jay were friends. Why all the sudden hostility toward him?" To tell you the truth, I was a little relieved that her attitude was directed at him and not me for a change.

"Please, Allen, Jay is a big-ass phony. He is not the friend you think he is." Cassie folded her arms across her chest. She was so angry that she wouldn't even look at me. "I really don't want him staying here anymore."

Well, damn, I didn't see that coming.

I scooted in close to Cassie and put my arm around her. Jay was my best friend and all, but Cassie was my wife, my woman. She was my life. I'm talking some Prince, "I would die for you" type shit. If she wanted him gone, then I would figure out a way to make that happen, but first I wanted to be sure it was what she really wanted. Maybe they'd had a little fight over who got control of the remote control or something and she'd get over it soon. I didn't want to kick him out if it could be avoided.

"Uh, did something happen I don't know about?"

"I just don't trust him right now." She got up from the couch and turned to me with hateful eyes. "And I don't trust you." She began rubbing her arms as if she were trying to erase my touch. "I don't trust men. I'm sick of men, and I just want to be left alone— by all of you." She looked like she might cry as she walked away.

"Cassie, what the hell is going on? What did I do?" I stood and reached out to her, but she ran off to the bedroom, slamming the door behind her.

"What the fuck?"

I'd never seen her so bothered, not since the night she showed up at my door after being beaten. There had to be more to this than just a spat between me and my best friend, and I was going to get to the bottom of it.

I took one step toward the bedroom, but before I could take a second, I heard a loud crash, then "U.S. Marshals! Don't move!"

A swarm of Robocops charged through my door, which they had just kicked down, and knocked me to the ground.

"Where is he? Where the hell is he?" one of them yelled in my face. The spraying spittle was the least of my problems, considering the big-ass gun he had pointed at my head.

"Who? What?" I wasn't able to think straight.

"Jay Crawford. Where the fuck is he?"

"Allen!" I heard Cassie yell. I looked over my shoulder just in time to see her being taken down to the ground. That's when, on instinct, I tried to get up to go to my wife's rescue.

"Don't you fucking move!" the spitter shouted, grabbing me by my collar. He pulled me nose to nose with him. "Now answer the fucking question. Where is Jay Crawford? We know he's been here, and we know he's been disguising himself as a woman."

Fuck! How the hell do they know that?

I looked over at Cassie, and all I could think was wherever Jay was, thank God he had taken all his shit before he left.

Jay

34

Spending the night at Tina's place and screwing her in every room had been a great distraction for the moment, but it didn't change the reality of my situation. I was now plagued with several dilemmas, the most immediate being where the hell I was going to stay now that I was back in Queens. As much as I hated the idea, it looked like I was going to have to go back to Allen's house—the last place I wanted to be after he tried to kill me and his wife tried to fuck me. I still couldn't believe she had blindsided me the way she did. After ten years in prison, I thought I had become pretty good at reading people, but if she had shown any signs, I totally missed them. I thought she was cool as hell, almost like one of the guys, until she tried to attach herself to my dick.

The weird thing about it was now that I knew Cassie had the hots for me, I understood why Allen had come after me with that hammer. Just thinking about it had me feeling like all the air had been sucked out of my lungs, and the closer I got to the house, the worse it got. I knew I had to man up and talk to Al face-to-face, but I dreaded telling him about his wife's indiscretions. That was one of those conversations that could go a few different ways. He could believe me and be pissed at his wife, he could believe me but somehow make it my fault and be pissed at me, or he could call me a liar and come after me with his hammer again.

I guess I would find out soon enough which way it would go. As much as I didn't want to, I knew I had to tell him. It was my duty as a friend to let Al know about the snake he was married to. Hopefully our friendship would survive the fallout.

I was so lost in thought that I almost walked into the worst possible scenario when I turned the corner on Allen's street. I was halfway down the block before I noticed not one or two but six black SUVs parked in front of his house. I was about seven houses away, far enough that the lone agent standing in front of Allen's house didn't notice me, but close enough that I knew I didn't want to be anywhere near there. I dipped into a landscaped yard with evergreens surrounding the house like a fence.

I moved a branch to peek through the trees, and my heart nearly stopped when I saw Allen and Cassie being led out of the house in cuffs. My adrenaline kicked into high gear and I took off, slicing my arm on a branch when I busted through the bushes on the other side of the yard. Running to the back of the next house, I went up on the porch and tried to open the back door, but it was locked. A dog started barking inside, so I bolted off that porch and hopped the back fence into the yard of a house on an adjacent street. Thank God I had left most of my stuff on Kyle's boat, because all those bags of women's clothing Cassie had bought me sure would have slowed me down.

The driveway was empty, but I still didn't want to take the chance of going near the house, in case there was a dog there too. Instead, I tried the door on the side of the detached garage, and luckily, it was unlocked. I slipped inside and shut the door behind me, collapsing against the wall as I tried to catch my breath and slow my racing heart.

The garage was full of lawn tools and boxes of junk. If I weren't afraid of making too much noise, I would have torn that place apart. I was beyond furious that someone had turned me in. There were only a handful of people who knew where I was staying, so the list of possible suspects was small.

Tina had been to Al's place, so it was possible she could have called, but after our conversation last night, I didn't believe she would. If any woman hated me enough to turn me in, it was Kenya, but she didn't know where I was staying, so I could cross her off the list too. Cassie was also pretty pissed at me after I turned her down the other day. For a second I thought she might have ratted me out just to make sure I didn't tell Allen about what a ho she was. But then I realized that she couldn't have reported me without implicating herself and Allen for harboring a fugitive, and she was smarter than that. Kyle was loyal to the end, so he wasn't even on my list in the first place.

That left only one person who could have called the feds: Wil. That son of a bitch had been on my back ever since I escaped. Shit, he had even tried to blame me for not being around for Steph all these years, like that was the reason for the pictures. That disloyal motherfucker probably decided he didn't want to ask his uncle for the money even after he promised he would.

I sat in that garage, feeling angry and disappointed in my friend all at the same time. I had thought we were all tight enough that I could rely on my boys to help me out until I could clear my name, but Wil had stabbed me in the back. What made it even worse was that I didn't know where to go now that the feds were on to me. If they went to Allen's house, then they'd probably been to Kyle's too.

After a few hours, it was dark, and I figured it was time for me to move on. I didn't know where I was going, but it wasn't safe for me to stay in Allen's neighborhood now that the marshals had been there. I cracked open the door and peeked outside. It was dark, and there were no lights on in the house, so I figured it was safe enough to go.

I took a deep breath and then raced out of the garage, passing through several yards until I got to the corner. Luckily, a bus was just pulling up. Without checking the route number on the front of the bus, I hopped on as soon as the doors opened. I had no idea where I was going, but now that Allen's block was hot, I only cared about getting far away from there.

Kyle

35

"Shit. Not again," I mumbled under my breath when I turned down my block and saw the caravan of black SUVs scattered in front of my house, blocking my driveway. I pulled up to the curb, threw my car in park, and quickly headed up the walkway. I was met by Deputy Franklin, who was coming down my front steps, followed by several other deputies whose attitude changed the second they saw me.

"Mr. Richmond." Franklin stopped in front of me and extended his hand.

"What are you doing here?" Needless to say, I did not shake his hand. I had tunnel vision at that point. My mind was on one thing: Why the fuck was this guy at my house again? Okay, two things, the second being Lisa, who was probably packing to leave my ass as we spoke. She'd been on the brink, and this was just enough to send her over the top.

"Where's my wife?"

"She's fine." His feelings didn't seem the least bit hurt about my lack of pleasantries. He just eased his hand back down to his side and slipped it into his pocket. "You're right. No need to pretend like we're friends. I'm here on official business. We received a very credible tip that Jay Crawford has been right here in good old Queens the whole time me and my men have been gallivanting all over Texas looking for him."

"Well, I don't know where this credible tip came from," I was quick to say, trying to step past him. His men closed the circle. "But I can assure you that Jay is not in my house."

"Relax. I believe you." He was wearing this stupid smirk on his face. "However, we did search your house just in case."

My jaw tightened. I'd seen enough during their last visit to know how careless cops could be when searching someone's house. As a matter of fact, I wouldn't be surprised if they messed up shit on purpose. I suddenly had visions of couch cushions ripped open and china cabinets turned over. I didn't know how much longer I was going to be able to stand there and not go check on my wife—and our possessions.

"So my question to you," Deputy Franklin said, "is: Have you seen him?"

He waited on my reply, but I treated it like a rhetorical question and simply waited on him to continue speaking. I didn't want to jump the gun and say anything that might make me look like I had something to hide.

When he got tired of waiting for me to speak, Franklin continued. "Not here, of course, because like you said, he's not here. Which doesn't necessarily mean he hasn't been here. He's clearly just not here now. But anyway, have you seen him...anywhere?"

"What you see is what you get, Deputy," I said through a tightened jaw. He stood there staring at me for a moment, probably trying to read my facial expressions, so I remained stoic and stone-cold still.

"Are you sure you want to play it this way, Mr. Richmond?"

he asked in a calm tone. I stood my ground and didn't so much as breathe. "I mean, this could get ugly."

He waited a few more seconds, but faced with nothing but silence from me, he nodded his head and walked away, pulling out a two-way radio.

I made a move to go into my house, but Franklin called out to another marshal, "Deputy Clarence, hook him up."

Before I could even think, the deputy yanked me by my right arm, and the next thing I knew I was being handcuffed.

"Kyle Richmond, you're under arrest for aiding and abetting a fugitive and lying to a federal officer," Franklin said.

"What? You can't prove that!" I said.

"Wanna bet the next five years on it?" Franklin challenged as they led me toward one of the SUVs.

Wil

36

"Hey, Mr. Duncan."

I looked up from my desk to see Clyde sticking his head in the doorway.

"Oh, sorry to disturb you, boss." He put his hand up apologetically and whispered, "Didn't realize you were on a call."

"I'm not," I said, placing the phone on the receiver. "I was just listening to my voice mail. What's up?" I was starting to really like Clyde.

"There's a guy outside who's insisting he has to talk to a Duncan. Well, he asked for Orlando, but he's not around. Then he wanted to see cousin Junior, but he's gone too. LC is out, so you're the only Duncan left."

"Did he say what he wants?" I asked.

"Nope. Didn't say much of anything. To tell you the truth, he doesn't look like the type of guy who'd be in the market for a luxury car."

"Interesting."

"You want me to send him away?" Clyde asked.

"Nah. Sounds like he's on a first-name basis with my cousins, so I better see what he wants. You can send him in."

"You got it." Clyde disappeared down the hallway.

I pulled open my desk drawer and popped a peppermint into my mouth. That had become a habit now that I was talking to customers all day.

"You Mr. Duncan?"

Clyde was right. The guy standing at the entrance to my office, dressed like he'd gone shopping in Lil Wayne's closet, didn't look like one of our typical customers. Still, I got up and reached out my hand, prepared to greet him like I would anyone who came to Duncan Motors.

"Yes, I'm Wil Duncan."

He smirked at me like the formality amused him. "I'm Mr. Cramer," he said without bothering to shake my hand.

"Nice to meet you, Mr. Cramer. How can I help you?" I asked.

He paused and stared at me. It felt like he was waiting on some kind of reaction, like I should have been familiar with his name or should have been expecting him.

He tilted his head to the side. "You said your name was Duncan, right?"

My forehead wrinkled in confusion. "Uh, yes, Wil Duncan."

He extended his hand and I thought he had finally found some manners, but when I went to shake it, he slipped a piece of paper into my hand.

I looked down at the paper, then up at him with a puzzled expression.

"You sure you're a Duncan?" he asked.

This whole situation was totally bizarre, and I was starting to get tired of this dude, whoever he was. "You wanna see my driver's license?" I asked, more aggressively than I should have.

My sudden lack of professionalism seemed to get his attention. He dropped the attitude, held his hands up in surrender, and began walking backward to the door. "Nah, man, I was supposed to give that to Orlando. Just make sure he gets it, okay?"

"Will do."

He left, and I unfolded the paper he had left with me. It said simply: 1000 Atlantic Avenue. An address, and nothing more. What the hell could be so important about this address that would make that dude act the way he had? I shrugged my shoulders and dropped the paper on my desk. I would give it to Orlando when I saw him.

My phone rang, so I sat down, ready to get back to work.

"Duncan Motors, Wil Duncan speaking," I answered.

"Wil, oh my God! They're at the door. I don't know what to do. Should I answer the door or should I—"

My wife was talking so fast I thought she was going to start hyperventilating. "Slow down, Diane. Who is there at the door?"

"They said they're federal marshals, Wil!" she said in a harsh whisper.

"At our door? At the house?" I stood.

"Yes. I don't know what to do."

I hoped like hell our phones weren't being tapped, because the way Diane was acting, anyone listening would think she sounded guilty of something.

"What do you mean, you don't know what to do? Answer the damn door. We have nothing to hide."

"But what if it's about Jay?" she asked. "And you know it

probably is. I mean, what else would it be about? You know he's still on the run. What do I tell them? What do I say?"

"Diane, calm down. You're acting like Jay is hiding out in our basement or something. Just tell them you don't know anything." I had purposely kept it a secret from Diane that Jay was at Allen's house. Now I was glad she didn't have that information, because she was nervous enough that she might have spilled something to the marshals if she knew.

"Calm down, huh? That's easy for you to say. You're not the one here who has to talk to them."

I heard them pounding on the door in the background. This was no friendly visit, that was for sure.

"You're right. I'm sorry. I wish I was there with you to handle this. Do you want me to come home?"

She sighed. "No, by the time you get here they'll be gone—I hope."

They started pounding again.

"I better go. I'll call you back after I talk to them."

"Do you want me to stay on the phone with you?" I asked, but it was too late. She'd already hung up.

I put down the phone and started pacing around my office. Diane's nervousness had rubbed off on me. She didn't know anything about Jay's whereabouts, but what if she said something that set them off and then something happened to her? With all the police shootings in the news lately, I was suddenly very worried about my wife's safety.

My phone rang sooner than I had expected it to. I ran back to the desk to answer it.

"That was fast. They're gone already?" I said, assuming it was Diane.

"You motherfucking son of a bitch!"

I had to pull the phone away from my ear because the voice was so loud. I waited a couple seconds until I didn't hear any more screaming before I put the phone back to my ear.

"What the hell are you yelling about?" I asked.

"You finally did it, huh? You finally called the police on me," Jay screamed. "You couldn't just ask your uncle for the money, could you? You had to rat me out!"

"Jay," I said calmly, not wanting to set him off any more than he already was. "What are you talking about, man?"

"You know what the fuck I'm talking about. You've been threatening to turn me in for the reward money, and so you finally did it. And you were supposed to be my friend, Wil. Supposed to have my back. This is real fucked up, man. Watch your back, you piece of shit, 'cause next time it might be me stabbing you in it—literally."

When he finally stopped talking, I lost it.

"Fuck you!" I said, completely stunned by the call. "You got the nerve to call me with this bullshit when I have the federal marshals at my door, harassing my wife because of your bullshit. Fuck you!" I gave him the finger even though I knew he couldn't see it. "And for the record, if I had called the cops on you, you'd be behind bars right now."

"Whatever, Wil!" was all he said before he hung up.

I dropped down into my chair, unable to get my thoughts together. Could this day get any worse?

Kyle

37

I felt like I was in the middle of an episode of *Law & Order*. Typical gray interrogation room with the typical double-sided mirror, where they can see you but you can't see them. I just knew that sooner or later, two assholes were going to enter the room and play the typical good cop/bad cop routine. I'd been sitting in there for two hours, no doubt so they could watch me through the mirrors to see if I was nervous. It was all so stereotypical, and it infuriated me.

"Well, guess what?" I shouted, losing control and yelling at the mirror. "I'm not your typical ghetto Negro." If they thought they were going to wear me down by making me spend hours in that place until I gave in and ratted out my best friend, they were sadly mistaken. I knew the law well enough to know that I didn't have to talk to them without my lawyer present. I'd already made it known that I wanted to call him.

I started pacing in the small space. Feeling myself about to lose control, I tried to regain my composure. "They're just trying to sweat you, Kyle," I told myself. "Get yourself together. They're just trying to sweat you." I sat back down, determined to show them that they were not going to break me. That I wasn't scared.

Finally, the door opened and Franklin walked in.

"I told you guys I want to speak to my lawyer," I said, hopping up out of my seat. So much for staying calm.

"Sit down," Franklin ordered, sounding like my legal rights were a mere annoyance to him.

"I don't have to sit down," I stated defiantly. I wasn't about to let them start treating me like a bitch.

"Sit down." His demand was delivered with a threatening tone this time.

I had to remember that even with onlookers on the other side of that mirror—hell, even with a camera recording everything—this cop could mop the floor with me. He could break my neck, paralyze me for life, and only suffer suspension with pay until a judge working for the same state he worked for found him not guilty. Fuck that! I sat my happy black ass down.

Franklin sat across from me, folded his hands, and gave me that trademark smug look I'd become familiar with. "First of all, this game you are playing is not going to work. You've been arrested for harboring a fugitive. Do you know how much jail time you can get for that? And let's not even talk about lying to a federal officer."

"Lawyer. I want my lawyer."

"You'll get your lawyer when I say you get your lawyer," he said, throwing his weight around. "Now, I know Jay Crawford is your friend. You guys have been friends a long time. You love him, but he's not a good guy. He's a rapist."

As much as I wanted to stay silent, I couldn't. Hearing him say that about my friend burned me just as much as hearing Lisa doubt Jay's innocence did. "He's not a rapist."

"You know he is. My God, a jury of the man's own peers know he is. He served ten years for the crime."

"He didn't do it." I stood firm.

Franklin leaned back in his chair. "Look, Kyle, don't you want to get out of here?"

"Of course I do."

"Go home with your wife?" Franklin's tone had softened. It almost sounded sympathetic. I guess he was playing both roles, that of good cop and bad cop.

Wait. Did he just say with *my wife instead of* to *my wife?*

"Where is my wife?"

He smirked, no doubt satisfied that he'd finally struck the right nerve. "Don't worry about that for now. Like I said, you want to go home, right?"

I held myself back from calling him the motherfucker that I wanted to, and simply said, "Yes."

"Fine. Then just tell us where your friend is. We'll drop all charges against you, then you're out of here. Just like that." He snapped his fingers. "Hell, I'll even make sure you get the reward."

He made it sound so easy.

"Imagine all the women out there you'll be protecting."

I shook my head. "You don't know Jay like I do."

"I know that you'll be a hero for helping to get a rapist off the streets. Not only will you be a hero to everyone in this town, but imagine what your wife and kids will think of you." He leaned in and winked. "You'll get blow jobs even when it's not your birthday."

I had to admit, he was probably right about that. Me dropping the dime on Jay would be exactly what Lisa wanted. She was fed up with all this bullshit. Not only would it make her day, but it would make our marriage much better, because right now, things weren't looking good on the home front.

I opened my mouth to speak, when the door cracked open and a head popped in.

"Deputy, his lawyer and wife are here," a suited-up cop said.

"Fuck!" Franklin said under his breath.

Relieved that my wife was not in custody, I had to chuckle. "You heard the man. My lawyer is here. I'm done talking." I pressed my hands against the table and stood up slowly, triumphantly, and headed toward the door.

Not inclined to allow me the last word, Franklin shot back, "By the way, we have your friend Allen and his wife in custody. Let's see if he breaks under the pressure."

I slowed my steps but refused to turn around and look at him. Still, he knew he had my attention, so he added one more thing: "If you do see Jay, give me a call. Your wife has my card."

I'd had it with this guy trying to use my wife as a threat. I turned around and faced him, my eyes narrowed with pure disdain. "If you have any more questions for me or my wife, you can call my attorney."

That only caused him to smirk again.

"And far as my friend Allen is concerned, his lawyer is my lawyer, so you might as well cut him loose now and save yourself the grief."

Franklin jumped out of his chair and took a few quick strides until he was practically in my face. "You have a lot of mouth for a man who could be behind bars right now, Mr. Richmond. I'm cutting you some slack because I like your wife and I think you're a genuinely decent person who is caught in his friend's shit. But I'm running out of patience."

Wil

38

"Can I get a Corona?" Kyle asked the waitress as he slid into the chair across from me. Allen, who had just taken the seat to my right, put up two fingers to let her know he wanted one as well.

Kyle waited until she was halfway to the bar before he leaned in and said, "Did they get you too? Your text message sounded urgent."

"Yeah, I would consider having a dozen marshals knock on your door and scare the crap out of your wife urgent." I had a little attitude in my voice, but I guess I should have added a little more bass to let them know I wasn't kidding, because Kyle sat back in his chair and laughed. Allen rolled his eyes at me, shaking his head.

"You find something funny?" I asked.

"First of all, is Diane okay?" Kyle asked. He sounded genuinely concerned, so I relaxed a little.

"Yeah, she's all right. She's just not used to dealing with cops. They were only there about five or ten minutes. Once they figured out she didn't have any information they could use, they left her alone."

Allen let out a snort that pissed me off, because what happened to my wife was not a laughing matter. "You got a problem, Al?"

"Wil, I'm glad Diane's okay, but compared to what me, Kyle, and my wife went through last night, her little visit sounds like a walk in the park." Allen was about as emotional as I'd ever seen him. "So, yeah, that shit is funny and sad at the same damn time."

"What's he talking about?" Allen had a tendency to talk in riddles sometimes, so I turned to Kyle for an explanation. He was still sitting back in his chair, although he wasn't smiling or laughing anymore. "What the hell happened?"

"We were arrested last night," Kyle replied.

"Arrested?" That shocked the hell out of me. "Arrested for what?"

"Harboring a fugitive," Kyle replied rather calmly. "And in my case, lying to a federal officer."

"Get out," I mumbled in disbelief as I shifted my eyes back and forth between them, hoping to see someone break into a smile and tell me they were just joking. Their stern expressions remained unchanged. "You're serious, aren't you?"

"Serious as a heart attack," Allen said. "Someone tipped off the marshals that Jay was staying at my house." He was so angry he was starting to tear up. "And they weren't as nice to me and Cassie as they were to Diane. They broke my door down and slammed me and my wife to the ground. I had to watch those bastards grope her like she was some street ho."

I probably should have offered some sympathy to Allen for what happened to his wife, because in truth, it really was much worse than what Diane went through, but I was too mad to even go there. There was only one thing on my mind, and as far as I was concerned, one person responsible for all of this.

I turned back to Kyle. "I told you guys this was going to fucking happen. Eventually Jay's gonna get us all locked up."

Kyle shook his head. "My lawyer thinks it was just a scare tactic, because if they really wanted to, they could have held us. They don't have solid enough information, so they were just on a fishing expedition."

"Well, that's a relief," I said, but Kyle sure didn't look relieved. He was staring at me skeptically.

"What I don't understand is why they didn't arrest you along with us," he said.

"Yeah, Wil, why didn't you get picked up?" Allen snapped.

I shrugged my shoulders, although the same question had entered my mind when I heard they'd been arrested. "I don't know. Maybe it's because I was innocent. Maybe because I never harbored a fugitive or helped finance him while he was on the lam."

I wasn't saying anything that they didn't already know. It was no secret that I was not with the program when it came to helping Jay. If those pictures of Steph hadn't surfaced, I wouldn't have gone near him at all.

"Yeah, maybe," Kyle said, looking perturbed. "But how did the cops know that? And how did the cops know Jay had been wearing a dress?"

"I don't know, Kyle, but it wasn't me."

"Then who was it?" Allen asked, obviously not convinced. "Only the three of us and Cassie knew Jay was at my house, and you were the only one who threatened to turn him in for the—"

"Don't even go there," I said, cutting him off. "You know I said I'll ask my uncle for that money."

"Wil," Kyle said, getting to the point in a straightforward, even tone, "did you call the marshals on Jay?"

He stared at me, and I looked him straight in the eyes as I answered. "No, Kyle, I didn't and I wouldn't. You have my word."

He stuck out his hand. "Good enough for me."

Allen wasn't quite ready to put the issue to rest. "Well, if it wasn't Wil and it wasn't you, me, or Cassie," he said, "then who could it have been? Because someone told the cops."

"Unfortunately, my friend, there was one other person who knew." He had a pained expression on his face. "And that was my wife, Lisa."

Allen

39

I was on the subway headed to work after a weekend where Cassie and I had spent time recovering from the ordeal of being arrested. Thank God Kyle's lawyer had been able to get us released as fast as he did, or we might have been sleeping on benches in lockup all weekend, which was probably the marshals' intent. Instead, we got to go home to our own bed, where Cassie was more than happy to let me have her every which way, all night long. Whatever she had been mad about before the marshals showed up at our door, it seemed to be all but forgotten by the time we were released.

It was a little crowded on the subway, but still enough seats to go around. I was about to sit down next to this young guy who had these huge holes in his earlobes and what looked like quarters inside the holes. It was painful to look at. Then I caught sight of two empty seats together and sat down just as the train took off. I looked straight ahead and allowed all thoughts to escape my mind. I didn't want to do shit or think about shit. This was about the only time nothing was required of me.

Not long after the train started moving, the door between cars opened, and someone stepped into the car. The person squeezed into the seat next to me—or rather, practically on top of me—and the smell alone made me turn to look at whoever was invading my personal space and offending my senses.

"Man, I am so glad to see you," he muttered. "I knew what time you usually left for work, but I wasn't sure I'd be able to find you on the train."

It was Jay, wearing a flowered dress and some old-lady shoes, looking and smelling like a homeless transvestite. The amazing thing about New York City commuters is that a man looking and smelling this bad barely generated a second glance from the people sitting around us. Still, I spoke in a low voice through clenched teeth so that our conversation wouldn't be overheard.

"Where the hell have you been? Do you have any idea what happened to me and my wife because of your ass?"

"Man, I've been on the streets trying not to be seen. I was on my way back to your house when I saw all the cars outside. I watched them taking you out in cuffs. I'm sorry, Al. I never meant to put you through any of that." His apology sounded sincere, but I wasn't quite ready to accept it yet after everything Cassie and I had been through. My life was pretty predictable and uneventful before Jay came back around, and part of me was regretting ever having let him stay with us.

"Don't apologize to me; apologize to Cassie," I said. "She was a mess after everyone left."

He let out a *harrumph*. "Apologize to Cassie?" he said dismissively.

"Yes, apologize to Cassie," I snarled. "After everything she did for you, I think she deserves at least that much."

"Fuck Cassie. She doesn't give a shit about me—or you, for that matter."

His statement was so out of line that I wasn't even sure I had heard my boy right. "Man, watch what you say about my wife. She was nothing but good to you." I looked down at his outfit. "Shit, she probably bought you the dress you got on now."

Jay leaned forward with his elbows on his knees, looking me dead in the eye. "Look, I'm gonna tell you something, and I need you to just be quiet and listen."

I folded my arms and waited, thinking there was nothing he could say that would excuse the way he had disrespected my wife.

"Cassie tried to seduce me."

I was struck silent for a minute. I didn't know whether I wanted to hit him for speaking some bullshit like that about my wife, or laugh at him for coming up with such an obvious lie.

"It's true," he insisted. "Cassie tried to have sex with me."

"Man, that's my wife you're talking about," I warned him.

"I know, and I know it hurts to hear this, but your girl tried to get at me."

"She's not my girl. Like I said, she's my wife."

"And I could have had your wife's pussy had I wanted it."

I clenched my fists. The only thing stopping me from punching him in the face was the fact that it would draw too much attention to us on the train. God forbid something jumped off and the cops were called. At that moment, it wasn't so much that I was worried about Jay being caught and sent back to jail, but that I was afraid of what would happen to me if I was caught with him.

"Look, Jay. I don't want to talk about this. Matter of fact, I shouldn't even be around you right now." I stood up from my seat, ready to get off at the next station, which we were approaching.

Jay stood up too and grabbed my arm. "Nah, you sit down. I'll go. But I need you to give me all the cash you have on you right now."

Was this guy for real? First he told me my wife tried to fuck him—even though, with his history, I wouldn't be surprised if he was the one who tried to hit on her—and now he wanted me to pay him? And that's just the look I gave his ass too.

"Come on, Al, man. We're boys," he said desperately as the train slowed.

I shook my head as I pulled out my wallet. As pissed as I was at the moment, our decades of friendship wouldn't allow me to leave him to fend for himself without a penny in his pocket. I might not want him around me, but I didn't want my friend to suffer, either. As the train came to a stop, I removed my cash and handed it to Jay. He tucked it into his bra.

"Thanks, Al. Tell Kyle I need to talk to him. At our fishing spot, tomorrow at five." The doors opened and he darted off the train, leaving me to stew in what he had said about my wife.

Kyle

40

"You still don't believe me, do you?" Lisa asked as she closed the refrigerator door. She placed a head of lettuce on the cutting board, pulling a knife out of the drawer to start making dinner.

I remained silent as I leaned against the kitchen counter, taking a sip of my beer. I'd been home for a few days, and I couldn't eat or sleep from wondering if my wife had been the one to tip off the cops. I honestly didn't know what to think anymore. The whole situation was eating away at me. Lisa had never given me a reason to not believe her before, but that was then and this was now. Before, she never really had a reason to lie, but now she did. She knew that if I found out she'd tried to have Jay captured, it would put a wedge in our marriage, not that there wasn't already one there.

She started chopping aggressively, seemingly taking her frustration out on the lettuce. "I said I didn't call the police on your convict friend, but the way Jay is tearing our marriage apart, I can't say I'd be sorry if they do catch his ass."

Mad or not, saying stuff like that wasn't necessary. She'd made her mind up about not helping Jay the minute he went on the run.

She didn't care about his side of the story, nor did she want to hear it. It sure didn't help that Franklin had become a reoccurring visitor, and my actions only reinforced her belief that I was putting my friendship with Jay before everything and everyone else in my life. Still, I defended him.

"Not cool to say that, Lisa," I said as I watched her place the lettuce in a metal colander.

She swiftly turned and faced me. "What's not cool is my husband standing here calling me a liar dead to my face." She spun back around and began rinsing the lettuce.

"What? Would you rather me do it behind your back?"

Lisa paused, but she didn't turn and snap back at me. I could tell her feelings were hurt.

Now it was me who was saying unnecessary things. "I'm sorry," I quickly apologized. "I know you didn't call the cops on Jay." Now who was lying? I wanted to believe Lisa, but there was a little part of me that wasn't so sure.

Lisa had always been like a mother lioness. When she felt someone was endangering her family, she went into protective mode. I hated to say it, but if she felt that turning in Jay was protecting her family, then she'd do it in a heartbeat. And who was I to blame her? That fierce protectiveness was one of the things that had made me fall in love with her in the first place. Still, Jay was like family to me, so I was torn.

"Who knows," I said with a sigh. "Maybe that chick Ashlee found out where he was and called the cops." I took another swig of my beer. It made me feel better to redirect my suspicions from my wife to that crazy-ass broad.

Just then, my daughter entered the room, so we halted our conversation.

"Hey, Mom, Dad," she greeted, making her way over to the fridge.

"I'm making salad and there's baked chicken in the oven," Lisa said to her. "I bought some of those Hawaiian rolls that you and your dad like."

"Oooh, yummy! Call me when it's ready." My daughter grabbed a couple grapes from the fridge and popped one in her mouth. She passed by me on her way out of the kitchen, and something caught my eye.

"What's that on your back?" I said.

She damn near choked on a grape. "Huh? What?"

"What the hell is that on your back, Kiki?" I said in a little-girl-don't-play-with-me tone.

Lisa stopped what she was doing and turned her attention toward us as I set my beer down on the counter and walked over to my daughter. She was wearing two layers of tank tops, neither of which fully covered the image on her back.

"What the hell?" I said as I looked at the heart tattoo with initials scripted in the middle of it.

"It's a tattoo, Dad," she said, sucking her teeth and pulling away from me.

"I know it's a tattoo, but when...why?" I could hardly get my words out. "You didn't ask no damn body if you could get a tattoo."

"Really? I'm twenty years old," Kiki said. "I'll be twenty-one soon. Most of my friends have had theirs since senior year of high school."

"I don't give a damn about your friends. You are my daughter," I said. I turned her by the shoulders so my wife could see what had me so upset. "You see this, Lisa? She has the initials T.M. in a heart. Not only did she get a tattoo, but she got that boy's initials engraved on her body." Her latest boyfriend, who she'd only known a few months, was named Tyrell Morris.

She jerked away, offended. "I love him, and he loves me."

"So did he get a tattoo with your initials, since he loves you so much?"

She opened her mouth, but nothing came out. She stood there looking stupid.

"Mm-hmm. Thought so," I said.

Even if in that moment she had an epiphany about what a stupid thing she'd done, she wasn't about to let Daddy know that he was right and she was wrong. So instead, she stormed out of the kitchen.

"Don't be mad at me!" I yelled. "Be mad at yourself."

I turned to Lisa and muttered, "That girl," expecting her to agree with my disapproval. She simply shrugged.

"What do you want me to say?" She went back to preparing salad.

"Nothing. I don't want you to say nothing about the fact that your twenty-year-old daughter is marking up her body with some dude's initials who won't even remember her last name this time next year," I said, feeling disgusted with the whole situation.

Just then, something hit me. "Oh my God!" I pulled out my cell phone and walked out of the kitchen so Lisa wouldn't hear my call to Wil.

"Hey, Wil," I said when he answered, "didn't that woman in the pictures with Steph have a tattoo?"

"Yeah, a heart with the letters DJ in the middle. Why?"

"If we can find out who DJ is, then maybe we can find the identity of the woman in the picture."

Wil wasn't exactly impressed. "Talk about finding a needle in a haystack. But if you think it's worth looking into, I'll talk to my cousin and see if there's anything he can do."

Allen

41

The longer I sat on that train, the angrier I felt. I'd been thinking about Jay's story all day at work, and now on the way home, I still couldn't get it off my mind. One minute I was pissed at Jay, the next minute it was Cassie, then last but not least, myself. I wouldn't have to be thinking about any of this if I had just told Jay his fugitive ass couldn't stay at my house.

Given that Jay had betrayed me in the past with Rose, I wouldn't put it past him to try to sleep with Cassie too. I loved my friend, but he definitely had a selfish side to him, and when it came to getting pussy, he didn't always think through the consequences before he dove in. Then again, I wondered, if he had tried to get with Cassie, why would he bring it up to me at all? Why would he come find me on a train to tell me about it if he was the instigator?

If that was the case, then I had to ask myself if it was possible that Cassie had really offered it up to my friend. I thought about all the clothes she had bought for him, how she seemed to be by his side on the couch every day when I came home from work, and how eager she had been for me to let him stay there in the first place. Was there more to that than just helping out a guy who was like family? I didn't want to believe Cassie could be unfaithful to me, but I also couldn't deny that my wife was a very sexual person.

"Fuck!" I said in an outburst, slamming my fist against the seat. The young girl sitting next to me flinched. "Sorry," I apologized, hands up. "It's just one of those days."

She nodded her understanding with a slight smile, then shifted to get as far away from me as she could in the confined space of the crowded train. I couldn't blame her. I felt like I was going to lose it any moment if I didn't get home and get Cassie's side of the story.

By the time I finally got off the train and made it to my front door, I felt like I was on the verge of a panic attack or something. My hands were trembling so badly that I could barely get the key in the door. I headed right to the living room couch, where I knew I'd find Cassie sprawled out in her usual position, watching television.

"You tried to come on to Jay?" There was no greeting, no beating around the bush, no nothing.

She sat up and said, "Baby, what's wrong? What are you talking about?" She tried to reassure me with a smile, but I could see nervousness in her eyes, which only intensified my anger.

"Don't play with me, Cassie. You heard what the hell I said. Did you try to fuck Jay?"

"Is that what he said?" she shot back indignantly.

"Damn it, Cassie." The way she avoided answering my question didn't make me confident in her innocence.

"He's lying, Allen." Cassie approached me and put her hands on my shoulders. "He's just jealous that you're happily married and free, and he's mad that I rejected him. Because you know what the truth really is? He tried to come on to me." She put her arms around my neck and tried to kiss me, but I leaned back. I wasn't completely convinced.

"Why didn't you tell me then?" I pressed.

"Because he was your friend. So much was going on already. I figured he'd move on to his next hideout and we wouldn't have to worry about it." Cassie started to stroke my neck the way she knew I liked it. "But nothing happened. I would never do something like that to you. I love you."

She started placing little kisses around my face and along my neck, and I felt myself weakening. Then she whispered in my ear, and my whole world fell apart.

"I swear to God, Allen, I never offered to give that man a blow job."

I pulled away and locked my eyes on hers.

"I didn't say anything about you offering him a blow job."

"Allen, I—" From the look on her face, I could tell that she realized she'd just fucked up.

"You're a liar, Cassie," I said, fuming. "And a whore."

"How dare you call me a whore!" She shoved me hard.

On instinct, I pushed her back. My hands balled into fists, but I stopped myself from swinging at her. Even as furious as I was, I would not put my hands on a woman.

"Go ahead, big man. Hit me," she challenged.

"You're not even worth it." I relaxed my fists and headed up the steps. I had to get away from her, and if she knew what was good for her, she'd stay away from me.

I undressed and went into the bathroom, where I turned on the shower, extra hot. Standing under the spray, thinking about the mess that my life had become, I wondered how the hell it had gotten to this point. How was it possible that the woman I loved with all my heart was really a traitorous bitch? By the time I stepped out of the shower and slipped into some sweat pants and a wife beater, I was feeling cleaner, but not necessarily better about my marriage.

The sound of a police siren caused the tension in my muscles to instantly return. Were they coming back to search the place for Jay again? After the day I'd had, I did not need that type of bullshit. I looked out the bedroom window to see a cop car with lights flashing pulling into my driveway.

"Oh, man." I rushed out of the bedroom to see if I could stop them before Cassie let them into the house.

I was too late. They were already in my living room, and as soon as I came down the stairs, my backstabbing wife said, "There he is, Officer. That's him right there."

"What the..." My words trailed off as one of the two officers came toward me, pulling a pair of handcuffs from his waist. "Whoa, what's going on here, Officer?"

"Sir, we got a call about a possible assault. Your wife says that you hit her."

I looked to Cassie. "Are you serious? I barely touched you. That wasn't even a shove."

"That's not true." Cassie lifted her shirt to show the bruises she'd obtained yesterday after tripping over one of the hundred shoe boxes she had scattered around the house. "Look at these bruises! Does this look like he barely touched me?"

"I didn't do that," I protested. "She tripped over some boxes. She's trying to set me up." The officer looked at me skeptically, so I repeated, "I didn't do it."

"You can't leave me here with him. He's crazy. He'll kill me," Cassie said adamantly, pointing at the hall closet. "Look in there. That's where he keeps the bat he's always threatening me with."

"He's not staying," the officer stated clearly, pulling the bat out of the foyer closet. "Sir, please turn around. I'm going to have to place you under arrest for domestic violence."

"Wait a minute. You can't do this. She's lying!" I shouted.

"I can and I am," the officer said forcefully before he whipped me around and handcuffed me. He then began pushing me toward the door.

As I walked by Cassie, I saw a smirk on her face. It was probably the same one she had the day we got married, only I was too blind then to have noticed it.

Wil

42

I'd been riding around for almost an hour, trying to blow off a little steam by putting my company car through the test of the winding curves of the parkways between Queens and Brooklyn at 100 miles an hour. I wasn't usually this reckless, but I'd finally had my conversation with my uncle about the $50,000 we needed to get Stephanie's pictures, and he refused to loan me the money once I told him what it was for. Surprisingly, his reason was similar to the one Jay had used when we talked about it on the boat.

"Giving money to a blackmailer is like giving a stranger your bank card and PIN. Eventually they're going to take you for every dime you own," he said, chuckling as he walked toward the door to leave my office. "You and your friends sit tight and let me take care of this. You'll have a much better outcome in the long run, and more money in your pockets."

"Take care of it how?" I asked doubtfully. "We're supposed to deliver the money tonight."

He turned and gave me an icy stare. "There are advantages to being a Duncan that you haven't even imagined, young man. But

209

then again, you don't really wanna be a part of this family, do you? So don't ask what you don't want to know. I said I'd take care of it."

His words kept ringing in my ear, until I felt like my head was going to fucking explode. I had to get the hell out of there. I was no good to anyone at the office anyway. I needed to go for a drive or something until I could get my thoughts straight, and where better to go than to take a drive to 1000 Atlantic Avenue?

That address on the piece of paper that strange guy at the office had left for Orlando had me curious. Sure, the address had nothing to do with me, but driving out to Brooklyn to check it out would give me something else to focus on so I could take my mind off of Steph and those pictures.

I found the address and pulled over to park on Atlantic Avenue. From the outside, it didn't look like much. A big tattered FOR LEASE sign was hung on the front of the building, and although there were awnings over a few of the doors, nothing seemed to be open. To be honest, it looked like the place was abandoned.

I turned the car off and sat staring at the building for a minute, wondering if maybe Orlando was looking for some new warehouse space. It sounded like a simple enough explanation, but if it were true, then why did that guy come to my office acting like he was on a damn spy mission or something? My gut told me there was more to this.

"Why do you care what this place is?" I asked out loud, trying to talk myself out of doing the inevitable. Part of me understood that if I didn't turn around and take my black ass back to the office, I might not ever go back. Working for my uncle had been great, better than expected, but if I stumbled on something that changed my mind about the family business, I would not be able to go back with a good conscience, no matter how much I needed the job.

So far, I'd been able to work for the Duncan family business without any guilt. I mean, I was just helping customers who were shopping for cars. If there was truth to the rumors I'd heard all my life, I didn't see any evidence of it at Duncan Motors—and I sure as hell didn't go looking for it. Everybody knows that if you keep looking for something long enough, you're sure to find it, and I didn't want to find anything that would mess up my employment. So I kept my head buried in my work, collected my salary, and went home to my wife with a clean conscience every night. Until now.

There was no talking myself out of this one. I was here now, and I couldn't resist the urge to get out of my car and find out more about this warehouse.

The large doors on the front of the building were covered by metal grates and secured by padlocks, so I went around to the back of the building. Maybe there were some windows I could peek in, so I could satisfy my curiosity and then get the hell out of there.

There was a nondescript white box truck parked in the back, a dumpster, and just like I'd hoped, a few windows. I walked over and pressed my forehead against the glass of one window, hands on either side of my face, to see if the place was as abandoned as it looked.

It was a big warehouse, big enough for two Duncan Motors trucks to be parked in there. Maybe Orlando had already rented the place, I thought. I saw the man who handed me the note back at the office. I quickly ducked back down.

I walked over to another window and looked inside, where I saw a few guys moving around. I recognized two of them from the service department. That was weird. Why would they be over here in Brooklyn if they worked in the Queens dealership?

While I was busy trying to figure that one out, another guy came into the warehouse, and this one was heavily armed. *Oh, shit!* I ducked down before anyone spotted me at the window. I had definitely seen enough. I didn't know exactly what they were doing in there, but it had nothing to do with selling luxury cars, and it damn sure had nothing to do with me.

I quickly headed back to my car and started it up. With my heart racing, I looked into the rearview mirror to make sure no one was on the sidewalk who might have seen me there. I was about to put my car in drive when I felt the hard metal against the side of my head.

"Don't fuckin' move."

Oh, shit! Why didn't I keep my head in the fucking sand?

Kyle

43

Where the fuck was Wil? I'd been waiting on him for over an hour, and I refused to believe he was going to be a no-show. He knew what was at stake: Steph's reputation and future. The blackmailer had called Kenya with a time and place to exchange the money for the pictures that night, but as of now, I didn't even know if Wil had managed to get the loan from his uncle. Why the fuck wouldn't he answer the phone? I'd called him repeatedly, but every call went straight to voice mail.

"Kyle, the girl at the front desk said I could come on back."

I looked up to see Kenya entering my office. She appeared frazzled.

"Kenya, come in. Have a seat." I pointed to the chair across from my desk.

"I can't sit," Kenya said. "I can't sit still. I can hardly even think. I haven't been able to get in touch with Wil. He's supposed to drop off the money tonight." Kenya looked both hopeful and desperate at the same time.

"Yeah, I know," I said. "I've been trying to get ahold of him ever since you called. He was supposed to come pick up the rest of the money from me."

"The rest? I thought Wil had all the money. What the hell are you talking about, Kyle?" She was alarmed. I saw tears forming in her eyes. "We gotta get this done. My baby..." The tears began rolling down her face. "Her life is going to be ruined."

I handed Kenya a tissue from the box on my desk.

"Thank you," she said as she took one and wiped away her tears. Then she held her hand out to me. I grabbed another tissue and tried to place it in her hand.

"No, not that. Give me the damn money. I know how to get the rest."

I stared at her with a puzzled look on my face. I didn't want to be rude and ask, but I wondered how the hell she was going to come up with that kind of money. Then I realized what she was saying. She was still thinking about turning Jay in.

"Oh, no," I said. "I'm not about to let you—"

"Just tell me where he is, Kyle, and I'll get the reward. It's the least he can do for his child."

I stood up. "Kenya, he's on the run. I don't know where he's staying. And even if I did, you wouldn't get the reward soon enough. They're expecting that hundred thousand tonight."

"Then what am I supposed to do? Who is going to protect my baby? Wil sure as hell can't, and from the looks of it, neither can you." A fresh wave of tears flowed from her eyes. "This is my daughter's future. It will be ruined."

I really hated to see her like this, and I definitely felt like crap that I didn't have the full amount to put in her hands. "We'll work this out," I told her. "I'll go meet the blackmailer myself and give them what I have. I'll try to negotiate another thirty days. By then I can come up with the rest of the money."

She stood up and wiped her tear-stained face with the back of her hand. Poor woman looked exhausted. "I sure hope you know what you're doing, Kyle," she said.

Me too, I thought, although I didn't let her know that I was anything less than one hundred percent confident.

"Everything is going to be fine," I said to her. "Go home and try to get some rest. I'll call you later." I gave her a hug and she left.

I picked up the phone and tried to reach Wil again. That money from his uncle was our best bet to resolve this whole thing quickly. I got his voice mail again, and I realized that unless he called me back soon, I really was going to have to go meet this blackmailer and hope that twenty-five thousand would be enough to buy us some more time. The more I thought about it, though, the more I realized I did not want to go meet this person. My life was complicated enough lately. It was time for Jay to step up to the plate and help his kid, whether or not he was on the run.

Allen had sent me a text while he was at work yesterday, telling me that a friend wanted to meet me at our old fishing spot. I had known immediately that he was referring to Jay, because we had designated a spot near the water in Baisley Pond Park as our "in case of emergency" meeting place. I checked my watch and saw that it was almost four o'clock, only an hour from the time I was supposed to meet Jay there. I left my office, telling my secretary that I would be out of the office for the rest of the afternoon.

An hour later, I sat in Baisley Pond Park, staring at a frog on top of a giant lily pad in the pond. It was a weekday, so the place wasn't as crowded as it was known to be on the weekends.

"Everything all right?" Jay said as he came up behind me.

Feeling paranoid, I looked around to make sure he hadn't been followed. There was no one in sight. "Yeah, if you don't include the fact that Wil is MIA."

"What the fuck?" Jay said. "Isn't he supposed to—"

"I know, I know," I said, cutting him off. "It's supposed to go down tonight."

"Well, is it?" he asked.

"I have part of the money," I said as I slid him the briefcase I had stowed under the bench. "It's your daughter, so I think you should deliver it."

"Only part of it?" Jay asked.

"Yeah, Jay," I said, irritated by his attitude. "That's my twenty-five thousand. You're welcome. Now, I just told you Wil isn't answering his phone, so you're gonna have to work with what we got."

"How the hell am I going to get those pictures without all of the money?"

He was still complaining, but I was relieved that at least he wasn't trying to back out of meeting with the blackmailer. He was taking on that responsibility. Maybe there was hope for him as a father yet.

"I'm sure you'll think of something. Tell him we need more time."

Jay sat silently for a minute, I guess trying to wrap his head around this whole mess. After a while, he said, "I'm gonna need a car."

I reached into my jacket pocket and pulled out an envelope for Jay.

"More cash?" he asked as he took it.

"Yes, five hundred cash and five hundred on a prepaid credit card," I said. "You should be able to get you a taxi or something." I pointed at the envelope. "The address where you're supposed to go is written on there too. It's down the street from where my very first store used to be. You remember that alley?"

"Sure do." Jay stood up from the bench. "I'll see you in a few hours. Good looking out."

"Yo," I said to him before he left. "You keep your eyes open and be careful. I got a weird feeling about this."

"Yeah, so do I."

Jay

44

I went down to Guy Brewer Boulevard and found an African dollar-cab driver who wanted to make some real money. I slipped him a fifty, then told him I had another fifty for him when the job was finished. From that moment on, I had a personal driver.

"Hey, I need to make a stop up the block real quick. I'll throw in a little extra for it," I told him as he was driving to the first address I'd given him, which was fake. I knew better than to give the actual address of the meeting spot to the driver. I was trying to cover my tracks.

"No problem, as long as it's on the way. It's your lucky day," my driver said with a laugh.

"Yeah, right. That's funny," I said under my breath. As far as I was concerned, my luck had run out ten years ago.

"Right there," I said when I saw the Chinese carryout place a few buildings up.

There were no open spaces, so he double-parked out front. "How long are you going to be? I'll circle around."

"Not long," I said, opening the door and grabbing the briefcase. My plan was to get this over with quick.

"Cool. If I find a spot, I'll pull in, so look around for me when you come back out."

I went into the restaurant and took a quick look around to make sure there were no cops in the place before I walked up to the counter. "Let me get a beef and broccoli and a pork fried rice to go," I told the guy behind the counter.

He wrote down the order and told me "Ten minutes."

I nodded. "Do you have a restroom?"

"In the back."

I headed down the long hallway he'd pointed to, but passed right by the bathroom to go out the door that led to the dumpsters in back of the restaurant. Stepping outside, I checked my surroundings again. With the feds in the local area still searching for me, I was on high alert at all times. I didn't see anyone, so I pulled my hoodie over my head and walked north, in the direction where I was supposed to meet up to get the pictures.

I thought I heard a noise coming from behind me, but when I turned around, there was nothing there. Turning to walk again, I saw a guy coming from between two buildings in front of me. I slowed my pace but kept moving toward him.

"You have something for me?" the guy asked, stopping in front of me.

"I sure do." Before that fool knew what hit him, I lifted the briefcase and smashed his fucking face in. Blood squirted out of his nose, and when he raised both hands to cover it, I kicked him in the gut with the force of all my pent-up rage. Once he was down, I went to work making sure he wasn't getting back up, just in case he had a gun or a knife. I'd always been good with my hands, but I'd been in enough fights in jail to know exactly how to dominate this guy.

"Ugggh." He was curled up in a ball, clutching his stomach.

"You think you gonna fuck over my kid and blackmail me?" I took a break from punching him to kick him in the back. As he lay writhing in pain, I searched him for a gun but surprisingly found nothing. I then reached into his pocket and pulled out his wallet. When I found his ID, I read his name and address out loud so this motherfucker would know he couldn't hide from me.

"Okay, Preston Brown from 123rd Street in Queens Village, I want every last copy of those pictures—matter of fact, I want the damn camera they were taken with too—before you get a fuckin' penny. And you better believe if I don't get them, I will hunt you down and tear your fuckin' face off."

"What pictures? I don't know what you're talking about," he said, crying like a little girl.

"Don't play with me," I snapped, kicking him again. I saw a nearby trash can lid and picked it up, raising it over my head. Dude was gonna learn to quit fucking with me. I had truly been pushed to the limit.

He put his hands up defensively. "Wait, please," he begged. "I swear to God I don't know about no pictures. She just told me to come get the money from you and she would give me a cut when I brought it to her."

"She would?" I repeated, lowering the trash can lid, because something inside told me this guy was not lying. "Who told you to come here?"

It occurred to me that it could be the other woman in the pictures. Her face was hidden in every one, and maybe that wasn't a coincidence. Maybe she was the blackmailer and had purposely sent only the pictures that kept her identity hidden.

"I don't know, man. Some fine-ass light-skin broad," he said, wincing. I could tell it hurt him to even talk.

The woman in the pictures was light-skinned. So far the evidence was pointing to her being the blackmailer, but I still had another suspicion.

"This fine-ass broad have a name?" I asked.

"I don't know, man. I was just waiting for the bus and this lady comes up to me and asks me if I want to make a quick grand. I don't need to know your name if you gonna give me easy money like that."

"What did she look like? Light skin, and what else?" I wanted to punch him in the throat just for being a stupid ass, but I needed to get what little information he seemed to have.

"Tall, thin. And she had blonde finger waves in her hair," he said.

The woman in the pictures had long black hair, so either she'd changed her hair since those pictures were taken, or she wasn't the blackmailer. But I knew someone else with light skin and finger waves, and so he'd confirmed my first suspicion about who'd set my daughter up.

"Where is this lady now? Where are you supposed to bring the money?"

"Back at the bus stop in front of Starbucks up the block. I'm supposed to text her when you hand over the money, and then go meet her."

"Give me your fucking phone."

He was smart enough to hand it over without an argument. I threw it on the ground and smashed it under my foot. *Let him try to send that text now*, I thought.

Then I picked up the briefcase and stepped over the guy on the ground, warning, "Remember, I know where you live," before I took off toward the Starbucks. I had to see for myself if it was her.

Coming out onto the sidewalk from between two buildings, I could see the Starbucks a few stores down across the street. But when I saw the NYPD car parked out front, there was no way in hell I was going near that place. I ducked under the awning of a dry cleaner's and stood there watching the coffee shop, trying to decide what to do. I couldn't go near Starbucks, but I didn't want to leave until I knew for sure that it was Ashlee who was in there waiting for the money.

I got my answer sooner than I anticipated when that bitch came strolling out of Starbucks, chatting with a cop with a coffee in his hand. I couldn't believe my eyes. This whole thing was a setup— not just of my daughter, but of me too. I didn't know how Ashlee had gotten those pictures of my daughter—hell, it could have been her with a wig—but she had probably been hoping that I would be the one showing up with the money that night. As soon as she got the text from the guy in the alley, she would have sent those cops over there to arrest me. Then she could chalk up a double win, taking a hundred grand from me and collecting the reward money for my capture. Well, that crazy bitch wasn't getting shit that night, I thought as I raced back to the Chinese restaurant, hoping like hell my cab driver was still waiting there for me.

Wil

45

I opened my eyes to total darkness and realized there was something covering my head. There was sweat running down my face, and my head hurt like a bitch. When I tried to move my arms and then my legs, I couldn't. I didn't know how long I'd been there, but I vaguely remembered a guy almost as big as me pointing a gun at me right before everything went black. He must have knocked me out.

All of a sudden the bag was snatched off my head. I blinked a couple times to adjust my eyes to the light. My vision was blurry, but I could feel someone standing behind me. I began twisting and jerking, struggling to break the ropes that confined me to a wooden chair.

"You a nosy-ass nigga, ain't you?" I heard a male voice roar from behind me. "What the fuck was you doing creeping around outside?"

"I was just looking." I stopped straining against the ropes, feeling out of breath from the effort. "Look, my name's Wil Duncan," I said, hoping my name would afford me some protection. "Someone had mentioned one of our trucks was over here. I just came to take a look." It was a lie, but maybe they'd buy it.

"Man, I been working for the Duncans almost ten years, and I ain't never seen this nigga once." This came from a second guy, with a deeper and more threatening voice. He slapped me hard upside the head. "Who the fuck are you?"

"My name is Wil Duncan," I repeated.

"Bullshit!" He hit the other side.

"Yo, man, hold up," the other guy said. He began to search me for ID but wouldn't find any because I'd left it at the office in my suit jacket. "What if we're wrong? What if he really is a Duncan? They're gonna kill us if he is."

"I've heard of Orlando, Junior, Rio, Paris, you know what I'm saying? They even got a brother named Vegas I used to work with, but I ain't never heard of no goddamn Wil. That nigga is lying." He was trying to convince his partner, but I could sense the doubt in his words; even more so, I could hear the fear.

"If you a Duncan, where did you come from? We ain't never heard of you," the first guy said.

"I'm LC's nephew. He just hired me not too long ago. I work in customer service at the home office. I'm telling you, I'm a Duncan." Being nosy was what got me in this predicament in the first place, but perhaps being a Duncan could get me out of it. In order to convince them, I had to play the part right, so I put some menacing bass in my voice. "Why the fuck do you think I was driving a Ferrari? You don't think my cousins are gonna come looking for me? I'll tell you what: If you don't untie me real quick, then when I do get out, I might just kill you myself."

My threats definitely didn't have the effect I wanted. The bag was placed back over my head, and the two of them moved away to talk about what they should do.

"Yo, I think we fucked up," the first one said. "I think this dude just might be a Duncan. Which means we're fucked. What the hell are we gonna do?"

"I think we better call somebody," the second guy said.

They left me sitting there, sweating under that bag for at least a half hour. One of them went outside to make a call, but I smelled cigarette smoke, so I knew someone was still in there with me. The caller came back in, but neither one of them said a word, not even in response to me when I started yelling again about being a Duncan.

Suddenly, I heard a crashing sound, as if instead of turning the knob to come in, someone had busted the door right off the hinges.

"Take it off! Take that fucking bag off his head!" I recognized the voice as Orlando's. Thank God.

Once again I felt the air on my face and the light hit my eyes. When my vision cleared this time, I saw Orlando and Uncle LC standing in front of me.

"What the hell did you idiots do?" Orlando yelled. He snatched up one of the men who, I might add, was twice his size, pointing a gun to his head. After everything that had happened that day, I was not even shocked to see that my cousin was carrying.

"You okay?" Uncle LC asked as he untied me.

"Yeah, I think so," I replied, even though I wasn't okay. I wanted to cry like a bitch because my head was hurting so badly. My uncle helped me stand up.

"You two are some lucky sons of bitches that nothing happened to my cousin," Orlando said as he pushed the guy to the ground.

"We're sorry... sorry." The second guy held his hands up in defense, looking scared to death that Orlando was going to handle his ass next. Given the fact that he said he'd worked for the Duncans for ten years, I guess he knew what Orlando was capable of—something I was just now seeing with my own eyes for the first time.

The other man turned to me. "We're sorry, Mr. Duncan. Real sorry. If there's anything we can do for you, just let us know. We don't want no problems." It's hard to describe, but both men looked at me with a kind of respect laced with fear that I'd never seen or felt before.

"It's all right," I said, almost feeling bad for them.

"Let's get him to the car," Uncle LC said.

"You all right to drive?" Orlando asked, handing me my keys once we were outside.

"Yeah, I can drive," I said, just wanting to get the hell away from there.

"What were you doing here, Wil?" my uncle asked, his face stern now that we were out of sight of his underlings.

"Curious, I guess," I said. My head was still aching, so I didn't have the energy to come up with a cover story even if I'd wanted to. "What is that place, and why are our trucks in there?"

Orlando glanced over at my uncle, who just kind of shrugged. "Is that something you really want to know, or are you just curious? Because being a Duncan is about knowledge, Wil. Knowledge is power, while curiosity...curiosity killed the fuckin' cat. Which one do you prefer?"

Kyle

46

As I sat on the bench thinking about recent events, I felt as if my life had been flipped upside down. This time last year, no one could have told me that I'd be caught up in the shit I was caught up in now, with a best friend who had escaped from prison and a wife who had dropped the dime on my best friend. That didn't even include the fact that I was locked up behind that shit, plus I was dealing with someone blackmailing Steph, who was like a daughter to me. I mean, this was some shit you'd see in the fucking movies, not in the life of a dude who runs a beauty supply business. I just wanted this nightmare to be over, because I didn't know how much more I could take.

I was momentarily pulled out of my dark thoughts when Jay came and sat down beside me.

"How did it go?" I asked him. I'd been waiting in the park for him so that he could give me a report about his meeting, and hopefully the pictures. I wanted to destroy them, take them out to the middle of the water on my boat, then set them on fire and let them burn before releasing them into the water. Yeah, that sounded a little dramatic, but hell, if I was going to feel like I was in a fucking movie, I might as well play the lead action hero. In reality, we were in the age of digital photos, so even if we burned a few paper copies, we could never be one hundred percent sure all digital copies were deleted. That thought discouraged me, and the look on Jay's face brought my mood down even more.

He exhaled and stared down at the ground. He couldn't even look me in the eyes. "It didn't," he said.

"What do you mean? What the hell happened?" I had not just sat in a bar across the street a half hour and thrown back two shots expecting to hear this news. I thought we would be celebrating a victory for once. "Please tell me you went to the drop."

"I did, and I had to beat the crap out of a guy when I got there."

"A guy?" I asked. "So it wasn't a woman?"

"Oh, there's a woman involved, but she wasn't in the alley." I could see the tension in his jaw, and his forehead was creased with aggravation. "Kyle, Ashlee's behind this whole thing. We thought she'd go after Jordan, but she went after Steph."

"You sure it's her?"

"Bro, I've never been so sure about anything in my life. Saw her with my own eyes."

I shook my head. "I can't believe she's got it out for you like this. You'd think taking ten years of your freedom would be enough."

"Not for Ashlee. She's psycho. She offered some dude a thousand dollars to meet me in an alley and get the money while she waited down the block to sic the cops on me."

"Fuck!" I said, feeling a pressure build up behind my eyes like my head might actually explode or something. "What are we gonna do, Jay? Those pictures are going to hit the Internet like wildfire."

It was a question neither one of us could answer, so we sat there saying nothing, lost in our own thoughts.

The silence was interrupted a few minutes later by my ringing phone. I looked down at the caller ID and saw a number I didn't recognize. That made me nervous, but I felt I had to answer it in case it was Wil or Kenya and there was still a way to stop her from leaking those pictures.

"Hello?"

"Thank God, Kyle." I recognized the voice, but it definitely wasn't Ashlee.

"Allen? What number are you calling me from?"

"Kyle, you gotta get me outta here, man. Cassie had me arrested for domestic violence."

"What? Are you serious?...I'm on my way." I hung up, shaking my head at the never-ending shit train. "Fuck, if it ain't one thing, it's another."

"What now?" Jay asked.

"Not only is Wil missing," I said, "but Allen's been arrested."

"Arrested? For what?"

"Whipping Cassie's ass, I think."

"Really?" A smirk slowly emerged on his face.

"Why you got that look on your face?"

"Let's just say it probably ain't even go down like that. Knowing the snake that she is, she set his ass up."

"Seems to be a lot of that going around these days. What aren't you telling me, Jay?"

"It will all come out soon enough. For now, just go down there and get our boy outta that jail."

"Yeah," I said, standing up on shaky legs.

"Yo, you all right?" Jay asked. "You don't look so good."

"I don't know, man. All this shit going on, and now this on top of it, I swear I feel like I might just lose it or something."

"Kyle, you gotta keep it together. You're the glue for all of us right now. We don't need you going off the deep end like your old man did."

"Yeah, you're right. Don't worry. I'll be fine." I tried to laugh it off as I walked away from him, but truthfully, I was starting to scare myself.

Allen

47

I never made it into a cell the day the marshals had hauled me in, but I was in one now. I was sharing a pissy-smelling jail cell with six dudes. One looked like he ate heroin for breakfast, and another one was so big he looked like he might eat me for breakfast.

"Motherfucker!" I said out loud. I just couldn't control myself anymore as I paced back and forth in the holding cell. "I can't believe this shit is happening. I could kill that bitch."

"Yo, homie, simmer down, son," said the heavyset guy. "I heard what the judge said. Your bail is only two hundred dollars. You'll be out of here in no time."

"Two hundred bucks," said another guy in the cell. He sucked his teeth. "Sit down, bitch-ass nigga."

"It ain't even about the bail. I ain't stressing on that," I said in my defense. And I wasn't. Thank God, I had gotten ahold of Kyle and he was on his way to get me out. "It's my wife. She played me like a piano." I punched a fist into the palm of my hand. "I could kill her ass right now."

"Pssst, come here. Settle down, man," the heavyset dude said again, waving me over to the bench.

I really did need to sit my ass down somewhere before I lost my mind. I was thinking about some really vicious things that I wanted to do to Cassie, things that could put me behind bars for life.

"Just have a seat, man. Let me holler at you for a minute."

I stopped my pacing, exhaled, and then went and sat down.

"You didn't mean what you said about wanting somebody dead, did you?" he said in a whisper.

"The hell if I didn't. Like I said, I don't need bail. I need a hit man."

"Shhhh." He put his index finger over his mouth. "What're you trying to do?"

I took a good look at him. He looked pretty serious as he waited on me to respond.

"Why? You know somebody?" I asked, testing the waters.

"How much you talking?"

I paused for a moment to process the fact that this conversation was really happening, and he wasn't joking. But what was crazier was that I was seriously contemplating it myself. The woman that I married, that I had loved with all my heart, had flipped on me in the blink of an eye. First she tried to get with Jay, and then she lied to the cops and had me locked up. I don't think anyone in my life had ever hurt me this bad—or made me this angry.

Just then, I heard my name being called. I looked up to see a guard at the door. "That's me." I jumped off the bench and started making my way to the door.

"You made bail," the guard said.

"Hey," the dude called out to me from the bench. "If you're serious about that, you can always find me at Joe's Bar over on 132nd Street."

232

I nodded at him, then exited the cell.

The guard processed me out, and as I left the building, Kyle was outside waiting on me.

"Damn, man," Kyle said. "We got Jay trying to run from the jail and your ass running to it. What the fuck happened?"

Kyle

48

"Why don't you just stay at my house for a couple days until you figure things out?" I said to Allen as we drove.

He just sat there, shaking his head repeatedly, like he was in shock or something. I could only imagine what he must have felt inside, a man who couldn't go lay his head at the place he called home—the place where he'd worked hard to pay all the bills and maintain it. I couldn't even pretend that I knew what he was going through. All I could do was be there for him and at least offer him a bed.

He tightened his lips and closed his eyes as if trying to calm himself down. "I appreciate it, but fuck that. That's my house. My momma left me that house. That bitch needs to get the fuck out. Besides, you and your old lady got enough going on as it is."

I'd never heard Allen call a woman a bitch before. That right there let me know that it was not a good idea to take him to his house, knowing there was a chance that Cassie might be there. After all, where else would she have gone? As far as I was concerned, he'd found her ass on the streets, so that was the only place she could go back to. With the way Allen had spoiled her rotten, I couldn't see her willingly walking away from any of it.

"I don't think that's a good idea, man," I told him.

"Take me to my house, Kyle," he said adamantly.

"Look, I'll take you there, but if Cassie's there, you don't need to stay there. You can't stay there. Just grab some things, or I'll grab them for you, and then we're out. Agreed?"

Allen didn't respond. He just sat in the passenger's seat with a tight jaw, flexing and unflexing his fists.

"Agreed?" I was not going there until I had his word.

"Yeah, yeah, sure," he said, obviously only agreeing to shut me up.

"I mean that shit, Allen. Neither one of us needs any more problems with the law right now. As a matter of fact, you need to call the police to meet you there so that she doesn't try to pull no shit this time."

I could tell Allen was considering my words because this time when he said, "Yeah, okay," he added, "you're right." He held out his hand. "Let me borrow your cell."

I pulled my phone out of my pocket and gave it to him. He called 911, but since it was a nonemergency, they transferred him to the local police precinct.

"Yes, I, uhh, have an order of protection against me placed by my wife. I need to go to my home to get some things, so I was wondering if you could send an officer to assist me." There was a pause, and then Allen gave them his address. A few seconds later, he ended the call and handed the phone back to me.

"They're going to meet us there," Allen said. "Let's go."

No sooner had we parked and I turned the car off than a police car pulled up behind us. We got out of the car.

"Officer, thank you for coming," Allen said as the officer approached.

"It was pretty smart of you calling us before you came here and tried to get your things without us," the cop said. "I've seen the end result of situations when that didn't happen, so again, I commend you."

"I just want to get her out of my house," Allen said. "That's all I want, Officer. No trouble, just her gone." Allen was getting a little riled up again as he spoke.

"You called in saying you wanted to remove your items from the home, sir. Now you want your wife to leave?" the cop questioned.

"Yeah, that's right," Allen answered indignantly. "I want her lying ass outta my house."

"Well, hold up," the officer said. "Let me go talk to your wife and see what's what. You just wait right here until I get back. Okay?"

When the cop went into the house, I turned to Allen and asked, "What the hell was that about? You said you were coming to my house. You try to get her kicked out now, you're just stirring up a hornet's nest."

"Whatever, man. I changed my mind. That bitch lied on me, and now she's got to go."

As riled up as he was, it wasn't worth arguing with him about it, so we just stood there without talking until the officer came back.

"All right, sir. I'm going to escort you inside to get some of your things, but then you have to leave," the officer said.

"I have to leave? This is my house," Allen said a little too forcefully. "My mother left me that house."

"Well, your wife just showed me an ID with this property as her address. Right now, she's a legal resident with an order of protection against you, and she was here first. If you want her out, you're going to have to legally evict her, so until then, I'll escort you inside to get a few things, but then you have to go."

"That bitch!" Allen yelled.

"You're going to want to calm down, sir, before you lose the chance to go in and get anything," the officer warned.

"Come on, Allen, you heard the officer," I said, trying to calm him down before things got out of control between him and the man in blue. "Just get some things to tide you over for a couple days and come on back to my place."

Realizing he'd run out of options, Allen surrendered. "Sure."

We followed the officer to the door. When we walked inside, we saw Cassie in her usual spot on the couch, music playing, television going, and a bottle of wine and two glasses on the table. It looked like Cassie was having a celebration since Allen had gone to jail. When she saw Allen come in, she smirked at him and leaned back so her robe opened to almost completely expose her breasts. That was one low-down woman.

It was bad enough that she was taunting him like that, but when some dude came down the stairs in his boxers, I thought Allen was going to lose it.

"What the fuck, Cassie? I'm gone half a day and you got this motherfucker up here in my house?" Allen yelled.

I put a hand on his shoulder. "Al, be cool, man. She ain't worth it." I shifted my eyes in the direction of the cop, hoping to remind Allen that law enforcement was present and he was skating on thin ice at the moment.

Allen shrugged my hand away. "Hell nah, man. I ain't calming down. This the same dude that used to beat her ass before she came crying to me and I married her sorry ass."

The guy in the boxers wore the same smirk that Cassie did. I suddenly understood Allen; now I wanted to smack the shit out of them just as badly as he did.

"Sir, let's get your things and go," the officer said. He kept a hand on Allen's elbow as he guided him past the couch, probably to remind him who was in charge.

As Allen walked by Cassie, he stared at her with daggers in his eyes. If looks could kill, Cassie would be dead, and then I would have two friends on the run to worry about—as if one weren't bad enough.

Wil

49

I shook my head with annoyance when I turned the corner and saw my garage door open. Once again my wife had left us vulnerable to thieves. I don't know how many times I'd told her not to leave the garage door open, but I guess she just liked hearing my mouth. I mean, it wouldn't have been so bad if our next-door neighbors hadn't just been robbed the very same way a few months ago, when one of their kids left the garage door open. The poor guy had his Harley rolled right out of his garage and down the block.

When I turned into the driveway and parked my car, I noticed that Diane's car door was still open.

"What the fuck?" I yelled out loud when I saw a very strange scene before me. Through the rear window of her car, I could see Diane's head. There was a pair of legs sticking out the open car door, but they weren't my wife's. They belonged to a man.

I jumped out of my car and started running when I heard my wife screaming, "Get off of me! Get the fuck off me!"

"Then just give me the keys, bitch!" the guy yelled back.

Jesus Christ, that son of a bitch was carjacking Diane!

I ran up on him so fast he didn't even notice me coming until it was too late. I pulled my leg back and then swung my foot right between his fucking legs. The impact of my foot connecting with his balls damn near folded him in two. He froze up as if he'd been tased.

I pulled him off Diane, yelling to her, "Get in the house!"

"Wil, thank God!" she said, coughing, trying to catch her breath. "He tried to steal the car. He was going to kill me."

"I know, baby. It's all right. I'm here. Now get in the house," I told her.

As Diane passed by me and ran to the house, I saw that her eye was starting to swell. It would probably be black-and-blue by morning. That son of a bitch had hit my wife, and he was going to pay now.

I was consumed by rage. "You wanna hit somebody?" I put my hands around his neck and squeezed. His lower body was on the ground, with his head and shoulders against the bottom of the car. "You wanna hit women, huh?" I kept my grip on his neck with one hand and smashed my other fist into his eye. Then both hands were back on his neck, and as I tried to choke the life out of him, I began beating his head against the car. With every bang of his head, I called out another curse at him.

"Motherfucker!" *Bam!* "Fucking piece of shit!" *Bam!* "Low-life cocksucker!" *Bam!*

"Wil?" Diane was calling my name. I could hear her voice coming from the front of the car. "Wil?" I heard her say again. Whatever she wanted could not have been more important than kicking this motherfucker's ass.

"That's enough! Stop it!" She now stood over me.

Diane's screaming finally pulled me out of the zone I was in, but it was too late—for the guy anyway. I looked to see blood from his head splattered all over Diane's purse, which sat in the front seat. I noticed her keys were still in the ignition. That explained why she hadn't run into the house and called 911. She didn't have her keys. Instead, she'd stood there and witnessed me beating this guy's brains out.

When I looked down at him, I saw blood and brain matter splattered all over. I looked up at Diane. She was trembling, with tears settling in her eyes.

"Wil," she said. "I think he's dead. You killed him."

Allen

50

Any other time, I wouldn't have been able to wait until the end of the workday. That was before I had only my buddy's boat to go to instead of my own home. Kyle had wanted me to stay at his house, but with everything going on, I wanted to be alone, so I opted to stay on the boat instead. Now that I had a place to stay, I didn't want it. Don't get me wrong, I was grateful that Kyle let me stay on the boat. I just couldn't shake the fact that Cassie was over there living in the home my mother broke her back working to pay for.

I tried to put it out of my mind, and sometimes I was successful, but whenever I thought about it, I'd pop off. I'd lost count of how many coworkers I had to apologize to for snapping at them. I knew that everything was going to work out eventually. I just had to keep it together until this whole mess was over with.

That reminded me: I needed to make some phone calls to get this eviction process rolling.

Before I could pick up the phone to dial, it rang. "Verizon technical support. This is Allen," I answered.

"Good afternoon, Allen. This is Jody from Human Resources

Services. I just wanted to confirm a couple things before we proceed any further with liquidating your 401(k)."

"Sure, go right ahead. What do you need to know?" I said before the words Jody had spoken really had time to set in. "Whoa, wait a minute." I stood from my desk. "Did you say liquidate my 401(k)? What the hell made you think I want to do that?"

"Uh, sir," she said, sounding offended by my outburst. "I got the e-mail and signed paperwork with your request to liquidate the funds. I just need to verify the account number your wife gave me."

"My wife!" The steam started to build.

"Yes. She's the one who confirmed the request and account with a phone call this morning."

"That bitch!" I said for the umpteenth time. I think I'd used the B-word more than Tupac and Too Short put together. My mother was probably rolling in her grave.

"Pardon me?" Jody said, sounding even more offended now.

I forced myself to take it down a notch. It wasn't this lady's fault that I'd married a backstabbing thief. "I'm so sorry," I apologized. "It's just that my wife and I are having some problems right now. I assure you I do not want my 401(k) liquidated. I don't want it touched. Do you understand?"

"Yes, sir. I'll cancel the request."

"Thank you. And again, I apologize." I was lucky she had called to follow up, or my retirement fund could have been wiped out without me even knowing it.

"You're welcome, sir, and I hope everything works out between you and your wife."

I ended the call with Jody and immediately called a taxi, which

243

would arrive in less than ten minutes. I went to my boss's office to tell him I needed a few hours off.

"Pardon me, sir," I said, sticking my head in his open doorway.

He raised his eyes from the paperwork on his desk, not looking too happy to have been interrupted. Either that or he just wasn't too happy with me. Maybe one of the coworkers I'd gone off on had said something to him.

"I'm sorry to interrupt," I said, "but I have an emergency and I need to leave for the day."

He raised an eyebrow. "You've been missing quite a few days already, Allen."

"And I'm going to have to miss one more," I said, slightly too aggressively. It caused him to lean back in his chair and look at me with an expression that said, *Go ahead and be insubordinate one more time and I will fire your ass.* That pretty much confirmed my suspicion that he wasn't too happy with me these days. It was time for me to take a different approach.

"Sir," I started again, "please allow me a few hours to handle a crisis. My wife and I are having problems, and I just found out she tried to cash in my entire 401(k)."

His eyes grew wide, and I knew I'd struck a nerve. He'd been divorced three times, so he was no stranger to money-hungry exes. "Yes, you need to take care of that right away. Is there anything we can do for you?"

"No, sir. I've got this, but thanks for asking."

"All right, then. See you tomorrow?" he said in a tone that hinted at a warning that I better have my ass in the office the next morning or I could be out of a job.

"See you tomorrow," I said as I rushed out to meet the taxi.

"Where to?" the cabbie asked me as I hopped in the backseat of the car.

"Joe's Bar. It's on 132nd Street," I said as I closed the door and he pulled off.

Wil

51

"You okay?" Orlando asked me as he sat at the kitchen table with me and Diane.

She was still quite shaken up. We were holding hands, and I could feel hers trembling in mine. The bruise on her eye was starting to darken. Every time I looked at her, I was filled with overwhelming anger. Why hadn't I gotten home just five minutes earlier? Then that asshole would have never gotten the chance to put his hands on her.

"Yeah, I'm okay," I lied. I was far from okay. I'd just killed a man—in front of my wife. How was Diane going to feel, knowing that she was married to a murderer?

Diane's reaction wasn't the only one I was worried about either. I knew that the law might view the killing as self-defense, but then again, maybe it would be seen as unnecessary use of force. Either way, it would most likely involve charges and a trial, and that was a risk I was not willing to take. That was why, when Diane wanted to dial 911, I stopped her and called my uncle instead. As a result, here I was, sitting with Orlando, while a couple of well-dressed thugs were out in my garage cleaning up the mess I'd made.

I had to admit that this situation really had me rethinking Jay's circumstances. I now understood the phrase "Things aren't always what they seem" in a whole new way. You really had to be there in a person's shoes to know how things went down. Otherwise, you were left to come to your own conclusion, and I had judged Jay pretty harshly, both in refusing to believe his innocence and in refusing to support his run. Now I got it. If I didn't have a family that could make this go away, I might have ended up behind bars like Jay. I couldn't imagine being locked away from my family for even one year, let alone the ten years that Jay had endured.

"How about you? You okay?" Orlando asked Diane.

She couldn't even speak, so she gave him a weak nod.

Orlando looked back at me. "I'm sure I'm probably wasting my breath with what I'm about to say, but just in case, I'm going to say it anyway. What happened here today, well, it didn't happen. The carjacker was never here. I was never here." He nodded toward the garage. "Those two guys out there were never here. Do you understand?"

"Yeah, man. I got it," I assured him. "Never happened."

"Good," he said and then looked to Diane. "You understand?"

Diane looked at me. The tears that had been settling in her eyes spilled over.

"It's okay, sweetheart." I squeezed her hand, urging her to get on the same page as us.

She wiped a fallen tear and then turned her attention to Orlando. "Yes, I understand."

Orlando nodded. "Wil, can I take a walk with you?"

"Yeah, sure." Orlando and I stood from the table. I looked down at Diane. "Are you going to be okay, baby?"

"Yes," she said, but I could tell she was lying the same way I'd lied to Orlando. It was visually apparent that she wasn't going to be okay any time soon.

I kissed her hand before releasing it, then nodded toward the exit. Orlando followed me outside to the sidewalk.

"I'm serious about this whole thing never happening," he reiterated as we started walking up the block. "She doesn't talk to her shrink, lawyer, or priest about this, or else you're going away for a long time."

"I get it. I know. Diane knows too. I'll talk to her again once she's over the initial shock of it all."

"Good, and by the way, I did a little research on that woman Ashlee you asked Pop to look into," he said, bringing up yet another stressor I had in my life at the moment. "Turns out that broad is crazy."

"Jay always said she was a psycho." Here was yet another reason for me to start rethinking my opinion of Jay.

"Well, he wasn't kidding. She's certifiably crazy, but she's got a rich daddy who's well connected in Texas, and he saves her from herself every time she does something over the top."

"Interesting. So do you think Jay's innocent?"

"If I didn't think it before, I think it now." His words surprised me. "Oh, and your boy Kyle was right about that DJ tattoo on the chick in the pictures. It's turned out to be more helpful than you would have thought." He reached in his suit jacket and pulled out an envelope. "Take a look at this when things calm down. It might just be the break your friend has been looking for."

"Thanks, O. For everything." I wrapped my arm around him in a brotherly hug.

"You don't have to thank me. We're family. That's what family does for one another. At least the Duncan family anyway." We turned to walk back to the house. "There's just one more thing I want to know."

"What's that?" I asked.

"Will you be at work on Monday?"

I halted my steps for a minute. I wasn't sure I could answer that right now.

Orlando stopped and spoke to me. "Look, I know there are some things you've learned about the family that you didn't want to know. Things that you shouldn't know. But like I just said, we're family. I think you see the importance of that now. Which is why, again, I want to thank you. Thank you for calling us, Wil, and not the police. With you being a Duncan, depending on who you're dealing with when it comes to the police, things might not turn out as good as you hope. Having the Duncan name can be like a double-edged sword sometimes. You know what I'm saying?"

"I think I'm starting to know what you're saying, cousin."

We resumed our walk.

"So does that mean we can still count on you to be a part of the family business? I mean be a *real* part of the family business? I think you've proven today you're understanding more than ever how this business works."

Orlando was right. As much as I hated to admit it, my call to Uncle LC instead of 911 proved one thing: In spite of what I thought about Uncle LC and my cousins, I was cut from the same cloth.

"See you Monday," I said to Orlando, and we headed back to the house.

Jay

52

I'd been watching this guy for three days straight. I had to make sure that when I approached him it was just the right time, when no one else was around who might recognize me from the news. Even if I was to get him alone, he could still drop a dime on me too, but after I gave him the information I had, something told me that wasn't going to be the case. Something told me he'd be quite sympathetic to my cause. After all, it could very well have been him in my position.

I watched him exit the building and hail a taxi, and I decided it was time to make my move. I approached him slowly just as he opened the door and got in the cab. Before he knew what was happening, I had slid in beside him.

"Um, excuse me," he said with a frown. "This is my cab."

I started talking fast, because I knew I only had a short time to convince him to hear me out before he would throw me out of the cab. "You probably don't know me, but I'm Jay Crawford. Your baby momma framed me."

He narrowed his eyes at me, and I felt my stomach start churning as I waited to see a sign of recognition. Either he would understand what I was referring to, or he would put my ass out on the sidewalk in a second. Or worse, he would know who I was and call the cops on my ass.

The tension was killing me, until he leaned forward and spoke to the driver. "Can you take me to Fortieth and Fifth?" Then he closed the partition and looked over at me. "Close the door, Mr. Crawford."

I let out a huge sigh of relief and swallowed the knot that was stuck in my throat as the cab pulled away from the curb.

"First of all, thank you...for letting me talk to you. But getting straight to the point, ten years ago, your baby momma had me locked up for a rape I didn't commit." I paused for his reaction.

He didn't look too surprised.

"Does that story sound familiar to you?" I pressed for confirmation.

He cast his eyes downward, so I continued.

"A friend of mine had some people look into her background, and your name came up several times."

His eyes darted back up at me, and he looked totally distressed, as if he was reliving a terrible part of his past.

"I know she tried to do the same thing to you." The file that Wil's people had compiled had documents showing that Ashlee had once upon a time accused her child's father of rape. The paper trail showed that eventually those charges were dropped and the record was sealed, which was why Kyle's investigators never got ahold of them. It would appear Wil's guys had a little more clout. Unfortunately, that's where the trail ended, but I knew who to approach for more information: the subject of the accusations, former NBA player Darrius "DJ" Jones.

"Why does this woman always seem to haunt me?" DJ was

finally able to say, echoing the sentiments I'd been feeling for the past ten years.

"Look, man, my life is on the line. Did she set you up or what?"

He looked at me sympathetically. He didn't ask for details, but it was safe to assume that was because he already knew what I was going through. "Okay, you're right," he said. "Ashlee tried to pull the same shit on me that she did with you. But I didn't trust her ass, so while she was trying to set me up, I flipped the script and set her up."

"How?" All of a sudden I wished I could have rewound the clocks and met this guy long before Ashlee ever had a chance to get me.

"Ashlee is crazy and I didn't trust her, so I had a nanny cam set up. It proved to be the smartest thing I ever did in my life."

Everything he was saying was music to my ears, and hopefully it was just the information I needed to get myself out of the predicament I was in. Being able to prove that Ashlee had pulled this exact same stunt with someone else was definitely grounds for a new trial.

"So the charges were dropped against you?" I asked, repeating the information I'd read in the file.

"Dropped and sealed. Her pops is a really powerful dude down there in Texas, and he didn't want anything leaking to the news about his crazy daughter. I don't even know how you found out about it."

That would explain why the paper trail ended.

"Yeah, well, the people who put me on to you are pretty damn powerful in their own right," I replied.

"They'd have to be to get those records unsealed."

"So make me understand this: She falsely accused you of rape, and you just let her get away with it because her old man is power-ful? I'm sorry, but that just doesn't make sense to me."

"It's a little more complicated than that, but let's just say I walked away with enough money to have severe memory loss."

"So he paid you off?"

He smiled with a look of victory in his eyes. It must have been a huge amount of money. Personally, I didn't know if there was any dollar amount that could stop me from trying to bring Ashlee down, but then again, I'd been sent to jail behind her lies. This guy had gotten off with no jail time and a clean record, so it was probably easier for him to forgive, or at least forget. He also had another reason.

"We settled. She's my kid's mother. What was I supposed to do?"

"Look, man, I'm not here to judge you," I said. "I don't care about money or anything else. All I want is my life back, and if that's going to happen, then I'm going to need your help. I'm going to need you to testify to all this in court on my behalf."

That smile he'd had on his face moments ago was wiped clean. "I can't." He shook his head adamantly. "I signed a confidentiality agreement. I shouldn't even be having this conversation with you."

"Come on, Darrius." I said his name as if he were one of my boys or something. I needed to make a connection with him to make him want to help me. "This is my life we're talking about. I spent ten years in prison behind her shit. I know you're not going to leave me hanging like this." I gave him the most desperate look I could muster up. I needed him to feel my pain. "You know I'm innocent, right?"

He thought for a moment and then exhaled. "Yeah, but they paid me a lot of money not to ever disclose that information. If

I talk, I have to pay it back with interest and then pay damages. Look, I'm sorry, but I can't, Jay." He hit me back with the same personal touch by the use of my name, even though that had failed to work when I did it. "I wish I could help, I really do, but..." His words trailed off.

The driver stopped the car and looked in the backseat through his rearview mirror. We had arrived at our destination.

"This is me," Darrius said, which meant I had run out of time to convince him to help. He reached into his pocket and pulled out some money, which he handed to the driver. "Here you go, partner. Take him wherever he needs to go." He got out of the car.

With him having retired from the NBA and now working as a commentator, it had been pretty difficult to make this moment happen, especially in the middle of play-off season. It had been my one shot at getting his help, and now it was all for fucking naught.

But how nice of him to pay the driver to take me wherever I was headed.

Which was nowhere.

Allen

53

It had taken me almost twenty minutes of staring across the street at the bar before I finally willed myself to go inside. When I'd headed out to this side of town, I was so fucking pissed at Cassie that I couldn't get there fast enough. Now that I was there, though, just like the previous two times I'd come, I was having second thoughts. I guess that was only natural. Who wouldn't have second thoughts about doing what I was thinking?

As all the wrong that she'd done to me entered my mind once again, the anger that washed over me helped me to gather my courage and finally cross the street.

"What the fuck have I gotten myself into?" I asked myself as I entered the shady-looking bar. The place was filled with so many derelicts I'm sure I stuck out like a sore thumb in my suit. I took a seat and stared up at the dusty liquor bottles behind the bar.

"Can I get you something?" the bartender asked. His huge body seemed to take up half the area behind the bar as he wiped down the spot in front of me while he waited to take my order.

"Let me get a Coke."

"A Coke? Is that it?" He smirked like he wanted to laugh. "You a cop? 'Cause nobody comes here just for a Coke."

"Nah, I'm not a cop, but I am looking for someone," I answered.

"Well, I'm the owner of this joint, so if the person you're looking for is here, has been here, or is expected here, I'm the one who can tell you." He flung the towel over his shoulder. "What's this person's name?"

"Uh, I don't know." I felt like an idiot. I couldn't even answer his first question. I sat there with a blank look on my face.

"A'ight then, what does he look like?" he asked, still cheerful.

Now, that I could answer. "He's kinda big, real big." I held my arms out to the side to indicate the guy's girth. "And he's not the most attractive man I've ever met."

"You trying to be funny? Sounds like you describing me," he said with a straight face.

"No, no, this guy's white. Dusty blond hair. A lot more rugged-looking than you."

"A lot of guys fit that description," the bartender said. "Look around."

He was right. The place was full of big, homely guys.

"Let's try this." The bartender leaned in, placing one elbow on the bar. "*What* exactly are you looking for this guy for?" He raised his eyebrows suggestively.

Oh, God, I thought. *Does this guy really think I'm in here looking to buy sex from some big white dude?*

The chime hanging on the front door rang out, and a man entered the bar. It just happened to be the person I was looking for. "There he is."

"See that. I told you I'd help you find him," the bartender joked as he walked away.

I waited a few minutes before I headed over to the table where my former jail companion sat down.

"Buy you a drink?" I slid into the seat across from him.

He did a double take. "Well, I'll be damned." He chuckled. "I really didn't expect to see you again."

"Look, I'm going to make this short." I didn't want to be there any longer than I needed to be. "Can you really do what you said?"

He shrugged. "Depends."

"On what?" I asked.

"What exactly did I say? Sometimes I have memory loss, and I would prefer you made things very clear." He sat back in his seat and stared at me.

This was a test, and to be honest, I didn't know if I could pass it. "I want you to . . . I want you to . . ." I looked around to see if anyone was listening. They weren't, but even if someone was eavesdropping, the patrons in this place struck me as the type of people who weren't easily shocked. I finally spit it out in a low whisper. "I want you to kill my wife."

"Well, that was straight and to the point," he replied, sitting up in his seat with a shit-eating grin. "But I still need to know one very important thing."

"What's that?"

"Do you want it to look like an accident, or will a simple mugging gone wrong suffice?" He chuckled again, like we were having a jovial little conversation. "Taking out the target is never a problem. I can do that with my eyes closed, but making it look like an accident requires considerably more skill and money. It also usually means more suffering, but some people like that." He was fucking laughing again.

My heart was racing and sweat beads broke out on my forehead.

This was fucking surreal. It was bad enough that I was hiring someone to kill my wife, but the thought that I had to decide how much she would suffer was too much, and I almost lost my lunch.

"You okay?" He handed me a napkin. "You sure you have the stomach for this?"

I wiped the sweat from my face. "Yes, I'm all right. So how much will this set me back?" I couldn't believe I was talking about this like I was purchasing a stereo system for my car. Had Cassie really made me this cold? Yeah, I guess she had.

"Again, that depends," he said. "One costs five thousand, and the other costs ten."

I leaned back in my chair and considered it for a minute. In that short time, I felt my heart rate slow and my sweating stopped. Just like that, I was becoming comfortable with the idea of being a person who snuffs out a life.

"Okay Mr.... What do I call you?"

"Just call me Mr. Bigg."

I nodded. "Okay, Mr. Bigg. I'll take the five grand option. I'm not spending any more money on that bitch than I have to."

Jay

54

My head was still spinning in disbelief when the cab driver pulled up in front of the Long Island Rail Road station in Jamaica, Queens. I kept thinking about the way that cold bastard DJ refused to help me. That fucking coward was going to leave me hanging out to dry for a crime he knew I didn't commit. I should have beat his ass before he got out of the cab, and I had every intention of tracking him down again. This wasn't over as far as I was concerned. The next time we met, he was either going to see things my way, or I would make him see the light, cellblock-three style, with my fists.

Well, at least I had something to look forward to, since I was going to see Tina. Her place had become my safe haven, my refuge. Since she wasn't part of my past, the cops didn't know anything about her, and her place wasn't even on their radar.

I climbed the stairs to the railroad platform on the westbound New York City side of the tracks. I was going east to Tina's house, but I always stood on the opposite side until right before the train came, so that if by chance someone spotted me, they'd think I was headed to the city.

As I stood on the platform, I had this weird feeling that I was being watched. I looked to my left. There were several people waiting for the train, but none who seemed to be paying me much attention.

I looked to my right, still unable to shake the feeling that someone was watching me. That's when I saw a cop. Our eyes met, and I glanced away in a hurry.

Damn, I wished I'd put my hood on. If I did it now, I'd look way too suspicious, so I just stood there feeling exposed. I glanced back to see if the cop was still checking me out. His eyes were glued to me. He pulled his radio from his hip and began speaking into it.

"Fuck," I cursed under my breath, then slowly began making my way up the platform, trying to appear casual. Maybe I was just being paranoid.

I took a peek over my shoulder and saw that the cop was shadowing me. I was not being paranoid. This cop had recognized me. There was only one thing I could do at this point. I sprinted off like an Olympian, knocking people out of my way.

"Hey, you! Wait!" I heard the cop call out.

His words were like fuel. I increased my pace that much more.

"Excuse me. Sorry," I said as I bobbed and weaved in and out of people, running downstairs to the subway entrance. I jumped over a turnstile, then ran across the subway station to a flight of steps that took me back out onto the street. I took only a second to look around and decide which way to run. I was in my old neighborhood, so I was familiar with most of my surroundings.

With the cop still on my ass, I headed down Parsons Boulevard. I prayed this old carryout was still up the way. It was the only building I knew for sure how to enter from the front and exit to the rear. I'd been a stock boy there when I was in high school.

Horns blared as I ran between cars in the moving traffic. One driver just barely avoided splattering me all over the street. It was such a close call that I felt the bumper brush against my jeans. I spotted the carryout place and darted inside. The clerk looked up when he heard the bell above the door chime, but I zipped in and out of that place so quickly that I was probably just a blur to him.

I crashed open the back door, ran into the alley, and headed left. I was hauling ass, breathing so hard I thought I was going to pass out.

"Police! Stop or I'll shoot!" He didn't even give me time to comply before I heard a shot.

I kept right on moving. If he wanted to keep shooting, he could, because I was not going back to jail. I cut a sharp right, picking up speed. Straight ahead was a dead end, marked by the same eight-foot-tall, rusty fence that had been there for years. I was prepared to hightail it over that fence. I sprinted and leaped up, giving me a four-foot start on the climb. It slowed me down a bit, closing the distance between the cop and me. If he let off another shot, I was dead.

Clearly he was one of those cops who loved a good chase. I imagine his adrenaline was pumping. Once I reached the top of the fence, I couldn't waste time climbing down it. I had to jump the eight feet. I landed in a frog position, then took off toward the same old abandoned building that had been there since I could remember.

I entered and was able to navigate my way around in the dark, with the only light seeping through from the broken windows and missing roof shingles. Heading to the stairwell, I went to the basement, running into what used to be the boiler room. I stuffed myself into the corner behind the old, broken furnace.

It wasn't easy, but I paced my breathing to a level where the cop wouldn't hear me. After a few seconds, I could hear footsteps. I stood stiff, holding my breath now. I thought my heart was going to burst out of my chest when I saw the beam of a flashlight, but thank God, the cop only peeked his head in and did a cursory search. He didn't see me in the dark corner, and he moved on to search elsewhere.

I was finally able to exhale, but that didn't mean I could relax. I was sure the cop would be calling for backup, if he hadn't already. It was going to be a long night hiding in this cramped room.

Allen

55

When I first saw Kyle's boat, I thought it was spectacular enough to live on, but I never thought for one minute I'd actually find myself living on it. What other choice did I have, though? I couldn't shack up with him and his family. He was starting to act a little strange lately, talking to himself and snapping at people for no reason, and I could also sense tension between him and Lisa. I wasn't sure whether I was the cause of it, but I was certain my being there wouldn't help the situation any. When I told Kyle that I was going to stay at a hotel until I could take back my house, he offered up his boat. Now it had been two long weeks of staying at the marina.

If all went well, I would be back at my house soon enough. I was actively pursuing my plan to get Cassie out of there.

"I changed my mind. I'm gonna go with option two," I said into the phone as I stood overlooking the deck.

"Cool, but it's going to cost you ten grand," Mr. Bigg said sternly. "So there's the matter of you getting it to me so we can get the ball rolling."

"What do I need to do to get the five thousand to you?" I asked. "Should we meet back at the bar?"

"Dude, are you trying to play games or something? What's with this five thousand shit? Did you not hear me say that option two will be ten grand?"

"I heard you, but I figured it was five up front and then the remaining five once the deed was done."

Mr. Bigg let out a sigh. "I swear to God if folks don't stop watching these crime dramas...This ain't no TV show. This is real life. You want your wife taken care of, then it's going to cost you ten grand—up front."

Perhaps I had watched *Law & Order* one too many times. On not one of those shows had I ever seen anyone pay a hit man the entire fee up front. "I give you all the money up front, then what kind of reassurance do I have that you're going to handle it?"

"Reassurance? Man, do you want your wife dead or not?" Mr. Bigg sounded eager to spill some blood, and that awakened something that I had buried deep inside—it was my conscience.

I was starting to feel remorseful for something that hadn't even happened yet. I could only imagine how I was going to feel after Cassie was killed. "Yes, I do, but first I want to know how it's going to happen. I don't want her to suffer badly or anything like that."

"You know what, dude? I ain't got time for this shit. When you're ready, and I mean really ready and not just talking about doing it, give me a call." He was fed up with me.

"Okay, okay. Don't hang up. I'll get you the money."

"What money?" I almost shit my pants when I turned to see Kyle standing there.

"Man, you scared the shit out of me." I fumbled the phone in my attempt to end the call and put it away.

"So, who was that on the phone?"

"No one," I replied, looking down to make sure the call was ended before I slipped the phone in my pocket.

Kyle stared at me for a moment, then stepped onto the boat. "Al, I've been knowing you for years. Something is going on, and apparently it has something to do with that phone call, because you're avoiding my question. So what is it?"

"Nothin'," I said weakly.

Kyle stood there staring me down. "Look, I know this situation with Cassie is pretty bad, but not as bad as your situation with Rose. I mean, what could be worse than your fiancée killing your mother?"

Kyle was trying to reason with me, but reminding me about Rose just intensified the fire within me. "It doesn't matter which bitch was worse. The point is, I've been taken advantage of my entire life, and I'm not ever gonna allow it again."

"I hear you," Kyle said. "You'll figure this out. You're a lot stronger than you think."

"I've already figured it out," I replied.

"Oh yeah, and how's that?"

"Let's just say that Cassie is going to have a little accident, and Mr. Bigg is going to see to it that things don't turn out so well for her."

Kyle's face fell. "You're hiring a hit man to kill your wife?" he asked. "Where the hell did you even find this Mr. Bigg?"

"I met him when I was in jail. He told me he hangs out in a bar called Joe's over on 132nd, so when Cassie pushed me too far, I just went over there and found him. Did what I had to do to get my mother's house back."

Kyle shook his head, looking disappointed. "Come on, Allen. This is crazy. I know you. This is not who you are. You can't do this."

I looked him square in the eyes and said, "I don't have any other choice. She's taken everything from me. Now it's time something gets taken from her, even if it means her life."

Jay

56

"You sure about this?" Tina asked as she pulled up to the curb near the town dock in Port Washington, Long Island.

I'd spent the last two weeks hiding out at her house, waiting for the heat to die down after my near miss with the police. After I'd lain on that floor in the abandoned building for hours, listening to cops' voices, sirens, and helicopters overhead, things finally died down around daybreak. Once the coast was clear, I made my way to a nearby cab stand and got the hell out of Queens. Tina had welcomed me with open arms, and even though I was pretty sure she had seen news reports about how the police were pursuing me, she never said a word to me about it in the two weeks I spent at her place. Even now that she was dropping me off, she still seemed concerned about me.

"Yeah, it's cool." I leaned over and kissed her, then exited her car. She was a good woman, and if my life ever became mine again, I was going to make her mine. "I'll see you in a few days."

She rolled down the window and waved as she pulled off. "Jay, please be careful."

I waved back and headed toward a bench, where Wil was already seated, eating potato chips out of a family-size bag.

"Hey, bro," he said, gesturing for me to have a seat next to him.

I did just that, leaning back and stretching my legs to look at the water. "Kyle's not here yet?"

"Not yet." He lifted the bag to offer me some chips. "But I wanted to talk to you alone anyway."

"'Bout what?" I asked.

He turned to me, looking sad. "Well, I just wanted to say I'm sorry, man, and that I owe you an apology for not believing in you." He reached over and pulled me into an unexpected man-hug. "I'll never let you down again."

"It's all right, man. Nobody believed in me."

"Nobody but me." The voice came from behind us, and I looked up to see Kyle standing there.

"He's right," Wil replied. "He did believe in you."

"Yeah, I know." I reached out and gave Kyle a pound.

"Sorry I'm late. I was just finishing up lunch with my wife when your friend called me." Kyle leaned against the railing. "So what's up? Your friend said it was important."

"It is. I'm going to need your help. I'm going after DJ again," I said.

"Have you lost your mind?" Kyle snapped. "It was hard enough the first time. That guy's a public figure who makes a living hanging around TV cameras. It's too risky. Besides, he already told you no." Kyle's negativity was what I would have expected to come out of Wil's mouth, at least before his apology. This time, Wil stayed silent.

"I'm not taking no for an answer this time," I said to Kyle. "That guy holds the key to my freedom, and he's gonna help me whether he wants to or not."

"Jesus Christ," Kyle said, sounding exasperated. "What are you gonna do, beat him into submission?"

"If I have to," I replied seriously.

Kyle raised his hands in frustration, like he wanted to choke me, but I didn't back down.

"Kyle, you don't understand. This man is holding my life in his hands."

Kyle ignored me and turned to Wil. "Will you talk some sense into this man?"

"What do you want me to say? Sometimes you gotta do what you gotta do," Wil answered.

I was satisfied that Wil was taking my side, but that good feeling was short-lived, because Wil's eyes drifted past me, and suddenly there was a look of alarm on his face.

"Oh, shit! Jay, you need to get the fuck outta here!" he said.

I went to turn my head to see what had him so worked up, but he gave me a shove and yelled, "Run, goddammit!" I could hear the fear in his voice.

Call it a black thing, but when other folks start running or someone calls out the order to run, we don't ask questions. We simply get to running. So that's exactly what I did. I jumped up and started running toward the street, but my instincts had me running straight into the arms of trouble. Parked at the entrance to the town dock were several black SUVs. The marshals were swarming out of the vehicles, heading toward me.

I pivoted, running in a different direction, but being on a pier, the only other direction to go was toward the water. By the time I slowed my momentum and came to a halt, I had reached the end of the pier. *Fuck!* After more than two months, now there was nowhere left to run. I looked over my shoulder and saw that the marshals were only about thirty feet away.

My shoulders were heaving up and down as I struggled to catch my breath, all the while telling myself, "I'm not going back to jail. I'm not going back to jail."

I turned around to face my captors. The marshal who yelled "Freeze!" as he approached me had to be the man in charge, because he was dressed more like a civilian and was the only one pointing a handgun at me. I glanced back toward the water, contemplating my only remaining option. There may not have been anyplace else to run, but there was still one place to go.

"Don't do it, Crawford. It's not worth it," the marshal said, reading my thoughts.

"I'm not going back to jail." I looked over the edge and realized that, just my luck, it was low tide and there wasn't very much water. Just big-ass rocks. I slowly raised my hands over my head, repeating my assertion: "I'm not going back to jail. I'm innocent."

"Not my problem," the marshal shouted.

In that moment, I understood why some people choose suicide by cops. These guys didn't care one way or another about the truth. They were given only one task: to put my ass behind bars again. My guilt or innocence didn't matter to them, and they weren't planning on leaving that pier unless they had me in handcuffs. If I surrendered and let them take me away, I'd end up dying in prison anyway. That was a long, drawn-out death that I could not accept, so maybe I should just speed that death along.

I dropped my hands back down to my sides. "You're right, so do what you gotta do. Kill me if you want." I turned toward the edge, looking down at the boulders that would break open my skull if I jumped down there. "Or I'll save you the trouble and jump, but I'm not going back to prison."

"Don't jump! Please, Jay, don't jump, man!" It was Wil who

called out to me, sounding panic-stricken. He moved in to stand next to the marshal, who kept his gun trained on me.

"Listen to your friend, Crawford," the marshal said.

"Don't jump, Jay," Wil repeated, taking a cautious step toward me. "Not without me."

Before the marshals could make a move to stop him, Wil took us all by surprise and planted his big body right in front of me.

"Get the hell out of the way!" the marshal shouted. "I'll get you for aiding and abetting. Move it, now!"

"I can't," Wil said, looking back at me. "He's my friend. I let him down before. I'm not going to let him down again." He stepped on the edge right next to me.

"Wil, are you fucking crazy?" I seethed at him through my teeth.

He let out a chuckle like even he couldn't believe the situation he'd found himself in. "You know what? I'm starting to think I am."

"Come on, you guys," Kyle said as he cautiously stepped up on the scene to stand near the marshals.

"Finally, one of your friends who actually has some sense," the marshal said.

"My life is real fucked up right now to say the least," Kyle said, speaking to us in a personal tone, as if the marshals weren't even there. "Right now, you guys are the only things that are keeping me going." He looked directly at me. "I've lost you once, for ten fucking years. If I lose you again, man, then I might as well die too." With a sudden burst of energy, he rushed over and joined me and Wil.

"Are you fucking serious right now?" the marshal spat. "I swear to God we'll kill you all if we have to."

Wil and Kyle looked at one another and gave a slight head nod. They didn't have to say the words, yet I knew that my friends were confirming to each other that they were both in this thing wholeheartedly.

Kyle said, "There are a lot of people taking video right now, Deputy Franklin." I looked around and realized he was right. There were several people standing around with their cell phones capturing this entire scene.

Kyle continued, "Either let us talk to our friend or, well, you heard my man. Do what you gotta do."

I can't describe the feeling that rose up inside of me. We'd always said we'd take a bullet for one another, but who knew that moment would actually present itself? And that they actually meant it? But this was my mess. I'd wreaked enough havoc in each of their lives in one way or another with my situation. I'd die for those fellas in a heartbeat, but no way could I allow them to do this for me. They'd done enough.

"What are you guys doing?" I turned my head and looked at each of them, hoping they could see the gratitude in my eyes.

"The same thing you're doing," Kyle said. "We're boys. You go, we go."

"I don't want you guys to kill yourselves because of me."

"Then step down, man," Wil said. "Because our word is bond. If you jump, Jay, you best believe we're right behind you."

Dammit, I couldn't tell if he was bluffing. I turned and looked over my shoulder at the edge of the pier once again. I had no doubt that prison would be worse than jumping to my death. I was never going to get out of that fucking place after all the new charges they would pile onto my original sentence. I'd never see the light of day. I'd never see my children as a free man again. Without that, I had nothing to live for. But Kyle and Wil did. I couldn't see them leaving their entire lives behind for me. Maybe once their punk asses saw the results of my landing on those rocks first, they'd reconsider. But I couldn't be sure, and I couldn't let them sacrifice their lives for me.

With that final thought, I turned my body all the way around to face the edge of the pier, placed my hands behind my head, and dropped to my knees.

"Get him!" Franklin yelled as the marshals stormed toward me and my boys.

They restrained Kyle and Wil as I was handcuffed by Franklin.

"Damn, those idiots really must love you," Franklin said as he pulled me up off the ground. "I've never seen friends like that before in my life." He led me back toward the cars.

"Yeah, I know," I said as a smile crept onto my face. "They do."

Kyle

57

As long as they had Jay in custody, the marshals weren't really interested in pursuing charges against me or Wil, so they had released us right there at the town dock. Thank God we'd gotten out of there before any of the bystanders could contact the local news stations. My business did not need the kind of publicity I would have gotten if the news trucks had shown up. Still, that was the only bright spot in an otherwise devastating day. I was heartbroken knowing that Jay was on his way back to prison. We'd all been through so much and had tried so hard to help him, so fucking hard, and in the end, he was right back where this all started. Everything was in vain. A thousand times I considered turning my car around to go find some hole-in-the-wall bar and drink the night away. I just wanted to forget everything. But I couldn't, because there was some unfinished business to tend to between me and my wife.

It was pretty quiet when I entered the house—not what I was expecting. I was half expecting to be hit in the face with a handful of confetti and then handed a glass of champagne. By now Jay's capture had probably been all over the eleven o'clock news, and I had no doubt my wife was ecstatic.

274

I headed to my bedroom and realized I was right about Lisa's mood, at least partially. There were candles flickering throughout the room, and rose petals scattered across the floor, leading to the bed, where Lisa was lying in a silky negligee.

"I don't want to fight anymore," she said once we made eye contact. "Let's go back to who we were just a few weeks ago, before..." She wasn't exactly celebrating, but she was making it very clear that to her, Jay was just a bad dream that was over, and we could get on with our lives now that he was locked away.

"You mean before Jay escaped?"

She didn't miss the bitterness in my tone. "Yes. Is that so bad?"

"So you don't want to fight anymore, huh?" I said mockingly. "How convenient now that there's nothing to fight about. Jay got locked up again—but I'm sure you knew that already."

"I'm sorry, Kyle." Lisa crawled down to the foot of the bed where I was standing. She got up on her knees and ran her hands over my chest, rubbing my shoulders and kissing my neck.

"Please forgive me," she moaned into my ear.

"I'll forgive you," I said. She smiled and then leaned in for another kiss. I pulled back. "After you tell me exactly what it is you're sorry for."

"What do you mean?" She sat her bottom on her feet. The fact that she put that distance between us and couldn't even look me in the eyes said it all.

"I know, Lisa."

I could hear her swallow hard. "Oh, God. You know what?" She was trying to sound dismissive, like I was being ridiculous. I might have been a little out of sorts lately, but I wasn't paranoid. I knew what she had done to my friend.

"Don't play with me, Lisa. I know that you overheard my

conversation with Jay's friend and you called Deputy Franklin to tell him where we were meeting. I hope you're proud of yourself, because you're the reason that Jay is on his way back to prison for a crime he didn't commit."

She exhaled, and her shoulders sank in defeat. "Okay, so I called Franklin. But I did it for us."

"You didn't just call him once," I snapped. "You called twice. Hell, the first time you sent them to Allen's home, and three of us got arrested."

She had the nerve to roll her eyes. "I mean, nothing happened. You were locked up all of two hours. They weren't going to do anything to you. Try to get you to rat out Jay, maybe, but nothing serious."

"Nothing serious? You're kidding me right now, right?" I threw my arms up in exasperation. "I'm a black man, Lisa. Any time you put me in the position of dealing with law enforcement it could turn into a big deal. Do you not watch the news? Do you not know what's happening out there to black men? The last place I ever want to be is in police custody." At that moment, I was overwhelmed by a desire to hurt her. "You fucking betrayed me. And you don't know what the fuck could have happened to me in that place."

"Stop cussing at me already," she snapped back.

"You're lucky all I'm doing right now is cussing at you," I seethed. "I swear to God I could—"

"You could what?" Lisa asked. "Go ahead, Kyle, say it. You could what? Divorce me?"

I glared at her for a moment, trying to rein in my anger somehow before I lashed out and hit her. To stop myself from doing that, I grabbed a pillow off the bed and started squeezing, to release some of my pent-up rage. She looked down at what I was doing to the pillow, and then looked up at me. I saw something in her eyes I'd never seen—it was fear. My wife was afraid of me.

Truthfully, I was a little afraid of myself. My anger had reached such a peak that there was no telling what I was capable of. It was better for me to remove myself from this situation before things turned ugly. I headed for the door.

"Wait. Where are you going?"

"To my boat," I said.

"But, but I—" She hopped up out of the bed. "I did all of this for us, Kyle." She held her hands up, signaling toward the rose petals and the candles.

"Then you did it all for nothing."

Wil

58

I couldn't believe that after four hours of me watching him, this guy was still at the same damn blackjack table. Any halfway-decent gambler knows that the only time you stay at the same table for an extended period of time is if you're hitting. Even then, you have to know when to walk away, when your luck is going to run out. I mean, had this guy never heard the Kenny Rogers anthem of all anthems about gambling? He was losing so bad it took everything in me not to go snatch his ass up from that table and say, "Enough already!"

Babysitting grown-ass men was not for me. Orlando, on the other hand, seemed used to this type of thing. He threw back a couple drinks while we waited. Hell, he even won a few bucks at the craps table. I was too focused. I didn't want to mess up and lose this guy. Trying to pick up someone's scent in a casino if we lost him wouldn't be easy. Then again, as shitty a gambler as this guy was, then perhaps not. He hadn't moved a muscle all night.

"Looks like our guy is about to move," Orlando said.

"About time," I said. "What are we going to do, stop him in the parking lot? Wait for him to get to his car?"

"No, he's not going to his car."

I nodded. "Finally deciding to change tables, huh?"

"No, bathroom break."

The gentleman stood, scooped up his chips, mumbled something to the dealer, and then walked away.

"Come on," Orlando said as we began following him. The guy dropped his chips into his pants pocket as he headed under a sign that read RESTROOMS.

Orlando shot me an *I told you so* look.

"How'd you know?"

"Son of a bitch drank three beers and had two shots. Weren't you counting?" Orlando chuckled. "I knew it was only a matter of time before nature called. Good sense and willpower might not have gotten his ass up from that table, but a full bladder will do the trick every time."

Orlando had a point there. I just couldn't believe he'd counted how many drinks this guy had.

We watched our mark enter the bathroom.

"You go in and make sure everyone who is already in there comes out," Orlando said. "Keep the dude in there until it's the two of you. Make small talk with him."

"What do you mean?"

"Ask to borrow a cigarette or something. I don't know. Just keep him in there. I'll wait out here to make sure nobody else comes in. Let me know when it's just you and him. Got that?"

"Got it," I said.

As I opened the men's bathroom door, one man was exiting. Inside, there was one guy at the sink, and our mark was already at a urinal, handling his business. All the stall doors were open, so I knew we were the only three people in there. I walked over to the sink and began washing my hands, messing around in the water until the other guy at the sink left. Then I went to the door.

"All clear," I told Orlando.

Orlando followed me back into the bathroom, locking the door behind us. Ol' boy was at the sink now. He finished washing, dried his hands, and then turned to exit, only to notice that Orlando and I were blocking his path.

Let me be the first to admit that I was a little nervous about all this, but I trusted Orlando. This may have been my first time at the rodeo, but I was sure that Orlando had roped many bulls in his day.

"Excuse me, fellas," he said.

"In a minute," Orlando told him. "We need to holler at you first." He spoke with authority so it was clear that it wasn't a request but an order. Dude looked from Orlando to me, then back to Orlando. He was a big guy, but I still don't think he liked the odds.

He puffed out his chest. "Pssht. Who the hell you think you are? You can't come in here and just—"

"I can do whatever the fuck I want when it comes to you," Orlando shot back.

He took a deep breath like he was preparing for battle. "Oh, can you?"

"Damn right I can." Orlando took a step closer. "You do know a man by the name of Juan Carlo Smith, don't you?"

This guy looked like he'd just shit his pants. The blood drained from his face. Still, he tried to play hard, like he wasn't scared.

He looked Orlando up and down. "I don't know you guys. Is this some kind of joke?" He stepped forward as if he was going to walk between Orlando and me.

Orlando closed the space between us. "You don't know who we are? Well, you better take the time to know us, because we're the people who just bought your three hundred thousand–dollar gambling debt."

The guy looked oddly relieved and a little confused at the same time. "I don't have to pay Juan Carlo anymore?"

"Nope, your debt to him is paid, so you can leave that blackjack table you've been at all night and go home and get some rest. And just so you know, Juan Carlo Smith was ready to put you in a body bag. I'm not quite at that point yet but I do want my money."

That made him uneasy. He broke out in a sweat. "Look, I'm gonna get you your money. I just need a little time."

"Good, 'cause I've come up with some pretty favorable repayment terms," Orlando said in a nonchalant tone. "And in the meantime, I need you to do me a little favor. You don't mind doing me a favor, do you?"

"What exactly do you need?" the guy asked warily.

This is when I stepped in. "All you have to do is tell the truth."

"The truth? About what?"

I took a step toward him and looked him dead in the eyes. "It's simple, DJ. You just need to tell the truth about Ashlee and how she set up my friend, Jay Crawford, the same way she set you up."

Kyle

59

"Kyle?" My secretary Anne's voice on the intercom interrupted my thoughts as I sat at my desk, staring at a picture of my wife and kids, unsure when I would see them again. I'd walked out of the house the day after Jay's capture because every time I looked at Lisa, my mind would become enraged and I just wanted to strangle her for her betrayal. For her protection and mine, I moved onto the boat with Allen. Still, my thoughts kept returning to Lisa. Believe it or not, as much as I hated her for what she'd done to me and Jay, I still loved her and I missed her. Crazy, right? I was one messed-up dude, and it was making it really hard to concentrate on anything these days.

I flipped the picture facedown and tried to bring my focus back to running my business. "Yes," I said through the intercom.

"Someone's here to see you."

"Who is it?" I snapped.

"Umm, a Mr. Anthony Davis," she said tentatively. Poor woman was probably a little shell-shocked by my recent unpredictable mood. I'd been so irritable that simply announcing a visitor was enough to set me off. I made a mental note to put a little bonus in her next paycheck as a sort of apology.

"He's not on my calendar," I said, though it was possible that I'd failed to write the appointment down. Lord knows my mind had been all over the place as of late.

"He's not on mine either," she replied, "but he said you definitely want to see what he has to show you."

"All right. Send him back," I said. He was probably just some salesman wanting me to carry his product in my stores. I could get rid of him quick enough.

As I waited for my visitor, I looked down at the checkbook on my desk, then back up at the invoice on the computer screen. Shit. I'd written two checks for the same damn invoice. No way should I have been trying to deal with money and numbers with my mind all fucked up. I ripped up one of the checks and threw it in the shredder as Anthony Davis entered my office.

"Kyle Richmond?" He was a white dude wearing a crisp white shirt and some khakis, carrying a black leather briefcase. It looked kind of small to be carrying hair care products.

"Yes." I stood up from behind my desk and extended my hand. "Anthony Davis?"

"Yes, sir." He approached me and reached his arm out, but instead of shaking my hand, he placed some papers in it.

"What's this?" I unfolded the papers.

"Those are court documents," he said as my eyes scanned the first couple of lines. "You've been served."

My mouth opened, but no words came out. I was stunned.

"Served for what?" I was finally able to force out in a barely audible tone. I could feel my pulse pounding in the side of my neck.

"I believe your wife is divorcing you," he said.

"Divorcing me," I muttered as I read further. "This is bullshit!"

I called out, flipping through the pages. Certain phrases jumped out at me: *Claimant requests $15,000 in monthly alimony. Half of the community business. House in the Hamptons. The Jamaica Estates house, the Porsche, and the boat named* Vanessa.

"Why the fuck is she going after my car and my boat?" This couldn't be real. She didn't just want half; she wanted everything. "This can't be right," I mumbled, shaking my head.

I looked up toward Mr. Davis as my words trailed off, but he was no longer there. Apparently, once he served the papers, his job was done. He'd turned on his heels and hauled ass out of my office. I went charging toward my door to catch up with the processor, but I tripped over my wastebasket and landed flat on my face, the papers flying out of my hand into the corner.

"Fuck!" I yelled out. "Fuck! Fuck! Fuck!" The fall hadn't hurt that much. As a matter of fact, it hadn't hurt at all, because by the time I hit the floor, my entire being had already been numbed by the cruel dose of anesthesia Lisa had concocted in the form of divorce papers.

I peeled myself up off the floor and went for my cell phone, dialing her number.

A recording came on instantly. *"The number you have dialed has been disconnected or changed. Please dial the number again or check with an operator."*

"What the fuck!"

All of a sudden everything was a blur, because my eyes had filled with tears. After twenty-something years together, Lisa had betrayed me in the worst way.

"Liar." The word crept from between my lips as I looked toward a small end table and caught sight of a picture of me and my wife in happier times. "Liar," I said again, stepping toward the table.

Wiping away my tears, I picked up the picture and stared at it. My hands began to tremble with anger. "It was all a lie. You lied. We were a lie." With each statement, my voice grew louder. "A fucking lie. My life was one big fucking lie!" I threw the picture across the room, where it slammed into the wall, the glass shattering on the floor.

The next thing I knew, I was flipping my desk, throwing my computer onto the floor, tossing my chair against the wall, and punching a hole in the drywall. Hurricane Kyle was sweeping through my office. I'd heard people talk about out-of-body experiences, and now I understood how very real that experience could be. I honestly felt as if I were standing off to the side, watching someone else destroy my office. I stood there watching without a fight, without even trying to salvage anything. If my marriage couldn't be salvaged, then I certainly didn't give a shit about anything else.

With my energy spent, I stopped tearing the place apart and stood before the catastrophic scene, taking it all in. My eyes zoomed in on what had catapulted it all—the divorce papers. Walking over to the corner where they lay, I knelt down and collected them in my hands. Tears streamed down my face as I read every word this time. It was real. Lisa was leaving me, and my brain simply could not comprehend that reality. I couldn't remember what life had been like before her. I couldn't even grasp what it would be like without her. Yet at the same time, in that moment I didn't care, because I hated her more than anyone in the world.

"Kyle? Kyle? You okay, man?"

No matter how many times I said those words to myself in my head, I knew things would never be okay. I couldn't see us coming back from this.

"Kyle, man. Everything is going to be okay."

It took a minute for me to realize that the voice wasn't in my head. It was real. I looked up to see Wil standing over me.

"Get up, Kyle. Come on, man. It's going to be all right."

He extended his hand to me. Behind him I could see Anne, as well as another employee, standing in the doorway looking terrified. My eyes shifted around the disaster zone that was my office. How long had I been tearing things apart for Wil to have made it over here? It had felt like a minute, but I must have been going crazy for quite some time.

"What happened?" Wil asked.

"He stormed out of here about two hours ago like a wild man. Then he returned and started throwing things. That's when I called you. He was passed out up until now," Anne explained. "I've never seen him like this, Mr. Duncan."

I couldn't wrap my head around anything she was saying. She was talking about hours, yet I remembered almost nothing of what had happened after the process server left. It was like I had blacked out and lost a huge chunk of time.

"Has he been drinking?" Wil asked.

"I don't know," Anne answered, "but I don't think so. He doesn't keep alcohol in the office. All I know is a man came to visit him, and then this started."

Wil pulled me up off the floor. "What's going on, Kyle?" he asked me, speaking in a gentle tone.

I sniffed, wiping the snot from my nose onto my sleeve. "She's leaving me," I cried. "Lisa's leaving me. She filed for divorce—but I don't care, because I hate her."

"It's okay, Kyle. It's okay," he repeated. "Come on. Let's get you back to the boat." Wil put his arm around me and guided me toward the door. "Let's get out of here."

Anne and the employee stepped aside as Wil led me out of my office. I turned and looked one last time at the destruction that remained behind me. Not long ago, I had hoped that Lisa would come to her senses regarding the situation with Jay, but it appeared now that ultimately, I was the one who had lost my senses. Even worse, I felt like I had lost my mind.

"Don't take me to the boat, Wil. I think I need you to take me to the hospital."

Allen

60

"In light of the new evidence brought before this court, along with the recommendation of the U.S. Attorney, Mr. Crawford, I am exonerating you of the charge of rape in the first degree and the associated charges, with the court's deepest regrets. The judicial system is a good one, but it is not flawless. I honestly believe you've been a victim of those flaws," said Judge Monroe, a fifty-something-year-old white woman who had presided over Jay's new trial. It was almost eight weeks to the day since he'd been recaptured, and thanks to a very public statement from Darrius Jones, along with revelations about Ashlee's mental health history and her outright refusal to testify in this trial, the judge and the U.S. Attorney really had no recourse but to let Jay go.

"Mr. Crawford, you are free to go."

There were cheers, and folks were joyfully hugging each other in the courtroom, until the bailiffs told us we had to clear the area. When we finally headed out of the courthouse, I felt like I was dreaming. I couldn't believe that he was actually free.

"In light of everything that happened today," Kyle announced to the group, "I'd like to invite everyone to lunch and drinks on me."

"Now that's what the hell I'm talking about!" Jay yelled out, grinning from ear to ear. He threw his arm around Kyle. "Love you, bro."

"Love you too, man," Kyle replied. I was glad to see him in good spirits, although he still looked a little catatonic and over-medicated after his breakdown a few weeks ago. I had to give it to Wil; he'd found him a good doctor. Thankfully, Lisa had agreed to put the divorce proceedings on hold until we were sure Kyle was back to his old self. I hoped that Jay's release would do some good toward reaching that goal.

"Hold up for a minute." Jay stopped at the top of the courthouse steps. "I gotta say something."

Wil joked, "Can't you see you got a bunch of hungry Negroes who want to eat before Kyle changes his mind?"

"I know that, Wil, and even though it's pretty obvious you haven't missed any meals lately, I'll be brief so your greedy ass can eat." Jay started out joking with Wil, but he began to choke up as soon as he addressed the whole group. "I know the past few months have been hell for you all, and most of that is because of me."

"Aw, man, no it hasn't," I said, patting him on the shoulder.

"Yes the hell it has," Kyle shouted out to lighten the mood. As lifelong friends, we were good at doing that for each other.

"Seriously, though," Jay said, "I have to admit that I didn't take into consideration any of your lives and how they would be affected by my escaping. But please understand that I wasn't thinking about just myself." He looked a little weepy. "I did not want my kids to have to live their lives with the stigma of their father being a rapist."

"Man, you trying to make us cry or what?" I said, placing my hand under my eye as if I were wiping away tears.

"Anyway," Jay said, "I really want to say thank you. Without y'all, I don't know where I'd be."

"In jail!" Wil shouted. "Your ass would be in jail! Can we eat now?"

Once again the small crowd burst out laughing as we started to descend the courthouse steps. Well, everyone but me, that is, because I was suddenly frozen in fear. In fact, I was so terrified by what I was seeing that I was tempted to run back into the courthouse.

"What the fuck is he doing here?" I mumbled under my breath. Somehow Wil heard me.

"You all right, Allen?" Wil asked, placing a hand on my back and nudging me forward. "You look like you seen a ghost."

No, more like the devil himself, I thought.

Mr. Bigg began climbing the steps toward me. He looked just as intimidating as I remembered, maybe even more so. I contemplated hauling ass into the courthouse to avoid him. I didn't want to be seen talking to him in public, especially since there were seven uniformed officers walking up the steps right behind him. With each step he took toward me, my heart was pounding harder, until I felt like it would pump right out of my chest. Things went from bad to worse when he turned around and started talking to one of the cops behind him. His demeanor wasn't one of a criminal being followed by officers; it was more that of a guy joking with his friend the way Jay and Wil had just been doing. When he turned around again, I saw him tug on a chain around his neck and slide his identification tag out from his shirt. My knees were so weak I almost fell to the ground.

Oh my God, he's a cop, I thought. *How the fuck is he a cop?*

"What's going on, Allen?" Wil must have sensed my fear. I couldn't even speak to answer him.

Mr. Bigg walked up the last step and smiled right in my face. Shit, this was not going to be good.

"You're a cop?" I asked.

"Yep, New York City's Finest," he said with a smirk. "Going on fifteen years."

He couldn't be there to arrest me, I thought in a panic. Last time I called him, I'd told him I changed my mind, that despite how much I hated Cassie, she was still a human being and I had no right to take her life. Truth is, I knew I wouldn't have been able to live with myself, so instead of killing her, I decided I'd fight her in court for my mother's house. The law was ultimately on my side, so while it might take a little longer than a murder would have, at least I would still be able to sleep at night when it was all said and done.

"You can't arrest me," I said, trying to keep the fear out of my voice. "I told you I changed my mind, and on top of that, no money exchanged hands."

"You're right," he said. I couldn't figure out why he was still smirking, but then he turned to look at Kyle.

"But that's not true in your case, is it, Mr. Richmond?" Mr. Bigg asked in his deep, threatening voice.

Kyle

61

"Kyle Richmond, you are under arrest for solicitation of murder."
The cop, aka Mr. Bigg, placed a hand on my shoulder and spun me
around.

No! No! No! This could not be happening. This had to be a
joke, I thought. The only problem was that as I looked around, I
realized nobody else was laughing, especially not the seven men
standing behind Mr. Bigg.

"What the fuck is happening?" Wil asked, confused as hell.
"Get your hands off him."

"What's happening is that your friend here hired me to kill his
wife," Mr. Bigg said, lighting up a cigar. "Only thing is, I'm a cop.
The one who's here to protect and serve his wife." He let out a
chuckle. "Oh, man. The irony of it all."

"That's not true. That can't be true," Allen declared.

I wished like hell that Allen was right, but the fact was, I had
tried to find Mr. Bigg the day after Jay was arrested. I was so damn
pissed at Lisa when I figured out that she had called the marshals
on Jay that I couldn't stay in the house with her, or else I would
have killed her with my bare hands. Instead, I went over to the bar

where Allen had told me Mr. Bigg hung out. I didn't find him that night, but I left my number with the bartender. It made me feel better just to play with the idea of having her killed. I truthfully didn't even think about it again, until Mr. Bigg called me back a few days later.

"You're a fucking cop." The words fell from my lips as I stared at Mr. Bigg, trying to understand what the hell was going on. I didn't want to believe that I'd been set up.

"Yeah, I'm a cop, asshole," Mr. Bigg said in a tone so angry that you would have thought it was his wife I was trying to have killed. "And like I said, you're under arrest." He nodded toward his men. "Cuff him."

"This is some kind of prank, right?" Jay said, forcing out a nervous laugh. "Which one of you is behind this?" He looked from Allen to Wil. No one answered, so he looked at me. "Come on, Kyle, you got your laugh. Playtime's over."

"This isn't a prank, this isn't a joke, and this isn't a game, is it, Richmond?" Mr. Bigg stared at me with cruel eyes. "What, cat got your tongue?"

One of the cops pulled out his handcuffs.

"Fuck! Come on, Kyle, stop playing," Wil pleaded. "Tell me they're not really arresting you. Tell me this is some bullshit, bro."

I couldn't even find the words to answer him. What could I say in a situation like this anyway?

"You know, there's something I don't understand, Richmond," Mr. Bigg said as he watched the officers cuff me. "You backed off after our first call, actually told me to stay the fuck away from your wife. So why did you come back to the bar two weeks later with the money?"

I struggled to make sense of what he was saying. Ever since the day I'd lost it in my office, my memory of recent events was foggy at best. I had no memory of having gone to the bar a second time, and I definitely didn't remember giving this guy any money.

"I don't know what you're talking about," I protested. I looked to Wil, who had been somewhat of a protector ever since I went off the deep end.

Wil picked up on my silent plea for help and stepped up to Mr. Bigg. "Look, man, he said he doesn't know what you're talking about. Why don't you let me call his lawyer and we can get to the bottom of this. He just left. I'm sure he can be back here in a few minutes."

Mr. Bigg shook his head. "You can have his lawyer meet us down at the station, but I don't need any help getting to the bottom of this. I have all the evidence I need on the video from the bar. People always pulling out their phones to video cops these days.... Well, technology works both ways, you know.

"Your friend here came in ranting and raving about his wife, something about a divorce, and then he gave me the money, said he wanted her dead. In my line of work, that's called solicitation of murder."

"But I wasn't myself that day," I said now that I understood the meeting at the bar took place after I got the divorce papers and blacked out. "I haven't been myself for a very long time."

"Tell that to the judge," he told me as they led me down the steps to a waiting police car.

Allen

62

"Is it me or does this beer taste like crap?" Wil said as we all sat at the bar, staring down at our untouched drinks. None of us said it, but I'm pretty sure we were all thinking the same thing: *What the fuck happened?*

"Yeah, I know how you feel." Jay pushed his beer to the side. "Kind of hard to celebrate your freedom when your friend has just lost his."

"Now I'll drink to that." I picked up my beer and took a sip.

"What do you think is gonna happen to him?" Wil turned to Jay, who shrugged.

"I don't know. Goldstein's one of the best criminal defense attorneys money can buy. With him having a breakdown and seeing a shrink, maybe he can get him off on an insanity defense."

"Let's start with hoping he gets bail," Wil said.

"Maybe we should talk to Lisa," Jay suggested.

Wil turned his whole body to face Jay. "Are you nuts?"

"Yeah, well, speaking of Lisa . . . I hate to sound selfish at a time like this, but something tells me that Lisa isn't going to allow her husband's friend to continue to stay on that boat." I looked at Jay and Wil. "So a brother may need a place to stay."

"Don't look at me," Jay said, finally picking up his beer. "I was going to ask if I could stay with you on the boat."

Wil sat there shaking his head. "Un-fucking-believable."

"And that, my friend, says it all." Jay took a drink.

"Go home, Allen," Wil said emphatically.

"You have no idea how much I'd love to," I said, "but Cassie probably has nine-one-one on speed dial waiting for my ass."

If I wasn't mistaken, Wil's lips parted into a mild yet mischievous grin. "I'm not so sure about that," he said cryptically.

Wil's actions didn't go unnoticed by Jay either, as he shot me a confused look.

"Wil, is everything okay?" Jay asked him.

Wil didn't answer. He took a large gulp of beer and then placed his glass down with a loud, satisfied "Ahhhhh."

I wished I was feeling as good as Wil seemed to be feeling. Hell, I wished I could be privy to what he was so relieved about.

Wil put his hands on the bar and said, "You know, fellas, I've really—I mean *really*—started to learn what family is…what family means. You should go to the ends of the earth and back for family, whether they are right"—he looked at me—"or whether they are wrong." He took another drink from his beer. "And you two are my family."

Jay and I shrugged, realizing we might never figure out the riddles Wil was talking in.

My cell phone started buzzing. I took it out of my pocket and answered it.

"Hello."

"Hi, Allen, this is Sue Smith with the public defender's office."

I was a little puzzled at first. Why would the public defender's office be calling me? Kyle had an attorney, a damn good one. I was hoping his ass hadn't done something stupid like fire his attorney.

"Yes, Ms. Smith, what can I do for you?"

Her next words stunned me. "I'm calling about your wife."

"My wife? Cassie?" I knew she couldn't see it, but I rolled my eyes.

"Yes, sir. She's been arrested. I'm going to need you to come to the 103rd Precinct."

"Arrested for what?" I raised my voice, and Wil and Jay turned to stare at me.

"Sir, your wife needs your support right now."

"Ms. Smith, what exactly is this about?" I asked, curious but not really interested in giving Cassie any kind of support.

"Well, your wife's car was pulled over. Apparently the police received an anonymous tip that she was carrying a large amount of drugs. And I must say, there was quite a bit of cocaine found in the trunk of your wife's car when the police pulled her over. She swears up and down that the drugs aren't hers, that she doesn't even do drugs. Any chance they might be yours?"

I pulled the phone away from my ear and looked at it, contemplating whether I should just end the call. Then I realized that if I hung up, I might look guilty. I put the phone back to my ear.

"Hell no, they're not mine. I don't do drugs, and I still don't understand the purpose of this call. I haven't spoken to or been near that woman in weeks. She's got a restraining order on me. Did she tell you that?"

"Uhhhhhh, no." She sounded totally confused. "You're the only person she asked me to call."

"That's because I was the only person in her life who would come running to save her ass. But this time, she's wrong. Tell her she made the wrong call." I hung up the phone and turned to my friends.

"Well, you're not going to believe this, but it looks like I can go to my own house after all," I told them.

"What happened?" Jay asked.

"Cassie was locked up for having a carful of drugs," I answered. Then I looked at Wil, who had that smug smile on his face again, like none of this surprised him.

"Wil, you wanna say something?" I asked.

"Nah, just glad to have you guys in my life." He raised his glass and toasted, "To family."

Jay

63

The way my hands were trembling, you would have thought that I'd drunk up all the caffeine in the coffee shop where I was sitting, but I hadn't even ordered yet. I was finally going to be able to see all my kids, and we weren't going to be inside a jail or a court-room. I'd waited ten long years for this moment. I didn't want to do anything else in life without my children.

"Dad!" The sound of a man's voice drew my attention to the door.

"Son." I stood to my feet and opened my arms. As Jordan walked over and I pulled him into a bear hug, I saw his mother walk in behind him. It had been almost two years since I'd seen Tracy, and she was still as fine as ever. I let Jordan go and waved to her.

"Hey," she said timidly.

"Hey, yourself." I took her hand in mine. "That's one hell of a rock you sporting there. Congratulations. Where's Mack?"

"He's in the car. I didn't think you'd want him—"

I cut her off. "Girl, go get that man."

A genuine smile spread across her face. "Okay, thank you, Jay. I'll be right back."

I watched her leave the coffee shop as my daughter came in.

"Hi, Daddy. Hey, squirt." She thumped Jordan upside his head.

"Hey, who are you calling squirt?" Jordan asked. "I'm taller than you."

She laughed as she put her arm around me.

"I love you, baby," I said to her, kissing her on the top of her head.

"I love you too, Daddy, and I'm so glad to see you again."

"You too." I looked at the door. "Is your sister coming?"

"Yeah. She said she would be here."

"Well, all right. Let's give her a couple more minutes to get here, and then we'll order something," I said.

We all sat down at the table, and it wasn't long before Stephanie arrived, followed by Kenya. I hadn't been expecting to see my ex, but I was glad that she'd come. There were some things I needed to say to her.

I stood up and hugged Stephanie. "Hey, baby girl."

"Hey," she said, leaving her arms tensely by her side.

"I'm so glad to see you." I hugged her tighter, attempting to hug that tension away, but she remained stiff, refusing to put her arms around me. I pulled out of the hug and stared at her face. We had yet to discuss the whole issue of her sexuality, but I needed her to see in my eyes that I truly loved her, no matter what.

"Hey, Steph," my other two kids greeted her.

She walked over to chat with them, leaving me standing across from Kenya. Staring at Kenya, I wasn't quite sure where her head was at. Before I went to jail, we couldn't hold a conversation without arguing. Now I was tired. I'd fought for one of the greatest and most important things I'd ever fought for in my life: my freedom. I was done fighting.

So before she could even start in on me, if those were in fact her intentions, I said, "I'm not trying to fight with you anymore, Kenya. I know I made a lot of mistakes in the past, but going forward, I'm going to do everything to make it up to you and the kids. I know it was hard on you all out here, and I'm sorry that I even got caught up in the situation I did. But like I said, those are past mistakes, and I'd like to put that behind me...behind us. Do you think we can do that?" I waited anxiously for her response.

"I don't want to fight either. I just want what's best for my kids." Her tone wasn't exactly warm, but at least she didn't sound angry.

"I know we're not married or anything, but can we get along and be cordial for the sake of the kids, like me and Tracy?" I gestured toward Tracy, who had just walked back in with her fiancé, Mack. Surprisingly, Tracy and Kenya had figured out a way to coexist. I was hoping they could do the same with Tina now that I had made a commitment to her.

"For the sake of the kids," she agreed and then, to my surprise, she smiled. I couldn't remember the last time I had an interaction with Kenya that ended on a peaceful note.

I turned to look at the kids. "But what in the world are we going to do with this one right here?" I pointed to Stephanie and smiled.

"Look, Dad, just so we can clear the air and go on to have a nice day minus the awkwardness, I'm gay." She looked at each one of us. "There, I said it. It's out there. I'm gay. And no, I wasn't keeping it a secret from you all. I wasn't scared. I just wanted to be sure. I wanted to make sure that I wasn't just gay for a day, but that I really liked women. That's not something you come out to your family about unless you're sure."

I paused for a minute to process what she had just said. I asked, "So, are you sure?"

She nodded. "And I'm not ashamed either."

"And I don't want you to be ashamed," I said. "But what about those pictures? They could ruin your hopes of becoming a teacher when they come out." As her family, we were going to love her regardless, but I wasn't so sure how she'd handle the world finding out about her.

"I never really wanted to be a teacher." She glanced over at Kenya, giving her a sad look. "Sorry, Mom."

"It's okay," Kenya replied.

Again I was surprised that Kenya was so calm about it. She had been so intent on Steph following in her footsteps, and the old Kenya would have flipped out after hearing that it wasn't Steph's dream too. I think this whole situation had taught us all a lesson about what's really important in life.

"And as far as that bitch Ashlee is concerned," Steph continued, "I've already done what I needed to do." She had a wicked smirk on her face.

Kenya and I shot each other a look, each wondering if the other was privy to what Stephanie was talking about. The look on Kenya's face told me that she was as clueless as I was.

"What did you do?" Kenya asked her.

"I put them out myself," Stephanie said matter-of-factly. "She's the one on the DL. Let's see how she handles the wrath of social media. That tattoo is just as identifiable as my face. Oh, and don't think I didn't take a few pictures myself when she fell asleep. After all, this is the age of social media."

I shook my head, amazed by how slick Stephanie had been in beating Ashlee to the punch, never once having thought that was the fire we'd needed to fight Ashlee with all along. But in the end, that's how Stephanie had chosen to fight, and needless to say, she'd won.

Epilogue

(Six months later)

I finished off the last of my lobster tail, savoring the flavor as I stabbed the last piece of filet mignon. This was my last meal before I was to turn myself over to the New York State Department of Corrections. I had chosen to spend my last night of being Kyle Richmond, the free man, with my boys, enjoying a few of the finer things in life, because all of that would change in a few hours.

If I had to find a bright spot, then this was it: At least I hadn't been sentenced to twenty years like I could have been. Instead, I had taken a plea deal and accepted five to fifteen years for solicitation of murder. Some said I was lucky to have been offered that deal, because the DA had me dead to rights on video. I couldn't say I disagreed with them, because I barely remembered committing the act. I just thanked God for my lawyer, who was able to get me bail in order to get my business affairs together, with the stipulation that I sought therapy.

During my sessions, I was diagnosed with bipolar disorder, something that unfortunately didn't surprise me. My father had suffered from untreated bipolar disorder for years, and it made our family life a living hell. I promised I would never let myself get that bad, so I took my meds faithfully, as if my dick would fall off if I didn't.

"That was the best surf and turf I've had in my life," I said, wiping my mouth with a cloth napkin, then laying the napkin across my plate, which I'd scraped clean.

"Yeah, Tony Roma's has always been your favorite," Wil said halfheartedly, like he was forcing himself to enjoy this moment.

I looked from Wil to Jay to Allen. Each one had a somber expression on his face. "Come on, fellas. We're supposed to be enjoying ourselves here." I took a sip of my wine.

"Are you seriously telling us to cheer up?" Jay said. "You're going to fuckin' prison, Kyle. Remember, I know what it's like. I spent ten years there, so forgive me for not haw-hawing and bumping elbows with you."

I exhaled. "I know, but sometimes we have to deal with the consequences of our actions." I looked directly at Jay. "You didn't do anything, and you didn't deserve to be in prison. I, on the other hand, can't say the same."

"Yeah, but that wasn't you," Allen protested. "You weren't in your right mind. Trust me, I've been there. I know what you must have felt like when you were hit with those papers. Shit like that can make you snap."

"And unfortunately I did," I said.

"But your own doctor told them you have issues," Jay said in my defense. "This just isn't fair." He pounded his fist on the table. "And I don't know how you're able to just lie down and take it. Appeal. Do something. I don't know; just keep fighting. Like I did. It took me ten long damn years, but I never gave up. I feel like you're giving up."

The frustration was plain on Jay's face. I placed my hand on his shoulder. "I know, man. I'm sorry. I'm sorry that I made choices to put me in this situation." I looked around at my boys and apologized to them all. "I'm sorry that just when we get Jay back and things look as if they're going to go back to normal, I turn around and fuck up. I'm sorry."

"It's all right, man," Allen said. "We got through it with Jay. We'll get through it with you too."

"You mean *we'll* get through it." Jay pointed to him and Wil. "Nigga, you know you ain't gon' make that trip to see his ass in jail. I can vouch for that."

Everyone laughed. Even Allen had to chuckle at that one.

"Fuck you, man," Allen said to Jay with mock indignation. "I have to admit that with all the bullshit that has gone down, it's taught me just how priceless friendship is. If it hadn't been for you guys, hell, I might be the one..." Allen's words trailed off, but I knew what he was going to say.

"You might be the one going to jail." I finished the sentence for him.

Allen nodded. "Yeah. I'm sorry, Kyle."

"It's okay. Like I said, I did it to myself." On that note, I pushed my chair away from the table. "I'm not into no long, emotional good-byes, so if you fellas don't mind, I'm gonna head out." I looked to Wil to make sure that was okay, since he was my ride.

"Cool. Don't worry about it," Allen said. "I got this." He pulled out his wallet and then looked around for the waitress to get the bill.

"All right then, fellas." Wil stood. "I guess we out."

Jay and Allen stood. I gave them hugs that threatened to become a little too emotional. Thankfully, the waitress came over and broke up our little good-bye session. Jay and Allen stayed behind and handled the bill, while Wil and I headed out of the restaurant to his car.

Wil climbed in the driver's side, I got in the passenger's seat, and then we were off.

"So you really want to do this?" Wil asked after he'd been driving a few minutes.

I nodded. "Yeah. Can I use your cell phone?"

"Mine is right there." He nodded toward the center console.

I picked up the phone and dialed. After the second ring, she answered.

"Don't hang up. Please just listen. Come tomorrow I'll be out of your life and you'll never have to hear my voice again. So please just listen."

I waited to see if there would be a clicking in my ear, but all I heard was silence. I guessed that meant Lisa was willing to listen to what I had to say.

"I don't know how we got here, how I got here, but I'm sorry. I'm really sorry, Lisa," I said. "I wasn't in my right mind. My doctor and everything he said was not a joke. It was real, and I'm getting help. You know about my father's mental illness history, so you know I'm not making this up. I know that doesn't excuse what I did, but I need you to know that you were my life, Lisa. I love you and the kids." I swallowed back my tears. "That's all," I managed to croak out without breaking down.

"As much as I hate everything you did, Kyle, and the choices you made, I will always love you." That's when the click came and the phone went dead. That's when I was no longer able to hold back the lone tear that slid down my face.

I placed Wil's phone back in the console.

"You ready?" The voice came from the backseat.

I turned to look at Wil's cousin Orlando. "Yep. I have no choice," I said.

"Cool." Orlando handed me a large manila envelope as Wil drove. "There are two passports inside, and euros and dollars," he explained. "Come morning, consider Kyle Richmond dead. Your name is Dennis Wilkerson."

I pulled out the contents of the envelope and looked through everything as Orlando finished explaining.

"We've already set up everything for you. Since you like boats so much, we got a boat at the pier to take you to Jamaica. From there you'll go to Europe."

Orlando rambled off a few more details before he asked, "Is there anything else you need?"

Wil asked for confirmation one more time. "So you're really going to do this?"

I nodded, unable to talk for fear my emotions would get the best of me.

"Then you know what this means, don't you?" Wil stopped at the red light and looked over at me.

I gained my composure, swallowed hard, then replied, "Yes. This means I'm the new man on the run."

About the Author

CARL WEBER is a *New York Times* and #1 Essence® best-selling novelist.

In addition to his writing, Weber is the founder and publisher of Urban Books, the largest African American publishing house in the country. He is also the CEO of Urban Books Media, which has written and produced four films adapted from his books: *The Man in 3B*, *The Preacher's Son*, *The Choir Director*, and *No More Mr. Nice Guy.* Weber has recently partnered with Queen Latifah's film production arm, Flavor Unit, to produce seven more films and two television series.

Weber graduated from Virginia State University and holds an MBA in marketing from the University of Virginia. He lives between Georgia, Los Angeles, and New York, where he is hard at work writing and producing his next film and working on his next best-selling novel.

356740566622209